The
Heiress's
Deception

OTHER TITLES BY CHRISTI CALDWELL

Sinful Brides

The Rogue's Wager
The Scoundrel's Honor
The Lady's Guard

The Brethren

The Spy Who Seduced Her

The Heart of a Scandal

In Need of a Knight
Schooling the Duke

The Theodosia Sword

Only for His Lady
Only for Her Honor
Only for Their Love

Heart of a Duke

In Need of a Duke
For Love of the Duke
More Than a Duke
The Love of a Rogue
Loved by a Duke
To Love a Lord
The Heart of a Scoundrel
To Wed His Christmas Lady
To Trust a Rogue

The Lure of a Rake
To Woo a Widow
To Redeem a Rake
One Winter with a Baron
To Enchant a Wicked Duke
Beguiled by a Baron

Lords of Honor

Seduced by a Lady's Heart
Captivated by a Lady's Charm
Rescued by a Lady's Love
Tempted by a Lady's Smile

Scandalous Seasons

Forever Betrothed, Never the Bride
Never Courted, Suddenly Wed
Always Proper, Suddenly Scandalous
Always a Rogue, Forever Her Love
A Marquess for Christmas
Once a Wallflower, at Last His Love

Danby

A Season of Hope
Winning a Lady's Heart

Brethren of the Lords

My Lady of Deception

Nonfiction

Uninterrupted Joy

The
Heiress's
Deception

Christi
CALDWELL

Montlake
Romance

Published by Montlake Romance, Seattle

www.apub.com

Amazon, the Amazon logo, and Montlake Romance are trademarks of Amazon.com, Inc., or its affiliates.

ISBN-13: 9781542048941
ISBN-10: 154204894X

Cover design by Michael Rehder

Cover photography by PeriodImages.com

Printed in the United States of America

To Jennifer and Jennifer:
Oftentimes being a mom of a child with special needs
is lonely . . . but then, if one's fortunate, one finds
friends and fellow mothers who understand more clearly
what this journey is. Friends who are there for you and
support you . . . who are there to listen through the
uncertain times and always cheer you and your child on
through the triumphs. I'm so very grateful to both of you
for your friendship. Calum and Eve's story is for you!

Prologue

Calum Dabney was dying.

And it was even more painful than his former gang leader, Mac Diggory, had threatened it would be.

Stumbling along the alley, Calum clutched at his right side; warm blood coated his fingers. His breath came hard and fast in his ears as he crashed against the side of the white stucco townhouse.

At fourteen, he'd been beaten, shot, and stabbed more times than even the Almighty himself had a right to survive. But borrowing support from the elegant building, he gritted his teeth through the pain and accepted the truth.

I'm dying . . .

On his birthday, no less. It was foolish, the staggering intensity, this need to survive. Since his parents' death when he was a boy of five, he'd lived first in an orphanage, beaten for the pleasure of the nurses caring for him. Then he'd escaped and found a ruthless home among the Dial's most lethal gang leaders. Calum had had an empty belly on most nights and had been forced to fight boys and men for scraps and coins. Mayhap it was a primitive need to survive that existed even in the basest beasts. But even with the misery of his existence, he still hadn't wanted to die then and certainly didn't now, since he'd found a family in Ryker, Niall, Adair, and Helena.

After all, even a starved dog snarled and fought for his last breath.

"I'm not a dog," he rasped. He was Calum Dabney . . . one of the best pickpockets in the whole of London and second-in-command of the Hellfire gang. The band of brothers he and Ryker Black had formed three years ago. It wasn't his time to die. He'd too many plans for the future. A future that involved climbing from the gutter and rising up. And security. And food. And a roof—he'd have a damned roof and a big bed and one of those fancy desks just like his late father once had . . .

With each reminder of his dreams, Calum dragged himself forward. He reached the end of the alley and stopped, frozen in the shadows. He breathed through his pain, waiting and watching. His gaze found the familiar mews. This place that had been an unexpected shelter nearly a year ago during a deluge and then became something more: a place where he'd come to escape the hell of St. Giles. The sight of the stables gave him a surge of strength.

The nighttime clouds stilled over the full moon hanging in the sky. With that cover, he darted forward, rushing to the mews. Holding one hand to the still-bleeding wound, Calum used the other to shove the stable door open. With all his remaining effort, he drew it closed behind him, and then he collapsed in a heap atop the hay.

A midnight-hued horse whinnied loudly and bent, nuzzling Calum with his cold nose.

"Hello, Night," he whispered to the familiar mount.

The tall creature neighed in greeting and then, as if bored by Calum's presence, resumed munching on hay.

Stars dotted Calum's vision, and he pressed his eyes closed, willing those flecks of light gone. If he gave in to the inky darkness, he feared he'd never wake up. That was what his brother Niall was forever saying about sleeping after a knife wound.

Calum shifted onto his uninjured side and gasped as agony burned through his body. Sweating from the pain and his exertions, he promptly closed his mouth. Silence saved and sound destroyed. *You'll get yourself killed* . . . Calum's lower lip quivered, and he focused on the self-revulsion at his weak response. For all the times he and his brothers had been stabbed, they'd withstood the pain and never cried. This was different. This time there was so much blood. With shaking fingers, he made to draw back the fabric of his shirt. He winced as the tattered garment peeled away, revealing the open wound. Then, sucking in a slow breath through his teeth, he quickly covered up the mark left by the Marquess of Downton's blade. Son of a duke, Lord Downton would one day be owner of the Mayfair mews Calum frequently visited. The ruthless bastard had caught him once before and promised him a hanging if Calum sullied his stables again. It had been one thing to disregard that long-ago threat, an altogether different one to rob from that same man in the street. Guilt and regret roiled inside.

It had been a careless mistake. Always nick from a nob in a crowd, when they were unsuspecting. That was the way. The *safest* way to pick a man's pocket. But the drunken gentleman exiting Diggory's hell had diamonds dripping, from the rings on his fingers to the buttons on his jacket to the cover of his timepiece. Calum had made an uncharacteristic misstep and found himself with a blade to his side for his efforts. He reached in the clever pocket sewn along the side of his pants. His fingers collided with a cool metal object, and he pulled it out.

Those exertions sent sweat dripping from his brow, into his eyes. He blinked back the stinging moisture and gazed at the heavy fob in his hand. Through the bloody agony of his side, he managed a grin. The piece was worth a damned fortune and had been worth the carelessness and risk.

Calum collapsed on his back and blacked out.

A faint creaking penetrated Calum's unconsciousness, and he struggled to open his eyes. The scent of cloves and mutton lingered in the air. Trying to piece together where he was, Calum shoved up on his elbows and gasped, remembering too late—the knife. The injury. His surely impending death.

"Calum." The faint singsong whisper, in those cultured tones, out of place in his world, pierced his frantic thoughts. "Are you here? I've brought you a birthday—"

A soft whir of air caressed his face as the familiar figure—a small one—sank down beside him. Little Lena Duchess, as he'd nicknamed her. He'd stumbled upon her in this stall in the middle of a rainstorm a year ago. Where any other lords or ladies would have turned him over to the constables, the small girl had run off and returned with leftovers from the evening meal. Little fingers captured his face in a surprisingly strong, if unsteady, grip.

"You're hurt." Hers was an accusation coated with heavy fear.

He marveled that she worried after him, when only his brothers and sister gave a rat's arse if he returned to the shack they called home. Not wanting her pity or tears or worry, he threw off her fingers. "I ain't hurt," he snarled.

Lena's lower lip quivered, and something moved in his chest. Setting down the plate in her hands, she swatted his arm. "What happened?" As one, their gazes went to the damning gold piece glittering in the dark.

He made a grab for it and, ignoring the burning in his side, stuffed the bauble awkwardly into his pants. *Did she recognize it as her brother's?* "It ain't your business." What would she know of stealing and surviving?

She knew nothing but a full belly, a pompous family, and what it was to be pampered.

Then with a fiery show better fitted to a girl on the streets and not a fancy nob's daughter who lived in the nearby townhouse, she unleashed her fury. "I'm trying to *help* you because you *are* hurt. And you know I hate when you use that fake way of talking. You don't talk like that, but you pretend you do and . . . Please don't die." Her lip trembled again.

The sight of it caused that damned weakening again. And this time the reply came not as a bid to salvage his street-pride but to stop that damned sadness from her enormous brown eyes. "I can't die," he said, reminding her of those words she'd given him when they'd first met and she'd pointed out the scar by his lip. "I have the mark of life." Or some such Greek nonsense she'd prattled to him about while he'd devoured a loaf of bread she'd once brought him.

"Lie down," she commanded with more authority than the constables who still hadn't managed to catch Calum. "What happened?" she asked, guiding him back atop the hay.

Breathing hard, he allowed her to help him down. "I nicked a piece and got stabbed for my efforts."

"One can't let oneself be caught unawares," she scolded. "You've told me that."

"I know," he gritted out. "I know." He expected that reminder from his siblings. Odd to hear a fancy lady spouting off on the rules of the street.

With determined little fingers, Lena pulled back his shirt.

He winced.

"I am sorry," she whispered, exposing the wound. He braced for her waterworks. Yet, she merely bit down hard on her lip and glanced searchingly about the room. "Oh, Calum."

"Isn't a lady supposed t-to cry over b-blood?" Pain lent a tremble to his voice, erasing all hint of the intended lightness.

"I'm not afraid of blood, Calum," she said, directing that reply to his injury. She paused briefly in her examination. "They bled my mama."

He furrowed his brow.

"When she was sick, the doctor would cut her and pour her blood into a dish."

He grimaced. There was no making sense of the nobility. Silly, loud garments and stupid ideas about healing. "That wouldn't make anyone stronger," he said automatically. He'd been cut in enough fights to know that bleeding weakened a person. "No wonder she died," he muttered.

The usually garrulous girl went silent, when she was always chattier than a magpie. He forced heavy eyes open. Lena stared vacantly down at his side. Pain wreathed her little features, and despite the cold exterior he presented to world, the sight of her suffering pierced through his own misery. Nine years old, and yet she, with her pixielike appearance, could have passed as a child of six. Little Lena Duchess had more courage than most men he knew in the streets. Sometimes, it was too easy to forget how innocent she remained to the true ugliness in the world. "I'm sorry," he said quietly.

She brought her shoulders back. "She's been gone two years. I'm all right." He no more believed that than he believed that nob's knife wouldn't end him this day. But he wasn't the boy to pry into another person's secrets. Not even the little girl he'd secretly taken to calling friend.

With determined little hands, Lena grabbed a napkin resting on the nearby tray. A tray containing food that would have had his belly growling on any other day. Now, however, he was incapable of focusing on anything but that stinging in his side. Lena pressed the fabric against the gash.

The air hissed between his clenched teeth.

"I'm so sorry," she repeated, glancing up.

It was a day of sorrys.

"It's foine—fine," he automatically corrected. In the streets of St. Giles, a boy with unblemished tones, and anything less than a Cockney accent, was marked as weak. She'd been the only person he'd shared his true accent with. "I'll be all right." He always was. The words danced on his lips, but his tongue fell heavy in his mouth, making a lie of that assurance.

"It won't stop bleeding." She shoved to her feet in a whir of white skirts.

He glanced up. "What—"

"You need hel—"

Calum shot a hand out, startling a shriek from her. He captured her small wrist in his grip. "No."

"But—"

"I. Said. No." How did his voice emerge so strong despite the pain wrenching at him?

Lena pursed her lips. "Fine," she muttered, and he released her. "But I need water and rags to mend your side."

Mend his side. Nothing short of a seamstress's skilled hand with a needle would help him now.

"No."

She settled her hands on her hips and glared. "Calum," she said warningly.

Calum opened his mouth to protest further, but another wave of dizziness hit him. He fell back.

Lena's quiet cry pealed around his muddled head. Then he heard the patter of her footsteps as she rushed from the stable. Giving himself over to the dark once more, Calum embraced the detachment that came with the darkness.

"Where is he?" The deep voice pulled him back to the moment, followed by Lena's answering reply.

"He is in here, Gerald. This way."

Dread swamped Calum's senses, blotting out the fog of pain. Calum frantically glanced about and took in the walls blocking him from escape. His palms moistened, and he struggled to his feet. The timepiece fell from his pocket just as the stable door opened.

The gentleman blinked in the darkness as he stopped, Lena at his side, blocking off the entrance. The man said nothing for a long moment. "You have done very well, Lena," the man murmured, something strikingly familiar in those tones.

Fighting through his panic, Calum tried to place it.

"Return inside while I see to *this*." Lena lingered. "Now," the man barked.

You little bastard, I'll see you in Newgate . . .

Oh, my God. Calum stared between the glittering fob and the lord with his menacing eyes. The same man he'd nicked, who'd stabbed him for his efforts. And that vital rule of his gang, the crucial one he'd ignored echoed around his mind—never trust anyone but one's family. Now he'd pay the ultimate price. Ignoring his pain, he glared at Lena. "You bitch," Calum growled.

She cried out. "No. I . . ." A footman proceeded to drag her away, and Calum forced himself to follow her retreating form until she'd gone. His friend. *You fool. You bloody fool.*

Rough hands dragged Calum to his feet, jerking him from that momentary escape. A hoarse cry tore from his lips at the force of that movement as pain lanced his side.

Bile climbed up his throat.

"You filthy guttersnipe," the man snarled, shaking him wildly. Another cry spilled past Calum's lips as the gentleman proceeded to drag him by the hair from the stables. "Steal from your betters, will you?" The nob punched him in the side, and flecks danced behind his eyes.

"Get him out of here . . . Newgate . . . see that he hangs . . ."

No!

Weakening, Calum slumped against the burly footman and fixed on a slow-burning hatred for the girl who'd betrayed him.

Chapter 1

St. Giles, London
Spring 1824

In relatively short order, Calum Dabney's beloved club, the Hell and Sin, had descended into chaos.

A fortnight, to be precise. It had taken but a fortnight for it all to unravel.

Who would have imagined it wasn't an outside foe that would wreak havoc on the club but rather their own, ever-shifting inner workings?

The piercing screeches of two serving girls, followed by the loud clatter of shattered glass and the clang of a silver tray, cut across the din of the large crowd.

Bloody hell.

Pulse hammering as it did in any battle, Calum stood surveying the crush of patrons. He instantly located them—the source of the chaos. Tamping down a curse, he rushed through the club. Gentlemen hurriedly stepped out of his way, cutting a path for him.

Calum skidded to a stop before the scantily clad women, just as the blonde beauty, a recent addition to the staff, backhanded the other server across the cheek. The crack of flesh striking flesh rose above the raucous laughter and encouragement from drunken gentlemen. "'e's moine, you doxy."

That charge was met with an indignant shout of fury from the other server; Marjorie launched herself at her attacker. Calum inserted himself between them. He caught a surprisingly strong blow to the cheek for his efforts. Giving no indication that they saw the second-in-command of the club attempting to separate them, the two determined servers reached around him. With their painted nails, each scrabbled to grab hold of the other.

From the corner of his eye, he detected the other part-proprietor of the establishment, Adair, coming up behind Marjorie. "Enough," Calum bellowed, restraining the lushly curved server, Deborah.

"'e's mine, Mr. Dabney," Deborah screeched, kicking her legs out before her, resisting as he pulled her away. The tip of her satin slipper caught Adair in the shin. The other man gave his head a wry shake.

"In my offices, now," Calum barked. "One misstep from either of you, and you'll both be without work." That sharp command cut across whatever momentary madness had gripped both women, and they fell instantly silent.

Cheeks flushed, eyes downcast, they marched before him, one neatly in front of the other. Calum stared after them, keeping an eye on Deborah's and Marjorie's every movement. One misstep following his pledge would be grounds for immediate dismissal. An employer was only as strong as the promises he made. As the second-in-command at the once greatest hell in London, Calum knew that.

Adair moved into position at his side. "What was this latest scuffle about?"

The two servers now gone, Calum glanced over. "The attentions of a damned patron."

Adair gave him a probing look. "Are you going to reinstate those services into the club?" he asked, his meaning clear.

With their brother Ryker Black temporarily gone, Calum had been filling in as head of the club, which meant these decisions fell to him. Ryker, as majority holder of the club, had made the decision to end prostitution inside the hell. It was a progressive idea, inspired by the man's wife, and yet, it had resulted in behind-the-scenes dealings between women looking to earn some coin on the side. Calum scrubbed at his chin. "I haven't decided."

"It would end the infighting," Adair pointed out. And earn them a significant revenue stream that had been lost since they'd ceased employing whores. That reminder hung unfinished, clear enough that it needn't be spoken aloud. In the time since Ryker had wed and Niall, their head guard, had up and married a duke's daughter, their club had been in a rapid decline. Members of the *ton* were content to toss coin down at their tables, but they were not fine with men of the underworld wedding their kind. Their profits had suffered, and the rival hell, the Devil's Den, had thrived.

Battling back his frustration, Calum moved on to the matter at hand. "See the patrons receive a round of free brandy," he instructed the other man.

"A waste of bloody brandy," Adair muttered.

"Better brandy than patrons," he said from the side of his mouth. As it was, in the recent months, they'd lost enough of both—too much. And with men, women, and children who'd once lived on the streets now dependent upon Calum and his kin for their very survival, pressure weighed heavily on his shoulders.

Leaving Adair to see to the floors, Calum started forward to deal with the two employees who'd caused a ruckus on his club floors. He set his jaw in annoyance. Here he was dealing with bickering women, when the overall health, wealth, and power of the Hell and Sin itself were now threatened.

"Mr. Dabney?"

What now?

Slowing his steps, he looked to David, one of the club's many guards.

"Sir . . . *Mr.* Dabney," David hastened to correct. "There's a problem."

Another one. "What is it?" he demanded impatiently. Since Ryker Black, the head owner of the Hell and Sin, had learned his wife was with child and hastily departed for the countryside, nothing but uninterrupted problems had been left in his wake. Calum had believed he'd never see the day anything or anyone would or could ever come before the hell. Recently married and now expecting his first child, Ryker had proved Calum wrong on that score.

"Problems with the bookkeeper, sir."

"I'm no *sir* . . . Oh, Christ." Calum wasn't a lord, sir, or any other form in between. He was a man who'd been orphaned at five and lived on the streets thereafter. "What is it now?" Now onto their second bookkeeper since his sister, Helena, had gone and married a duke, it was just another thread of inconstancy in the club.

"She's having another fit of the tears, sir. Claims she can't do her work today and has barred herself in her rooms."

Oh, bloody hell. Again. "That will be all," he said, dismissing the man. Calum did another quick search of the club, finding Adair speaking to the new head guard at the front. Adair paused midspeak and caught Calum's gaze. He jerked his chin.

Adair hurried over. "What?"

"Webster's locked herself in her rooms. See to her and get her back to her damned job."

Adair scowled. "Why in blazes do I have to deal with her?"

Because Calum didn't know what to do with a woman's tears and noisy blubbering. It unnerved him, when nothing unnerved him. In fact, he'd rather partake in a knife fight in possession of nothing but a dull blade than deal with the weeping Mrs. Webster. "Because I'm seeing to another matter," he settled for, neatly sidestepping the other man's question. Turning on his heel, he started for his office.

"I'd rather deal with the quarreling serving girls," Adair called after him.

"Indeed," he muttered under his breath. Not glancing back, Calum lifted a hand in acknowledgment. Even screeching and slapping Deborah and Marjorie were vastly safer than the latest bookkeeper to take up work inside the club.

Since the departure of Helena from the role of bookkeeper, change had come fast and furious to the club. Those changes only increased with Ryker's marriage, and the head guard Niall's recent marriage and brief leave from the club.

Calum started past the guard positioned at the stairway to his private office and climbed the stairs. Since they'd pooled their stolen funds and resources almost eleven years earlier to purchase the former bordello and transform it into a gaming hell, Calum, Ryker, Niall, and Adair had each taken on a role that best suited their temperaments. Decision making was by consent, with the majority owners having the overall decision . . . as had been the case with the post of bookkeeper and the role of prostitution. Calum had been content serving as second-in-command—until recently.

In his hiring of the bookkeeper, Ryker had been adamant that the person for the post would be a woman. That adamancy came from Lady Penny's belief that women should have control of their security and safety. And yet, Calum would have been the most experienced person for the post.

He reached the main floor and started for his office. Silence and the groaning of the floorboards served as the only sound. Calum entered through the doorway. Heads lowered, both women immediately sprang to their feet. "Sit," he commanded, striding deeper inside the spacious room. Situated along the back of the establishment, the room featured a row of floor-length windows that allowed light through the leaded panes, illuminating the tidy office. Where his brothers rejected the space in favor of another, Calum's brief stint in Newgate had given him an appreciation for open spaces. Or rather, it had given him an unholy fear of closed-in ones. He claimed a spot at his neat desk.

Steepling his fingers together, he peered over them. "Well?" he urged, when they remained quiet.

Both women spoke on a rush.

". . . 'e's moine, sir. Mr. Dabney. He's been caring for . . . This bitch . . ."

". . . Oi've been with 'im longer, sir. Oi . . ."

"Enough." His low, brusque command compelled them to instant silence. Directing a look at Marjorie, who'd not resorted to cursing, he urged her on.

The young woman with heavily rouged cheeks and charcoal-painted eyes cleared her throat. "He's my lover, Mr. Dabney. Lord Matthews," she clarified. "He pays me good coin." At his probing stare, she continued on a rush. "Oi never do it when I'm to be working," she clarified, going in and out of her Cockney. "And this one"—she jerked her finger at Deborah—"has been making advances at him."

Bloody hell. This was the dilemma Ryker, with his honorable intentions, had left Calum to deal with. The women worked as servers, as maids, and in the kitchens. Their wages were adequate, and they didn't have to pay coin for food or shelter. "Black was clear on prostitution inside this club," he said at last.

The two women fell mutinously silent.

"Those women who wish to earn their funds servicing gentlemen were encouraged to take employment elsewhere." Which a number of them had. He leaned back in his chair, layering his hands along the leather arms. "If you'd prefer to find work at another club so you can continue servicing patrons, then you are free to do so." He narrowed his eyes. "However, you are not free to remain here if you undermine the decisions of Black, me, or any other proprietor." Many people—patrons in the Hell and Sin and employees—had mistaken his affected calm demeanor for weakness. The truth was, it was just another careful layer he'd built to protect himself. Calum alternated his stare between them. "Are we clear?" he asked on a quiet whisper.

They both jumped. Swallowing loudly, they nodded.

A knock sounded at the door, and Calum tamped down a curse. Interruptions during meetings only hinted at trouble. "Enter," he called out.

The door opened, and Adair stuck his head inside. A look passed between them. It was that silent language their gang of five had learned on the streets that spoke of trouble, without relying on words. It had kept them safe more times than they'd deserved. "We are done here," he said, ending the meeting. Every moment they were away from their work, the less liquor was sold, and the less profit was made.

The two young women tripped over each other in their haste to escape.

No sooner had Adair closed the door behind them than he dropped the next crisis. "Webster's quit."

"Bloody hell." And just like that, Calum had a renewed appreciation for the seemingly easy order Ryker had accomplished inside the hell. "For what goddamned reason did she give?"

"You insisted she inventory the floors."

He swiped a hand over his eyes. "I told her she could do it from the goddamned Observatory," he muttered. Those wide windows with their clever mirrors had been put in at his insistence when they'd first purchased the Hell and Sin.

A wry grin hovered on Adair's lips. "She said she was sinning enough by simply being here, but she'd not be forced to bear witness to the evil we allow."

"She took on a damned post at a gaming hell," he barked. "What in blazes did she think she'd be doing?"

Chuckling, Adair settled his broad frame into the chair previously occupied by Marjorie. He propped his boots on the edge of Calum's desk.

"I'm glad you find the fact that we are now out a qualified book-keeper amusing," he groused, shoving the other man's feet back onto the floor.

Adair laughed again, and then his mirth faded. "What do you want?"

A competent—nay—skilled bookkeeper. A familiar head guard. His club back to the way it was before Helena, Ryker, and Niall had all gone and married members of Polite Society. "Find me a replacement," he settled for.

"A woman, as Ryker and Penelope insist?"

Calum would take a bloody Covent Garden pigeon, at this point, as long as it could successfully carry out the role. "I want the most qualified person you can drum up the quickest."

Adair hesitated. Did he intend to challenge Calum on breaking with the rules set forth on that position after Ryker had married? Instead, he just nodded.

In the meantime . . .

"Bring me the damned books," he grumbled. God, beyond tabulating the profits earned in a given week and month, how he despised the tedious record keeping. He'd a grasp on numbers, but he'd never possessed his sister Helena's natural acumen.

"As you wish." Adair hopped up and took his leave. In desperate need of a cheroot, Calum fetched one from inside his center desk drawer. Lighting it on the gold sconce behind his desk, he carried the small scrap over to the windows. He surveyed the streets below. With eyes sharpened from his time living on those very rough roads, he made out the figures lurking at the corners of buildings—waiting and watching. Pickpockets identifying a mark in the drunken gentlemen who'd no place in this dangerous end of London, but came here for that very reason alone. Calum took a long, slow pull from his cheroot and welcomed the calming of the pungent smoke as it filled his lungs. His gaze caught on a small boy who wove around the street. His dirty fingers effortlessly divested a bloke of his purse, and the street tough was gone without the fancy lord even knowing he'd been nicked.

Not even eleven years ago, Calum had been doing the very same thing. Committing any theft, short of murder, to secure the funds necessary to buy and then build their empire. Taking another pull, he tapped the ashes in a crystal tray that rested on his sideboard. He'd stolen enough purses to hang ten years to Sunday. As he knew the Devil was indeed real, Calum *also* knew that when he drew his last breath, he'd be paying for his crimes. Stealing from the fancy toffs, however, would not be the crime he swung for. He settled his stare on a pair of loudly dressed dandies climbing the steps of his club. The irony was not lost on him. Those same men he'd once fleeced now willingly handed over their fortunes, all for a day's pleasure at Calum's gaming tables.

No, those gentlemen who'd let a lad starve in the street weren't deserving of his—or anyone's—remorse. A little twinge struck his side, where a sharp blade had once pierced his flesh. *Steal from your betters, will you . . .* He closed his eyes as that old horror whispered forward, as it sometimes did. Terror weighted his chest, robbing him of air. *Stop.* Calum forced his eyes open just as the two patrons were admitted to his club. Giving his head a shake to force aside thoughts of the gentleman who'd come closer than anyone to seeing Calum hang, he fixed on that which was within his control—the Hell and Sin.

Taking a final pull from his cheroot, he ground the scrap into the tray. "Leave it on my desk," he instructed.

Adair's curse filled the room. "How in blazes did you hear me?"

It had been the age-old argument between them since they'd met as small boys, vying for superiority and survival.

"You've got a heavy footfall. Always did," he said, chuckling.

Adair dropped an armful of books in the middle of Calum's desk.

Calum winced, and this time it was his brother's turn to grin. "Knowing your love of the books, I'll leave you to it."

And with another smug look, Calum reclaimed the chair at his desk and grabbed the top ledger. Opening it, he scanned the neat columns Mrs. Webster had kept.

Bloody hell, I need a damned bookkeeper.

Chapter 2

London, England

Lady Eve Pruitt's breath came hard and fast in her ears; it matched the frantic beat of her heart as she sprinted across the darkened streets of Lambeth.

There had once been a time where lectures had been given by stern nursemaids and governesses on the need for measured steps.

But that had been before.

Before the death of her mother and father. Before her elder brother Kit's disappearance. Before Gerald's descent into total evil.

Your brother promised you'd be obliging . . . on the shelf, as you are. But I do so prefer a fight, my lady . . .

Terror and horror clutching at her insides, Eve quickened her steps. Dashing through an old rain puddle, she headed for a familiar, narrow alleyway. She reached that coveted place and collapsed against the wall.

Do not think of it. Do not think of it. If you do not think of it, it isn't real.

She squeezed her eyes tight as the memory of Lord Flynn's assault gripped her. His searching hands, the whiskey-scented breath as he'd taken her mouth. The slap of cold air as he'd yanked her skirts up.

A sob tore from her. Eve stamped her hand over her swollen lips to bury that damning sound. Dread pulsed in her veins, and all her muscles coiled tight, prepared for her assailant to emerge from the shadows like the demon he was.

"No one is here," she whispered. It was the reason she'd come. Her brother, in the midst of another of his wicked orgies, was far too drunk to hunt her down. His close friend, Lord Flynn, had been left in an unconscious heap at her feet after she'd clouted him over the head.

Eve fought through the dread and panic, coming back from it. *I'm safe.* That was—as safe as an heiress in possession of a sizable fortune could be from a brother and his reprobate friend who were determined to wrest those funds from her.

Her hands curled into reflexive fists at her side as fury flickered to life. She embraced it, welcoming the palpable outrage. For it gave her strength. It distracted her from the fate she'd nearly suffered this evening.

Do not think of him. Not again. Not now.

The distant sound of a horse's hooves filled the eerie night silence. *Run.* Springing into movement, Eve raced down the narrow passageway between the two buildings. She reached the back door and pounded frantically. That loud rapping thundered in the quiet. *Open the door.* Eve stole a frantic glance down the alleyway. *Open the door,* she silently pleaded.

And then the Lord apparently heard a second prayer of hers that night, for the familiar, wrinkled servant drew the door open. Surprise marred his heavily wrinkled features. Why should he not be startled by her appearance? It was late. Not an hour any respectable lady would be visiting Chancery Lane. And yet, Eve would rather sleep on the streets of Chancery than return home. "My lady . . ." Mr. Dunkirk's words trailed off, and his stare lingered on her swollen mouth, her torn décolletage, and the fingerprints on her arms.

Humiliated shame ripped through her. Never before had she longed for a cloak more than she did in this exposing moment. However, when presented with the option of donning a proper garment or fleeing her unconscious assailant, she'd opted for the latter. "M-may I see my offices?" she asked, her voice hoarse.

Cheeks flushed, the wizened servant stepped aside to admit her. "Of course. Of course, my lady," he said quickly, ushering Eve inside.

The click of the door shutting and lock turning eased some of the tension from her frame. It was an artificial sense of safety, and yet in this instance it was tangible and real. On numb legs, she followed Mr. Dunkirk through the familiar corridors of the Salvation Foundling Hospital. Where the sounds of laughter and children's chatter usually filled these walls, nothing but a fitting, eerie silence hovered in the air, punctuated by the soft soles of her leather boots. "If you'll wait here, my lady," Mr. Dunkirk said as he admitted her to the makeshift office that Eve called her own during the daylight hours, "I'll fetch Nurse."

"No," she rasped. "Do not. Please," she implored. "I—I . . ." *bring threat enough to this place in simply being here.* "My offices. I need my offices." Concern glinted in his rheumy eyes. "I merely wished to finish my reports," she finished lamely. Only a lackwit or madman would ever believe that, even with Eve's devotion to her bookkeeping at the Salvation Foundling Hospital, mere ordinary business brought her here in the dead of night. But then, how many other peculiar times had she fled Gerald's violent displays of temper, coming to this very place?

Studiously avoiding Eve's gaze, Mr. Dunkirk nodded. "Of course, my lady." With a slight bow, the old servant left.

Alone in the small office, Eve's legs gave under her. She shot a hand out, catching herself on a nearby shellback chair, and lowered herself into that seat. The books and ledgers neatly stacked as she'd left them earlier that morn represented a sliver of normality in her precarious world. Closing her eyes, she pressed shaking palms to the top of that pile. The leather was cool against her palms, a reassuring balm to this hellish night.

Originally, guilt had driven Eve to the foundling hospital. Guilt over the death of a boy she'd been responsible for seventeen years earlier. Over time, she'd accepted that remorse was a useless sentiment. It would never undo her actions in seeking help from Gerald. She could only work to see that other children didn't suffer the same agonizing fate. And so she'd come here and given the only gift she might contribute—her ability with numbers.

Now she sought solace in that same work. With shaking fingers, Eve opened the black ledger and lost herself in her work. It gave her purpose . . . and had for the better part of the year.

Seated behind the aged Carlton House desk, Eve frantically scraped her gaze over the page, pausing periodically to make a note in the far-right column.

Soaring costs of wheat . . . increasing number of children . . . must prepare for a . . .

This is not the greeting your brother prepared me for . . .

Her gut churned. "Damn you, Gerald," she whispered.

Her brother had grown desperate. Tonight's attack, encouraged by her faithless brother, was proof of that. But then, desperation made a person do desperate things, and the only funds between Gerald and dun territory were, in fact . . . Eve's monies. In one of his final acts of business, the late Duke of Bedford, knowing Eve would no longer be a debutante in her first bloom of youth, had set aside funds to tempt a marriage-minded gentleman. He'd not had the wherewithal to see that all he'd done in a final act of generosity had been to put a mark upon her for fortune hunters—and even more dangerously so, the ruthless son he'd left behind.

When she reached her sixth and twentieth year, the twenty thousand pounds reverted to her, and the decision of what to do with it and how to use it all fell to her. In the event she married, those funds would become her husband's. She steeled her jaw. It was an archaic arrangement her father had drafted on his sickbed. And though she'd loved her father for being a good, kind man, he'd given more credence to his son's wit than her own. What was worse, he'd been so fearful that Eve wouldn't make a match that he'd sought to sweeten the pot, as she'd overheard him discussing with his solicitor, Mr. Barry. Her fingers curled reflexively around her pen.

When she was nine years old, she discovered the depth of Gerald's evil. With the innocence only a child was capable of, she'd gone to him, pleading for help in saving the boy from the streets she'd called friend. Gerald had repaid her trust by having him dragged off to Newgate and hanged. That ruthlessness had extended to Eve in a whole new way this evening.

"Do not think of it," she urged herself in the quiet. "Do not think of him." She trained her gaze and every attention on the books before her.

Except, she'd let him back in her thoughts, and the menacing glint in Lord Flynn's ruthless blue eyes flashed behind her mind. Her stomach revolted, and Eve covered her face with her hands, willing him gone.

Do you know, I thought it would be a chore to bed you? But I do believe I've been wrong . . .

"Eve?" Snapped to, Eve dropped her hands and glanced to the doorway where Nurse Mattison stood. Nearly six feet tall, the unflappable nurse of thirty years had always had a Spartan-like strength around the children in her care. "Whatever has . . ." Her words trailed off.

Eve followed her stare to the ripped décolletage. Throat working, she made a futile attempt to right the gaping fabric. "I needed to finish my reports," she said blankly, no more believing the older nurse would accept that as truth than she trusted Gerald would leave Eve alone after this night. "Forgive me for disturbing you."

The other woman made a sound of protest as she slid into the seat opposite Eve. "Do not be silly," she chided.

Eve stiffened and braced for an onslaught of questions she was unprepared to answer. She couldn't share the details of the wicked party her brother currently hosted or . . . Her mind shied away from the details of Lord Flynn's punishing assault.

She continued to work, her pen flying frantically over the pages. All the while she felt Nurse Mattison's gaze on her. When Eve had come to this hospital a year ago and offered funds and her assistance, the woman had been skeptical. In time, when Eve had begun evaluating the head nurse's reports and books, they'd struck up an unlikely friendship. As such, this place had become a sanctuary from her uncertain world. And it was even more so in this instance.

"Do you know, I have served in three hospitals? In all those times, you are the only lady who's done more than pay visits to uplift the spirits of the children."

Eve paused midtabulation. Yes, she knew it. She knew it from her frequent visits and the time she spent reading to the children here. She knew it from the grateful smiles and words of thanks that fell too frequently from the mouths of those who called this place home. What they failed to understand was that since the illness and then passing of Eve's father, this institution had served as a de facto home. It had been the one place to give her purpose—and a sense of control, which her own life was so very much without. This place, where children who'd not a soul to depend on, found a home. And all that was on the cusp of being lost to the mounting bills. So how could the other woman appear so . . . so . . . calm, with ruin staring down the eyes of the noble institution? She mustered a smile. "It would take a good deal of conceit to believe that my presence would so uplift a person's spirits that they'd forget their empty belly or terror for the possible future awaiting them."

The candle's glow illuminated the sparkle in Nurse Mattison's eyes. "Then you do not properly appreciate just how dearly the children and the staff care for you." She gave her a meaningful look. "How much we all care for you." She paused. "What happened?" she asked quietly.

The pen slipped from Eve's fingers, splashing a trail of ink upon the otherwise perfectly tidy page. She shook her head tightly and proceeded to ramble on. "I have to see to the wheat reports. I fear it is even more dire than we thought." Not only had the foundling hospital seen a decline in donations and sponsorship from the peerage, they'd also taken in more children, which meant greater expenditures. "I'll just—"

"It can wait," the imperturbable woman insisted. "What happened, Eve?" she repeated.

Eve's throat worked. Since she'd come here, this woman had been like the caring, elder sister she'd never had. And yet even with that bond between them, she couldn't bring herself to share this. "I cannot . . ." Slowly, she lifted her head and met the other woman's gaze, pleading with her to understand.

Had there been tears or a hint of weakness in Nurse Mattison, Eve would have been reduced to a blubbering mess. Nothing but the woman's steely resolve met her gaze.

"You cannot remain there." The nurse set her mouth. She'd never been daunted by Eve's title, a duke's daughter, and that had only further earned her a spot in Eve's heart. "I'll not let you."

Nurse Mattison could have counseled all the commanders in the King's Army on resolve, and something in that gave Eve a renewed strength. In this, she was not alone.

"No," Eve concurred. In a bid to drive back the worry in the other woman's eyes, she added, "In three months, I'll turn my funds over as we agreed, and you'll offer me offices." So very much depended on those funds that she'd attain when she reached her sixth and twentieth birthday.

"Three months may as well be a lifetime, Eve," Nurse Mattison said with an uncharacteristic frown.

It was. After this evening's attack, Eve had little doubt Gerald would ultimately succeed in his attempts at getting hold of her inheritance.

She looked up, startled from her thoughts, when the nurse laid a fleeting hand upon hers. "We are grateful for all you've done. Let me help you."

"I can't remain here, either," Eve said as frustration propelled her to her feet. She began to pace. This would be the first place Gerald sought her out.

"No," the nurse confirmed. She reached inside her apron and pulled out a small envelope.

"What is this?" Eve asked, when Nurse Mattison slid it across the desk.

"I took the liberties of finding employment opportunities that exist for you." She nodded once.

Eve pulled the page free and blinked. *"A gaming hell?"*

Surely she'd misheard or misread. For seated in the cramped office, there was no other explaining or understanding why the nurse with a perpetual smile would send her to a . . .

"Yes. A gaming hell." Nurse Mattison echoed Eve's question.

She blinked. Had she spoken aloud?

"I was clarifying that you had, in fact, read my note correctly," the other woman explained with a gentle smile in her eyes. "I have received reports from numerous employment agencies, and this is the ideal option. As such, I took the liberty of securing a meeting for you."

Eve sat with her head cocked, studying the nurse. This was her plan? Of all the posts and positions or places she could find for her—*a hell?* Those dens of sin that her brother frequented more than a vicar did Sunday sermons.

"I'm sorry, Nurse Mattison," she began hesitantly. Because she was grateful. Truly. It was not every day a person would risk the wrath of a duke to help secret off that powerful peer's sister. Nurse Mattison, however, was not most people. A woman who'd followed the drum with her late father during the Peninsular Wars, she'd more strength and courage than any other Eve knew. "Are you suggesting I work inside a"—she dropped her voice to a scandalized whisper—"gaming hell?" What work awaited women in there was on their backs or in scant skirts.

"The Hell and Sin Club," she clarified. "And yes."

Eve emitted a strangled choking sound, but Nurse Mattison droned on and on about what she knew as a dull humming filled her ears. And in this instance, she felt very much the way she had when Gerald had held her head in Night's water bucket as punishment for aiding a street rough, after he'd discovered Calum in the mews.

Nurse Mattison wished to send her to not only a gaming hell but the Hell and Sin Club? The establishment that held the vowels and then some for her brother's weakness at those tables? "I'm not going there," she said blankly, shaking her head and dislodging the cobwebs there.

The nurse stopped midsentence, a frown on her lips. "Eve . . ." she began.

Eve leaned forward in her seat and touched the edge of the cluttered desk. That faint movement dislodged several papers, and they fluttered to the floor, forgotten. "It is a gaming hell, Nurse Mattison," she elucidated. She knew she repeated herself . . . but the matter certainly did bear repeating.

"I know that, Evie," she said gently, that term of endearment once used by her father. "But they're in need of help, and you require hiding. Your brother knows your dislike for them."

Dislike for them? More like hatred. Palpable, burning, twisting, seething hatred.

"It would be the last place he'd ever look," she said with more somberness than Eve ever remembered from her. "With the debt he's amassed to that club, he's taken to frequenting the Hell and Sin less." Less. Not altogether. It spoke of her brother's weakness for gaming. Even with that, however, the nurse was right. With the sizable debt Gerald had incurred at the Hell and Sin, he'd be mad to make himself a frequent visitor to that particular club.

Eve closed her eyes and ran her palms over her face. Damn Gerald for being a damned Judas who'd sell her for a bag of silver. Damn her other brother Kit for having gone off on matters of business, never to return. Tears pricked her lashes, and she blinked back the crystalline drops. She'd not shed another tear. What good came from weeping? None. It didn't fix a person's problems or erase hurts or create stability. Angling her head, she discreetly dabbed at her eyes. And damn society for leaving a lady with so few choices outside the bonds of marriage.

"It is just three months," the older nurse pointed out gently. Three months may as well have been three years for the peril she faced with Gerald. "And then you'll be in control of your funds."

Eve held the other woman's gaze. "Our agreement still stands?" Most any other person would wash their proverbial hands of Eve and her money to be spared the wrath of a duke.

"Our agreement still stands," Nurse Mattison confirmed.

That Salvation Foundling Hospital, where parentless children went to live, would be the recipient of her funds—all of them. As long as Eve was connected to that money, her brother would not quit in his pursuits. In exchange for her inheritance, Nurse Mattison had agreed to grant Eve permanent offices, rooms, and a post as second-in-command at the hospital. Eve twisted her hands. How was she to call home to a place that had seen her life shattered? Oh, it was certainly Gerald who was to blame . . . and yet taking shelter in the halls of that place . . . She grimaced and leaned forward. "My brother . . . Kit," she amended. She rarely allowed herself to speak his name, for when she did, the knifelike pain carved away at her heart all over again. Did she truly believe that if he'd been located and had found out the fate of their father, and now Gerald's intentions for her, he'd not return? No, only one thing could keep him away . . . Violently pushing aside that niggling truth, she fixed on Nurse Mattison.

The other woman gave her a pitying look, and Eve glanced away.

"Is missing and unaccounted for, Eve. I never knew your brother," she murmured, "but given the warmth with which you've spoken of him, I believe he'd want you to be safe at any cost." She stared back expectantly. Waiting. Her meaning clear.

The next move belonged to Eve. Opportunities for women were far and few between, and Nurse Mattison *had* proffered the temporary security she needed.

Eve stared out the lone window, overlooking the empty London streets. And yet . . . what choice did she have? Knowing how very close she was to attaining her majority, Gerald would not rest until she was ruined—or worse, committed—freeing those funds to his greedy, grasping hands. Releasing a sigh, she sat back in her seat. "What would my responsibilities entail there?"

The nurse smiled. "You would be their new bookkeeper."

"A bookkeeper," she echoed back.

The freckle-faced woman nodded, an ever-widening smile splitting her cheeks. "Given that you've handled the books for your family's estates and those at this foundling hospital, there is no better role for you."

Which she despised. Skilled at it though she may be, Eve still had at best a palpable dislike for math, and at worst, a decided loathing. It had been just one more responsibility she'd taken on when her father had fallen ill, and then kept up for the agonizing two-year period in which he'd wasted away and then drawn his last breath. That responsibility had continued in her hands when Gerald had ascended to the dukedom and driven to dust the legacy of wealth their father had left behind. Helping the children at the hospital, however, had fueled her, and because of them, she'd discovered an appreciation for those numbers that might help others.

The nurse's smile dipped. "It is the best I am able to do with such short time," she explained. "You cannot enter a nobleman's household as governess or companion."

No. Society well knew the Pruitt family. Obscurity could never be achieved in a townhouse in Mayfair or any other fashionable end of London.

"And more importantly, Eve, with the money your brother owes that hell, he's taken up at other clubs."

Bitterness stung Eve's throat. Those details about her brother's gaming pursuits had been splashed upon every gossip column so that even Nurse Mattison had discovered the truth.

"It is the last place His Grace will ever dare think to look for you," the nurse said.

It was. Because she'd spent the better part of four years berating and lecturing him for those pursuits that had left them bankrupted and jeered in society for his wastrel ways. Eve scrubbed another hand over her face. "Three months." It was a reminder more for herself, but Nurse Mattison answered her anyway.

"Just three months. And it is my understanding the proprietor, Mr. Black, is fair and kind with his staff."

An inelegant snort escaped her. That generous assessment went against everything those sinful establishments represented.

Drawing in a slow, purposeful inhalation, Eve stood. "I cannot," she said quietly, regretfully. There had to be another way.

Surprise stamped the nurse's features, and she quickly jumped up. "But—"

"My brother poses a danger, and yet, the peril would surely be far greater in an establishment filled with licentious men and their wicked pursuits." Memory of Lord Flynn's attack slipped forward. Her stomach muscles contracted, and she fought to stave off the remembered horror. "I can certainly outmaneuver my brother for three additional months." She spoke that assurance as a reminder for herself, only partially believing it.

"Eve," the other woman entreated. "We all do what we must in order to survive."

Something flashed in Nurse Mattison's eyes. So she was a woman who also had known strife. How much she knew of the nurse's spirit and life . . . and yet at the same time, how little.

Nurse Mattison persisted. "The post at the club will surely be filled soon, and then who knows how long it will be before I can find you an alternative place to go until you reach your majority."

Seeing the uncharacteristic worry in the nurse's blue eyes, Eve leaned across the desk and gathered her hand, giving a slight squeeze. "I thank you for your efforts and concerns, but I cannot go there," she repeated. Her gaze went to the wall clock just beyond her shoulder. Fifteen minutes past three. After his revelries, Gerald would no doubt be sleeping, as he always did. Eve stood. "I will be in touch with you should anything change."

Nurse Mattison looked about one wrong word on Eve's part from dissolving into a fit of tears. "Then you must at least remain the night here."

The following morn, when the sun crept over the London sky and the world stirred, Eve, escorted out by Mr. Dunkirk, climbed inside a hired hack.

A gaming hell . . .

That was the place where Nurse Mattison would send her for security and safety, when those establishments represented the furthest thing from either of those craved-for gifts. She'd seen her brother stumble in, stinking of too many spirits and cheap perfume, on too many nights. Now Nurse Mattison would talk of sending her to a place where there was a sea of those lecherous figures?

A moment later, the carriage dipped under the driver's weight as he climbed into his seat, and then they were rolling through the streets of London. Drawing back the tattered, long-faded, red velvet curtains,

Eve stared absently out at the foundling hospital. For her earlier bravado and assurances to the nurse that Eve could oversee her own safety for the next three months, she at least acknowledged the truth to herself—she was less convinced than she'd let on.

Having been born the son of a duke, and knowing he'd inherit the distinguished title, Gerald had lived an unrepentant life focused only on his own pleasures. His recklessness, however, had spiraled out of control, descending into new, dangerous territory once he'd gone through their fortune at his tables and in the arms of his mistresses. And given that Gerald had surely provided Lord Flynn the key to her chambers, she feared the other devious measures her brother would concoct as the days drew closer to her sixth and twentieth birthday.

The carriage drew to a slow halt outside her family's townhouse, and Eve sat on the bench, staring up at the white stucco residence. When her parents were alive, it had been a model of grandeur and elegance . . . a place visited by distinguished guests. Her mouth twisted in a macabre rendition of a smile. Now that *home* was nothing more than a symbol of depravity and shame.

Eve rapped once, and the hack driver instantly opened the door. With a murmur of thanks, she accepted his hand and rushed up the steps of the townhouse.

The butler, Sams, drew the door open.

By her estimation, she'd another one to two hours before her brother roused himself from his alcohol-induced slumber. Fueled by that reminder, she marched through the halls, seeking out her rooms.

Those same rooms where I was nearly raped . . .

Bile stung her throat.

Damn him. Damn Lord Flynn and damn Gerald for—

"Where have you been?"

A gasp burst from her lips, and she jerked around. Her heart sank.

Eyes bloodshot, hair disheveled, and a day's growth of beard on his cheeks, Gerald stood in the middle of the hall. *Bloody hell.*

"Gerald," she said in careful greeting. She folded her hands primly before her and stared expectantly at him.

He narrowed his gaze on her tattered gown, then strode over. More than a foot taller than her own five feet, one inch, he reveled in intimidating her. A girl with her head oftentimes dunked in a bucket of bathwater, she'd developed a healthy fear of him . . . until she'd come to discover that depriving him of her tears, pleas, and cries weakened him. "I asked you a question."

"Nay," she challenged, leaning back against the wall. She folded her arms at her chest. "You made a demand. I tend the books and oversee the household, but I'll not be subject to bullying." This was the first their paths had crossed since he'd sent Lord Flynn to her chambers, and she searched him for a hint of . . . something. Certainly not remorse. He was incapable of it.

"Well?" he snapped.

So, he'll pretend Lord Flynn didn't attempt to rape me last evening. The bastard. Tamping down the fury boiling under the surface, she strove for calm, arching an eyebrow.

A mottled flesh marred his cheeks. "Well?" he said again in a more conciliatory tone. "How many funds do I have for the month?"

Her lip curled in disgust. "With your latest expenses, we've exceeded more money than we presently have to pay the debt. As long as you insist on keeping your mistress, and membership at four clubs"— including the Hell and Sin, which owned fifteen thousand pounds of her brother's debt—"and drink and wager, then you are doomed."

His mouth tightened. "I am doomed."

"Yes," she pointed out. "You."

Silence met her pronouncement.

Vile curses burst from his lips and singed her ears. "By God, this is all your fault." He slammed his fist into the wall, and she recoiled. "You are sitting on twenty thousand pounds."

Heart racing, she schooled her features. *Do not let him see your fear. Do not let him see your fear . . .* "*My* twenty thousand pounds," she said quietly. "Left to me by Father."

"Left to your husband," he spat and proceeded to pace. "You are the only goddamned woman in the whole of England who won't do your damned duty and make a match. Flynn doesn't even care that you're homely as a horse."

Long ago, his insults had cut her to the quick. Over the years, she'd developed a stern protective shell against any of Gerald's slights. What would he say if he knew the real truth of what she intended with her funds? A secret only Nurse Mattison knew of.

"I rather think horses are beautiful. Do you know what else they are, Gerald?" She didn't give him leave to answer. "Loyal. They are loyal." She let the meaning linger in the air. Of course, too self-absorbed, he'd neither heard nor cared about that slight upon his character.

Her brother stopped his frenetic movements. He leaned forward. Malice and hatred glimmered bright in his eyes, and despite her resolve for courage, a shiver scraped along her spine.

This time, he turned his own question on her. "Do you truly believe you'll circumvent me?" he seethed. "When the only thing between me and Marshalsea is the funds in your name, I'd sooner see you committed as mad than claim them."

Another shiver snaked through her, chilling her from the inside out. For staring at him, the venom in his eyes, she saw he was very much the cruel young man who'd hauled an injured boy off to Newgate and then roundly punished Eve for having helped that boy. Only this man before her now spoke of a fate worse than death . . . and by God if she didn't believe that he would. "You wouldn't."

Except, how easily he could.

A ruthless smile turned his lips. "Oh, but I would. And it would be all too easy for a duke. You were never the same after you'd cared for your beloved papa. Went mad."

She tried to force out a tart, dry rejoinder—that would not come. She balled her shaking hands into tight fists. "You are a bastard."

"No," he said, matter-of-factly flicking a speck of lint from his wrinkled mauve sleeve. "I am a duke." He jabbed a finger across at her. "You'll marry Flynn. Have I made myself clear?"

"Abundantly," she said quietly.

After he'd gone, Eve stared at the empty hallway. Yes, it was indeed clear . . . just not in the way her wastrel of a brother believed. Stealing a glance about, she found her way to her rooms and the small bookshelf next to her bed. Eve plucked the copy of *Eighteen Books of the Secrets of Art and Nature*. An ache pulled at her heart for the loss of the only true family she had left. *It is a book that has all secrets for warding off pain and evil.* Smoothing her palm over the aged leather volume, she heard Kit's voice in her mind as clear as it was that day he'd given her the obscure tome. Her elder brother had been missing now two years, and Gerald had dispassionately determined Kit was, in fact, dead. She hated that it was the one time he'd likely prove correct. For nothing, not even his work for the Home Office, would have kept Kit away.

She stopped her turning on one page, homing her focus in on the words there.

It was to be the Hell and Sin Club, then, after all.

Chapter 3

St. Giles, London

She stank.

More specifically, Eve smelled of dates, figs, blackberries, and mulberries. Cooked, ground, and mixed into a heavy paste, she'd applied it to her hair for four days consistently. Given those particular fruit-based ingredients, one would expect a person might present with a *tolerable* scent, at least.

Alas, the concoction, when cooked, had left her with inky-black hair *and* a pungent odor. The offended looks she'd received from her hired driver had proved just how noxious she, in fact, was.

Of course, it certainly hadn't helped Eve's mixture that she'd been unable to drum up any of the requisite cypresses called for in the ingredients and had instead substituted the missing item with vinegar.

She wrinkled her nose. Yes, she offended even her own senses.

Then, mayhap that wasn't altogether a bad thing. Mayhap it would prove quite useful in going about her business inside the gaming hell. After all, she'd difficulty enough tolerating her own smell.

She bit down hard on her lower lip as all the anxieties swelled to the surface, blotting out the nonsensical musings about her dyed hair.

Eve peeked out the faint crack in the curtain. How much longer until she arrived? She peered out into the darkened night, searching for a glimpse of her surroundings. But for the one Season she'd suffered through seven years prior, she'd only ventured outside her family's properties when visiting the hospital. After her father had fallen ill, her entire life had become about caring for him, and she'd done so without regret. He'd been blind to the depth of Gerald's evil, even with the appeals she'd put to him; he'd been incapable of seeing bad . . . in anyone. It was that generosity of his spirit that also proved his greatest flaw and now saw Eve journeying to the streets of St. Giles to wait out the months until her birthday.

After a painfully interminable carriage ride, the conveyance rocked to a jarring halt. Eve grabbed the edge of her bench, catching herself.

She'd arrived. Eve peeked through the crack in the curtain at the white stucco building with the stone gargoyles out front. This depraved place of sin *would* have gargoyles.

Not for the first time since she'd spoken with Nurse Mattison about the post, reservations reared themselves. She flexed her fingers, stretching the quaking digits, and grabbed the edge of her curtain. What a sad day it was, when a lady was far better off in the dangerous streets of St. Giles than her own home. To give herself a task to focus on, Eve adjusted her braided bonnet made of straw and horsehair. Adorned in linen lace and silk ribbon, the hat—a gift given her by Kit from his travels to Sweden—had earned pointed stares five years ago when she'd first worn it. It was one of the last tangible connections she had to him. A ball of emotion wadded in her throat, making it difficult to swallow.

The driver drew the door open, slashing across her useless self-pitying. "Hurry up, ya. Oi got other customers to see to." He reached inside the carriage, and she recoiled.

I'm not ready.

"Just a moment, and then we can—"

The driver snorted. "Surely ya ain't looking for an escort?" The toothless driver laughed.

Eve frowned. Actually, she had thought he'd at the very least accompany her to the door. Or rather, she'd hoped he would. For even as she didn't expect the portly man who puffed when he'd opened the carriage door to offer much in the way of protection . . . the prospect of strolling through the streets of St. Giles seemed far safer with *someone*—even the aged driver—than no one.

"Oi said out," he snarled.

She managed a juddering nod. Eve dug deep for strength and reached for her valise.

She tossed her bag to the ground. It landed with a noisy thump. She grabbed the doorjamb to pull herself down.

Gathering the spectacles given by Nurse Mattison to aid her disguise, Eve popped open the wire-rims and perched them on her nose. She blinked through the heavy blur. Oh, drat. She couldn't wear these. She—

"Off ya go," the driver growled.

Eve climbed down and picked up her bag. As soon as her fingers touched the handle, apprehension set in. Noise spilled from the brightly lit establishment, while men stumbled in the streets toward the club. She glanced up and down the street and then, gaze trained forward, started down the path toward the Hell and Sin.

At her back, the rumble of the hack's wheels driving off into the night forced her to increase her strides. Shifting the valise in her hands, Eve reached the edge of the alley.

And for the first time, a different sort of trepidation held her immobile. She was . . . alone. Not a soul knew where she'd gone, and though that was the overreaching purpose of her taking on a post in the Hell and Sin, there was something eerily chilling about it at the same time.

Fueled by fear and the nervous energy pumping through her veins, Eve hastened her steps.

Ignoring the unidentifiable, high chirp of some nighttime creature, she knocked on the heavy door. Most ladies and all servants resorted to that obnoxious scratching. Given the animal-like quality of that grating rap, Eve had never, despite her nursemaids' and governesses' lessons, resorted to it. Nor was this moment any exception. At the stretch of silence, she pounded her fist hard on the panel.

The person on the other side wrenched it open, leaving Eve with her hand suspended midknock. Tall, dark, and in possession of a menacing black satin eye patch, the man looked her up and down with a coldness she'd grown accustomed to in her brother's eyes. His long, drawn-back hair and patched eye gave him the look of one of those menacing pirates Kit used to tell her of when he was home from Eton, and then Oxford. That soothing reminder of happier times with her brother cast off the chilling fear roused by this stranger. "I'm here to see Mr. Black," she explained. Dropping to a knee, she attended to the latch on her valise.

"Mr. Black isna here." The dark-clad stranger's gravelly brogue reply barely reached her ears.

She blinked slowly, staring at her cloth bag. She'd misheard him. "Mr. Black," she repeated for the man's benefit.

He made to shove the door closed, and she shot her arm out to keep that panel—one heavy piece of wood between her and disaster—from closing in her face.

"I am here for employment," she said, a strident edge creeping into her voice. "I have an appointment."

The stranger stared at her appraisingly with that same deadened expression. For a moment, she thought he'd knock her arm out of the way and bolt the door behind him. Shoving to her feet, she angled her shoulder, prepared for such an act.

"Oi don't ken any meetings."

"Are you the proprietor?" she shot back, desperation making her bold.

At that challenge, he narrowed his dark-blue eye.

Eve drummed up a smile—that had little effect. Then, with her slightly crooked teeth, pale cheeks, and freckled nose, she'd never been one of those women who held even a hint of appeal for gentlemen. Unnerved by the stretch of silence and the increasing likelihood that she'd be denied that meeting, she contemplated the slight gap between the guard and the doorway. If she feinted left and then darted quickly right, she might be able to make it past him. *And then what?*

In the end, the decision to admit or not admit her was made not by Eve or the surly stranger.

"What is it, MacTavish?" The towering man with pale-blond hair had an accent better suited to a ballroom than a hell.

Eve eyed him curiously.

"Mr. Thorne," he said in his gravelly brogue, "says she's here to see Mr. Black."

Eve gave her head a dizzying shake. "*No.* I said I was . . . I *am* here for employment." That brought the gentleman's direct stare back on her. He took in her coarse brown cloak and aged bonnet. "The bookkeeping position," she hurried to clarify. "Not as a—" She promptly closed her mouth. The ghost of a smile hovered on his lips, setting her briefly at ease. Clearing her throat, she sank to the ground once more, damning the spectacles that blurred her vision, searching for the latch. It gave with a satisfying click. Not taking her eyes off the two hulking strangers, Eve fished around for the packet given her by Nurse Mattison and handed it over. *My name is now Mrs. Swindell. I am Mrs. Swindell.* That reminder was a litany in her head as the guard collected the sheet. From beyond his shoulder, the din of the club spilled out into the alleyway, near deafening.

Through the spectacles, she stared at the hard stucco wall, blankly feeling an eerie connection to the structure. This was one of the clubs that her brother had lost a large part of their family fortune to. The servants who'd been released and the villagers without proper roofs all went without because of the monies that had been lost in this very hell.

Mr. Thorne folded the page and held it out. "You were expected days ago, ma'am."

At that finality, her desperation redoubled. She stuffed them back in her valise. "I was detained." Because in her arrogance she'd believed there was another way. One that did not include stepping inside this hell.

"Peculiar arriving at night," he said with far more cleverness than she needed in this instance.

As it was a statement, she met it with silence and a smile. Then his next words killed even the hint of false mirth.

"Mr. Black is not here."

She wrinkled her mouth. *Well, drat.* "Do you know when he's expected back?" And what in blazes was she to do until he returned? Hire a hack in these dangerous streets and make the return journey to her brother's home? Eve shuddered. That was not an option.

"Not for at least four months."

Eve choked. "Four months?" Her mind raced. How had Nurse Mattison not known the head proprietor was gone?

"Mr. Dabney is acting head proprietor in his absence."

Some of the fear went out of her. It hardly mattered who was in charge of the Hell and Sin . . . just that she could see him, secure her post, and hide away here until her birthday. "Then, I'll see him." Eve's impaired vision did little to conceal the twitch of Mr. Thorne's lips. At her own audacity, her cheeks warmed. "Uh . . . that is to say . . . may I see him?" *Now.*

For a long moment, the two burly strangers before her didn't move. Then Mr. Thorne gave the other man a look, and the smartly dressed guard stepped aside.

Grabbing her bag, Eve hurried inside.

"If you'll follow me?" Mr. Thorne directed over his shoulder, then set the path through the hallway.

Despite Nurse Mattison's rightful insistence on a disguise, Eve pulled her spectacles off to take in her surroundings. Gold sconces played off the red satin wallpaper; the vibrant crimson fabric spoke of its cost and newness. Unlike the faded and torn walls in her own home. They reached a stairway, and he reached for her bag.

Automatically relinquishing the burden with a murmur of thanks, she climbed the stairs ahead of him and waited. Mr. Thorne gestured down a long corridor. Making the remaining trek to Mr. Dabney's offices, Eve took in the incongruities of this place. Gold-framed portraits of flowers served as unlikely adornment to the garish wallpaper, the harshness of it offset by the delicate pink-and-white poppies captured on those canvases. They were odd pieces to be featured inside any room of a gaming hell. What did it say about the man who ruled this empire?

Mr. Thorne guided her through the club and came to a stop at one of three doors in the hall. He knocked once, then pushed it open. Her gaze immediately landed on the tall, towering bear of a man positioned with his back to them. Not glancing back, Mr. Dabney held a silencing hand up. His attention remained trained on the task spread out on the George III oval kneehole desk before him. She swallowed hard. Even with his palms layered to the desk, and leaning forward as he was, Mr. Dabney was easily the tallest, broadest, and most powerful man she'd ever beheld. His muscles strained the fabric of his black sleeves and jacket, demonstrating a raw, primitive power that sent her sidling closer to Mr. Thorne.

To distract herself from his heavy silence, Eve did a sweep of the spacious room. With its heavy, dark-wood furniture and leather seating, it had the look of a nobleman's formal office in a Mayfair residence and not a wicked gaming hell in the most dangerous of London streets.

Full windows with sapphire velvet curtains, now drawn back, lined the space, lending it an open feeling.

Just like the halls of this establishment, so too was Mr. Dabney's office an incongruity that didn't fit with the picture she'd painted of him.

Straightening, Mr. Dabney cracked his knuckles. "What is it?" he asked, still not bothering to glance back.

She puzzled her brow. He spoke as one who knew the identity of the room's occupants, sight unseen. Which was impossible.

"Adair?" Mr. Dabney demanded, impatience heavy in his voice.

Adair—Mr. Thorne—favored her with a wink. "The bookkeeper you were to interview last week has arrived."

The head proprietor turned the page of the book he now skimmed, then flipped to another. "Tell him—"

"Her."

"She is five days too late." In a dismissive moment, Mr. Dabney dragged over another book and proceeded to attend that next task. Her heart sank to her feet. Yes, she'd needed time to gather false references and perfect her disguise . . . all details that she could hardly share with this man.

Mr. Thorne gestured for her, but she remained rooted to the floor. The proprietor of this establishment still couldn't deign to glance at her. Could not spare but a handful of moments to acknowledge her presence. That realization dulled the unease and fear dancing inside and replaced it instead with a simmering outrage. She pursed her mouth. "You've filled the post, then?" she exclaimed, ushering in a new wave of thick, tense quiet.

"Regardless of whether or not I've filled it"—Mr. Dabney flipped another noisy page—"signifies less than the fact that I'd never hire a bookkeeper who arrived not one, not two, not three, but five days late."

Touché. It was an altogether fair point from the stranger. Any other time she would have concurred with his assessment. "You forgot four."

Mr. Dabney's fingers stilled at the top of his page, and he drew his back up. "What was that?"

She winced. At her side, Mr. Thorne emitted a strangled cough. *Oh, double blast, I'm blundering this.* "I assure you my services will prove worth the wait," she said instead.

That brought the bear of a man's head up. Still not around . . . but up, and she took strength from the dent she'd made in his composure.

She was aware of Mr. Thorne's fascinated gaze moving between her and his employer.

"I suspect your . . . *reservations* kept you from honoring that meeting," Mr. Dabney rightly predicted, a droll knowing that raised a frown. Damn him, this insolent stranger, for being correct. Need he present it as a bad thing that she'd been wary about setting foot inside a gaming hell? "Rest assured, madam, I've employed two women before you who've proven the need for a person who'll not wilt because of their surroundings."

Wilt.

She'd not wilted when her brother had buried her head in water. She'd not wilted when the care of her father, and of all the Bedford holdings, had fallen to her. She'd not wilted when Lord Flynn had invaded her chambers and attempted to rape her. Despite what this gruff, emotionless man might believe, Eve was made of far sterner stuff.

"Despite the rather ill opinion you have of women, Mr. Dabney"— he stiffened and slowly wheeled to face her, and Eve had to force herself to go on—"I assure you, I've never been one given to wilt . . ." Her words trailed off, and she stared at the man before her. He had a deeply crooked nose, hinting at a significant number of breaks, set among rugged features. There was nothing she should recognize about him, and yet . . . Eve cocked her head and sought to place just why she should know those eyes of dark chocolate and that equally dark hair, given to a faint curl. Then her gaze slid to his mouth. To be precise, the corner of his mouth. That slightly raised, white scar that slashed through the right corner of his lip. With a point at the top of the mark, it formed a diagonal *T*.

In ancient times, tau was a symbol for life—or resurrection.

Of their own volition, Eve's eyes slid closed as memories of that long-ago night assaulted her. His blood on her fingers, her appeal to Gerald, and then the hatred in her friend Calum's eyes . . . *you bitch . . .* The earth dipped and swayed, and the spectacles slipped from her grasp. They landed with a soft clatter on the floor. She dimly registered Mr. Thorne catching her arm and steadying her.

She'd believed it hadn't mattered who was in charge of the Hell and Sin . . . only to be proved so wholly wrong.

For standing before her, resurrected from the grave and very much alive, was the boy she'd unwittingly betrayed almost seventeen years earlier.

My God—Calum.

Chapter 4

The woman would *never* do.

Nor had that been the immediate, initial opinion he'd reached. At first glance, with her tart tongue, Mrs. Swindell had shown some mettle. Mettle, when every other woman who'd held or interviewed for the post had cowered and blubbered at the pressure of the assignment.

His reservation did not come from the stench of vinegar and Cook's dinner gone wrong that filled his office.

Rather, it came from the same intuition that had saved his arse too many times for a cat to live through—and the spectacles. It was also the young woman's spectacles. The ones that had slipped free of her shaking fingers and now lay forgotten at her feet.

The woman was weak. More than a foot smaller than his own six feet, five inches, her cloak hung big on her, giving her the look of a child playing dress-up. However, it was not her diminutive size that gave him leave to question her courage. Calum had known children who'd demonstrated a courage some grown men didn't possess and knew better than to form opinions from a person's size or gender alone. This one, however, stood trembling and silent, just as she'd been since he'd faced her.

He flicked his gaze over her once more, verifying that he wasn't incorrect in his supposition.

She recoiled. That hideous bonnet, with its long brim sides of lace fabric plastered to her cheeks, obscured her face, but he'd wager his shares of the club that terror lined the woman's features.

No, she wouldn't last a sennight. And then he'd be precisely where he was now—without a damned bookkeeper for the ever-changing club he'd been attempting to put back together since Ryker had left. This particular meeting had already gone on—he glanced across to the dinanderie-faced marble clock on his sideboard—ten minutes too many. At the waif's unending silence, Calum looked hopelessly past her to Adair.

The other man held his arms up and shook his head.

Calum silently pressed him.

Adair jabbed a finger in his direction. "You," he mouthed.

Oh, bloody hell. Calum had never envied Ryker for being the majority holder of the club, but neither had he truly appreciated just all the tasks he'd so effortlessly undertaken.

"I wish you all the best," Calum said, letting her down as easily as possible. He returned his attention to the damned ledgers. It wasn't that Mrs. Webster hadn't been capable with the books. She had. She had also deuced awful handwriting that made a man's eyes ache. Calum attended those columns. It did not escape his heightened senses, however, that neither Adair's nor the late-to-interview-bookkeeper's footsteps had marked their movement out.

"Y-you wish me the best?"

Her breathless hesitancy there only solidified Calum's previous opinion and confirmed his decision.

He scrubbed a hand over his chin and forced himself back around to confront the confounded woman. "Indeed." For he wasn't a heartless bastard. He again motioned to Adair, who took several quick steps forward.

The young woman spoke, bringing his brother to a sudden, jerky stop. "I—I've come for the post—"

"It was an interview, and you failed to come for the intended meeting," he interrupted, growing impatient. Her tones spoke of a person who'd not grown up in the streets of St. Giles, and though Calum appreciated better than anyone the desperation that came in being without work, he also knew that if one's security rested on meeting the Devil at dawn, one arrived an hour early. He opened his mouth to order her out . . . but made the mistake of looking at her hands.

Those small, still quaking, heavily ink-stained fingers she wrung together. That telling gesture spoke volumes about her anxiety. He winced, hating that this particular task fell to him.

Goddamn it. So, this was why Ryker had always been best served as the head. Tamping down a string of curses, Calum jerked his chin once. Adair instantly dropped the worn valise in his hand and marched out. He closed the door behind him with a soft click.

That faint sound seemed to penetrate the young woman's reverie, for she wheeled around. Coming over, Calum rescued the forgotten wire-rimmed frames. His nose twitched with the pungent odor that clung to her. At long last, Mrs. Swindell glanced away from the door. She gasped and then tripped over herself in her haste to get away from him.

He grimaced. "Are you afraid, Mrs. Swindell?" he asked pointedly. Surely, she didn't believe she could ever hope to have any post in his club if she was driven to terror just by his presence alone?

The woman took another staggering step backward. Again, her frenetic movements and palpable fear served as a pointed reminder why she was better off not wasting either of their time.

"Sh-should I be, Mr. Dabney?" her whisper-soft question barely reached his ears.

Calum sighed. "I suggest you sit," he said somberly, and the diminutive woman lurched past him, quickly settling her shaking form in the seat.

He started over to her chair.

She shrank into the folds, darting her head left and right. Odd, she'd the look of one contemplating escape, and yet she'd fight him still for the post of bookkeeper. Wordlessly, he held out her spectacles.

Mrs. Swindell hesitated, then grabbed them from him. She swiftly buried them and her hands in the brown woolen cloak hanging from her frame. Covered in scars and larger than most men, he'd grown accustomed to most men and women avoiding his gaze.

Calum claimed the spot behind his desk. As a young man of the streets who'd had to stab, steal, and kill in order to survive, he'd once been a street tough deserving of the ruthless reputation he'd received. Since he and his siblings had secured a home and built a fortune inside the Hell and Sin, however, Calum had—with the exception of the nightmares that sometimes gripped him—put that way of life behind him.

Though he'd developed a healthy cautiousness of *all* people, he was also able to distinguish those deserving of his hatred from everyone else. After all, he'd once been on the receiving end of a ruthless cruelty that had seen him in Newgate and nearly hanged. Being the recipient of a person's fears didn't make one stronger. It didn't make one a leader. It just highlighted the inherent weakness in a person.

To set the young woman at ease, Calum layered his hands on the arms of his chair, and in a nonthreatening manner, he settled back in his seat. "I don't intend to hurt you," he said matter-of-factly.

Mrs. Swindell froze in her seat. What caused a woman such as her fear?

Then, with trembling fingers, she untied the faded satin ribbons of her bonnet and pushed it back.

At first glance there was nothing remotely pretty about the woman seated opposite him. The midnight-black shade of her hair stood in startling contrast to her skin, highlighting the paleness of her gaunt cheeks. No, with her pert nose, dusted with freckles, and her slightly disproportionate lips, she was hardly one who'd ever be considered any kind of beauty. And yet . . . the saucer-size brown eyes staring intently back at him held him, momentarily frozen and silent. Her full lower lip trembled, and she captured the flesh between her slightly angled front teeth.

Reminding him all over again just why she'd never hold a post inside his club. Hiring women given to fits of tears and terror had failed them twice before. He'd not waste any more of the club's time with another cowering one.

"I cannot hire you," he said bluntly, getting back to the matter at hand. Many depended on him. Hiring the wrong staff would be a failing to those very people and the security they relied upon.

She wet her lips.

"The men *and* women who work in my club are strong," Calum said with the same blunt directness he'd give to any family member or employee. Whether she was fearful of him or not, he had neither the time nor inclination to dance around truths. "They have to be," he explained. "When we've hired anyone who demonstrated signs of wavering, those employees invariably failed." Weak employees and high turnover resulted in disorder at the club, slower service, and weaker profits. A man couldn't save men, women, and children who'd been starving on the streets without those precious coins. "I would be doing you"—he gestured her way—"and myself a disservice if I wasted either of our time with an interview, when we both know you'll never belong here." Her fine, cultured tones were proof enough of that.

As if to punctuate the end of their meeting, a knock sounded at the door. "Enter," he called out, grateful for an official end to the *interview*.

The guard, MacTavish, who'd shifted over to Adair's previous role of sweeping the club, entered. "Lord T—" MacTavish slid his gaze over to the woman intently studying their exchange. "*Patron* caught cheating, my lord. Dealing from the bottom of the pile."

Desperate lords attempting to fleece the club was a familiar, and for it, welcome *trouble*. Calum would far rather deal with those mundane gaming hell woes than the peril they'd known over the years from the rival establishment and gang members.

Calum nodded. The cowering woman seated before him momentarily forgotten, he called out orders for MacTavish. This end of the work was familiar. Comfortable. Turning away Mrs. Swindell? Well, that was an altogether different matter.

And damned if he didn't feel like hell for being the one to turn out the waiflike woman with desperation in her eyes.

Her mind racing at the same rapid beat as her pulse, Eve studied the man before her . . . this man who for a fleeting while had been the only friend she'd had.

When he'd turned about moments—hours—a lifetime—ago and squarely faced her, Eve had nearly been bowled over by the truth of his existence. In her mind and in her frequent nightmares, Calum was still the boy who'd visited her family's mews, the boy who'd been bleeding, snarling, and cursing her as he'd been dragged off to Newgate their last night together. That same boy she'd considered herself a little in love with as a girl, so hopelessly fascinated by his strength and resilience. As a form of self-torture, she'd relegated him in her mind to the role of unaged fourteen-year-old, frozen in time. Only he hadn't died. He'd survived and grown into a bear of a man.

And he has no idea who I am . . . Even with the hatred that had burned from his eyes seventeen years earlier, she'd been just a girl. Why should he remember her?

Because in going to Gerald, you betrayed him, and he nearly died for it . . .

While he conversed with the man, MacTavish, she used his distractedness as an opportunity to study him. As a boy, he'd been strong. Taller than both her brothers, and more terrifying for the glint in his brown eyes. It had taken, however, just one meeting to see that even snapping and snarling, he was very much like the stray pup she'd used to sneak down and feed.

Almost seventeen years later, there was a raw primitiveness to him that sent her heart into a quick double-time rhythm. Time had lent muscle, height, and strength to him. Broad of shoulders, and easily a half a foot taller than he was when they'd last met, he had the look of that all-powerful Zeus, doling out decisions and rulings for the mere mortals who set foot inside his world.

Only, his world was not the cold, dank streets of London, or Night's now aged and barren stall. It was the Hell and Sin. A successful gaming hell that had seen lesser men bankrupt.

Men like Eve's wastrel brother.

It was no doubt fate's ultimate vindication that they'd lost a large portion of their fortune to the man Gerald had hauled off by a constable. And perhaps she was the disloyal sister her brother had always professed her to be, for she found a palpable elation in Calum's rise and Gerald's fall. Calum had survived. Eve touched her gaze on every corner of his office, taking in the elegant surroundings that exuded fortune and strength. Nay, he'd thrived. He'd taken ash and turned it into an empire.

Whereas she would hide, counting down the days until she inherited funds left her by her father. There was no honor in how the peerage lived . . . and she was included in their shameful masses.

And now you sit before the very friend you once betrayed, seeking sanctuary. Guilt stuck painfully in her conscience. For, God help her, she was that selfish that she'd fight Calum for the post of bookkeeper anyway. Because when presented with the option of betraying him once again, in order to save herself, the need to survive burned strong with a life force.

Shame made it difficult for her to draw a proper breath.

"Tell Adair I'll be down shortly to deal with the situation."

The other man nodded, then hastily backed out of the room. He closed the door in his wake, again leaving her and Calum alone.

"If you'll excuse me, Mrs. Swindell?" Calum pardoned, climbing to his feet. "I've matters to attend."

Eve remained in her chair. Fiddling with the bonnet given her by Kit, she found a soothing comfort in the article. Once again, she searched Calum's stoic, rugged features for a hint of knowing. The hard jaw, crooked nose, and sharp cheeks may as well have been carved of stone. Then, to him she'd been a child and he on the cusp of manhood. He'd not truly seen her—not in the way she'd secretly pined for him as a girl. "I understand your initial . . . opinion of me wasn't a favorable one," she began, then promptly grimaced. If only he knew how very on target he'd been. Just not for the reasons he suspected. "And given my failure to come 'round and accept the post, the conclusion you arrived at is not unmerited."

"Mrs. Swindell," he said impatiently, shifting on his feet, "the position was never yours sight unseen. Nothing more than an interview awaited you here five days ago."

Eve frowned. When her father was alive and healthy, matters of business had been left to both Mr. Barry and his man-of-affairs. Her brother Gerald had never bothered with those important dealings. How peculiar to find a man who not only oversaw his affairs but conducted his own interviews. "Then interview me now," she said, setting the bonnet down on her lap. She folded her hands primly before her. "I am ready now." Because the alternative was to return to Gerald's townhouse, where only ruin awaited.

Calum chuckled, a deep booming laugh that shook his chest, and it was a surprisingly mirthful expression, absent of any wryness or mockery. "I am afraid it does not work like that, Mrs. Swindell." Given her insolence and his own power over her, she'd expect nothing more than a droll reply from him, instead of this gentle honesty.

"But why?" she countered, scrambling forward in a flurry of noisy wool skirts. She quickly grabbed her spectacles and bonnet, before they tumbled to the floor. "Why mustn't it? You are the head proprietor. You are responsible for decision making. You can do whatever you choose." It was a luxury and power afforded him that she'd never known—and never would, if her brother had his wishes met. In fact, it was a luxury often denied most women. "You are free to do as you please."

His smile slipped, ushering in a pitying glimmer in his eyes. She balled her hands, despising that sentiment.

"Do you know anything about instincts, Mrs. Swindell?" She hesitated, and with that slight pause, he carried on, preventing a reply. "A dog will sometimes meet a man, and with no seeming reason, growl and snarl."

Eve puzzled her brow, attempting to follow. Had he just compared her to a dog?

"We're not vastly different from a starving dog in the street. If one listens to one's instincts, one is invariably proven correct."

"And you've so much experience in being correct?" she countered, the tart rebuttal flying from her lips before she could call it back.

Another one of those dangerous half grins that tripped up her heart danced on his lips. "I'm not concerned with the number of times I've been proven correct, but rather the one time I was proven wrong."

Another knock sounded at the door. "Enter." His booming voice echoed off the walls, and a familiar apprehension gripped her. He'd made up his mind, and this interruption sealed her fate.

The guard MacTavish stepped inside. "Fight's broken out on the floor now, Mr. Dabney, over the accusations of cheating. Threats of a duel."

He shoved back his chair, and she knew by the fiery glint in his eyes that she'd been relegated to the place of forgotten thoughts. "We are through here, Mrs. Swindell," he said, coming quickly around his desk. Calum shed his jacket and tossed it aside, displaying the rippling power barely concealed by the fabric of the blanket garment.

Her pulse skittered another dangerous beat.

"MacTavish, see to Mrs. Swindell," he ordered as the guard stepped aside, allowing him by.

And just like that . . . it was done.

She stared blankly at the metal clock behind Calum's desk and, to keep from giving over to fear, fixed on the rhythm of the passing seconds. *Now what?* Eve pressed her eyes shut. *Damn you for letting your own reservations about this place keep you from the security to be found here.* She'd allowed her aversion to anything and everything related to those clubs her brother lost monies at to overcome her need for security. After all, what better place would there have been to hide than in this hell? It would be the last place her brother or Lord Flynn would ever suspect. In short, she would have been hiding directly under their noses.

You fool . . .

"Ma'am?" the guard's impatient query cut across her frantic musings and brought her eyes snapping open.

She couldn't leave. She—

Her gaze fell on those books atop Calum's desk.

Why do you have to?

That dangerous whisper slid around her mind. Smoothing her features, she forced a smile into place and stood. "Thank you for your assistance, Mr. MacTavish. If you could gather my valise." She pointed to the bag at her feet. He followed her gesture. "And my bonnet." With a spring in her step, she hurried to hand off the article. "I'll gather the books." *Now, which dratted books?* Racing her gaze over the surface of his desk, she settled for all six ledgers. Grunting over the weight of them, she met Mr. MacTavish's befuddled expression with another grin. "If you'll lead the way?"

"Lead the way where?" he blurted, eyeing the valise and bonnet in his hands as though he'd been handed Satan's scepter.

"My rooms," she said as though schooling a child. *How am I this calm?*

"Mr. Dabney didn't mention which ones would be yours."

"Oh, no," she said somberly. "He was concerned with addressing the situation on his floors. Mr. Dabney indicated I would be in the available room farthest from the gaming hell floors."

MacTavish hesitated for a long moment. His gaze did an up and down of her person, and through that suspicious search, she held her breath. And then—"Follow me, ma'am."

Follow me?

Not wanting to linger and risk him asking any probing questions, or worse, have Calum Dabney return and find she'd made off with his books, Eve hurried after him. What fate awaited a lady who stole from a gaming hell owner? Newgate . . . he could toss her in Newgate and return the favor. *Which he'd no doubt enjoy if he discovered my relation to Gerald.* Shivers iced her spine. He wouldn't. He couldn't.

With each step that brought her away from Calum's office and closer to her temporary rooms, her sense of victory mounted.

"Here we are," MacTavish muttered, and let her inside the rooms.

Eve blinked, struggling to bring the room into focus through the darkness. Eager to be free of his and anyone's company, she entered and found a nearby table. She released the burden in her arms. "Thank you, Mr. MacTavish. That will be all," she assured him, as he set down her bag.

"I can send one of the maids fer ya—"

"No," she squeaked, and then masked that high-pitched reveal with a cough. "I am quite fine. Quite capable of caring for myself." Which was only partially accurate.

Seeming as eager to be rid of her as she was of him, MacTavish rushed from the room and pulled the door hard shut behind him, leaving her alone in an inky darkness.

An eerie silence clung to the small chambers, the sound of it ringing loudly in her ears. Moving over to the bed set up at the center of the room, Eve slowly claimed a spot on the edge of the mattress. With the weight of the lies pressing down on her, she lay on her back and stretched her arms high above her. All earlier thrill of victory at escaping discovery and being sent out in the middle of the night receded, when presented with the reality of what she'd just done.

She'd purloined Mr. Dabney's books, lied to one of his burly guards, and commandeered rooms inside his private suites.

Eve slapped her hand over her eyes. "Think, Eve, think," she said into the quiet, the sound of her voice breaking the deafening still, somehow empowering. Calum Dabney had formed one opinion of her—one that was far from favorable. There was just one way that she might secure the post of bookkeeper. Her gaze, of its own volition, slid over to the stack she'd deposited at the front table. She slowly smiled, and with a renewed purpose, she jumped to her feet.

She'd at best a handful of hours before he discovered what she'd done.

Enlivened, Eve marched over, gathered the ledgers, and carried them to a nearby desk.

Not allowing herself to think of the second act of duplicity she'd committed against Calum Dabney, Eve pulled out the shellback chair and set to work.

Chapter 5

Not even twelve hours after sending away Mrs. Swindell, with her horribly unfortunate-for-a-gaming-hell name and odd odor, Calum felt like hell.

Only this time it was not solely guilt for turning out that faintly pleading young woman.

Seated at the breakfast table in the kitchens, Calum took a sip of his coffee and winced. Ignoring that sting of discomfort, he proceeded to read the front of the *Times*. Where most men attended those pages for the gossip contained within, Calum over the years had taken to studying them for their clients. A proprietor of any establishment was best served knowing when one of his patrons was on the brink of desperation. It always paid to stay a step ahead of them. He skimmed the useless stories and names, then stopped abruptly when his gaze collided with one familiar nobleman mentioned at the front and center of the page.

> The Duke of Bedford remains bereft at the loss of his sister.

Calum started. Little Lena Duchess. He'd not allowed himself to think of that girl in more years than he could remember. She'd be—his mind worked—nearly six and twenty years now. Pushing aside thoughts of her, he continued skimming through the article.

> His sister now missing for more than a week, the duke wears his heartbreak upon him at any ton function . . . The brokenhearted Duke of Bedford has vowed he will not rest until she is returned to him . . . Such devotion has also earned the notice of countless matchmaking mamas . . . None, however, who possess the fortune that gentleman requires . . .

Calum finished the article about the ruthless bastard who'd had him imprisoned all those years ago and the sister he'd now apparently lost. Devotion and heartbreak? From the Duke of Bedford? He snorted. There was a greater likelihood the Devil had developed a soft spot for mankind, everywhere.

"You look like hell," Adair drawled, bringing Calum's attention up. Tearing a piece of bread with his teeth, he waved the uneaten portion at Calum's swollen eye. As though Calum needed him to point out the injury in question.

Eating breakfast with the other guards who sat around discussing club business, Calum took care to not show that he also felt like hell. After his meeting with Mrs. Swindell, Calum's evening had been spent breaking up a fight between the once great fighter, Sam Storm, and a more than slightly insulting Lord Pemberly. "A fist to the face will do that," he muttered, shoving aside the paper. Especially one errant blow thrown by that skilled fighter.

Adair picked up his utensils and carved a slice of sausage. "Ah. I wouldn't know anything about that."

The guards seated around the table erupted into laughter. Allowing those men their mirth and ribald jesting, Calum took another sip of his coffee.

"Did you read that?" Adair asked around a mouthful of food. His earlier brevity gone, he nodded to the copy of the *Times*. "About Bedford," he clarified.

"I did," he said in even tones. Outside of the monies owed the Hell and Sin by that reprobate, Calum didn't give ten damns on Sunday whether the man had lost his sister or how society spoke of the dissolute bastard.

"It's all that's being whispered about at the gaming tables. Apparently, this is the reason he's been such an infrequent visitor here."

Calum snorted. "The only reason he's been visiting less is because he knows we're on the cusp of calling in his vowels." And anyone who doubted different hadn't been the recipient of that heartless Duke of Bedford . . . *I'll see you swing, you guttersnipe.* His gut clenched as the memories of that night flooded forward. He quickly shoved to his feet.

Adair looked up. "I can see to the floors," his brother offered, nodding at Calum's swollen eye.

Early-morn hours were the quietest at the club, when patrons slept off a night of excess in either their private suites or homes. Calum, however, wasn't one who deferred responsibility, and certainly not because he'd taken an unintended blow to the face. "I'm fine," Calum muttered. He lied. He felt like he'd been dragged facedown along the cobblestones of St. Giles. Lifting his hand in thanks and parting for his brother, and then the other guards, Calum started for the gaming hell floors.

Passing through the labyrinth of the establishment, he followed the winding halls that led to the gaming floor. Calum reached the quiet floors. The fragrant hint of cheroot smoke lingered in the air still, as it always did, the scent familiar and soothing for it. But for a handful of the most notorious wastrels, the tables sat empty of patrons. The scantily clad women who'd given up their posts as prostitutes for that of servers flitted about the hell, dusting the already-gleaming mahogany tables. Even with the quiet, his head pounded.

"I told you I'm fine," he said out the corner of his mouth.

Adair cursed and moved into position at his side. "How in hell do you manage that?"

"Skill," he muttered. He'd not mention that those street skills of using one's every sense had only been further heightened in the five days he'd spend in the bowels of Newgate prison. In those dark, dank cells, to keep from descending into madness Calum had focused on the squeak of rodents and the shuffling footfalls of ruthless guards. Fixing on anything but his own terror had kept him sane.

They fell into a companionable silence, both continuing their perusal of the quiet hell. A sharp bark of laughter thundered around the room from Lord Langley's table, only exacerbating the damned pounding in his head.

"I take it we are still without the services of a bookkeeper?" Adair put forward, breaking the calm.

Again, the wide-eyed Mrs. Swindell's visage slid forward, as did a damned guilt he didn't want to feel. After he'd suffered a knock to the head, he'd sought out his rooms, tended his bruise, and quite contentedly fell into a heavy sleep. He'd not had to think about the small creature with her wide, terrified eyes—until now. "Did you expect I would hire her?" he challenged, arching an eyebrow.

"You?" Adair snorted.

Calum looked over.

His brother flashed him a sheepish grin. "I thought you might," he admitted.

Calum scowled. A man was only as strong as other people trusted he was. The moment one showed any frailty, one's days in St. Giles were numbered.

"I said *might*," Adair reminded him.

Rolling his shoulders, Calum continued to scrape his intent stare over the hell. Calum wasn't Ryker Black—he had a sliver of a soul left—but he'd still not forsake his family and those dependent upon him to help a stranger. A stranger who also happened to arrive five days late for her interview, and who'd believed he'd ever hire a person for that important role sight unseen.

Adair sighed. "If it is any solace, I didn't want the task of turning her out, either."

No, that did decidedly not do anything to assuage the guilt.

"You interviewed her, I take it."

Calum gave a curt nod.

"All the while knowing you couldn't ever hire her. Not after failing to arrive for an interview, and arriving five days late, at the height of the action inside the club."

All correct. He gritted his teeth. Would his brother not let the damned matter of Mrs. Swindell, with her atrocious name and equally atrocious bonnet, rest?

He'd really rather talk of anything other than the quaking woman with desperation in her eyes. Calum knew desperation. It hollowed out a person's soul and filled one inside out with an icy dread. Just a glimpse of her after she'd pulled off that god-awful bonnet had revealed Mrs. Swindell knew a thing or two about desperation.

"Was she capable—"

He silenced Adair with a hard look.

"There is another candidate for the post scheduled for a meeting on Friday," his brother wisely demurred. "Mr. Cleverly." A vastly better name than Swindell. "If, in the meantime, you'd rather I oversee the task, I will fill in that role." Again. Just as Adair had after Helena had left the hell—first for a London Season, and then forever, when she'd become the Duchess of Somerset.

Even so, Calum considered the offer. Generously considered it. Alas, Adair had already served his time as bookkeeper, and filling in as head guard of the hell was equally as vital. "I'll see to it. You've enough with the guards." Calum cracked his knuckles. "We won't be without a proper bookkeeper forever." In the meantime, Calum would see to the task. He'd served as second-in-command to this club since it was purchased and established. To him, however, that role—regardless of who held the majority shares of the hell—had been of equal importance. A man was only as strong as the person at his side. It was why, when some men of the streets shut out the world and relied on only themselves for survival, Calum had not. His siblings had saved him too many times for him to believe he didn't need anyone in his life.

What mattered, however, were the people whom you entrusted yourself to. Calum had learned the peril of being lax. It had taken but one misstep. He flexed his jaw. And he'd nearly swung from the gallows at Newgate for that folly.

The guard at the entrance drew the door open, admitting a pair of patrons.

Elegantly attired in black satin cloaks and equally black hats, they might as well have been any other gentlemen inside the Hell and Sin. Calum thinned his eyes, honing his focus on just one of those nobles— Lord Bedford, with his eyes downcast and shoulders slumped. Fancily dressed gents approached the young duke and patted him on the back. The man's pathetic showing at feigned grief was worse even than a kid's Punch and Judy show.

If he were a believer in fate, Calum would have conceded that Bedford's sudden appearance was that lady's way of validating his silent thoughts from before.

"What is it?" Adair demanded. Then, when you'd hidden in dank alleys, utter silence the only barrier between you and discovery at the hands of men you'd fleeced, you became adept at knowing another person's thoughts.

Not taking his gaze off the Duke of Bedford, Calum gave his chin a slight jerk. "Apparently, the brokenhearted duke has nursed it sufficiently to spend some time here," he drawled, watching as that powerful peer moved through the crowd. With a day's growth of beard on Bedford's face and his cheeks flushed, only a damned nob would take his drunkenness for sorrow over a missing sister. "Keep a particularly close eye on him," he said, evading his brother's piercing stare. "He's in fifteen thousand to us." Triumph tasted sweet on Calum's lips just speaking those words aloud. He watched as Adair took himself off, and then, as stealthily as he'd picked pockets in the streets, he wove around the pillars and tables, his eyes seeing everything.

Calum's attentions, however, were reserved for one. The duke and his companion took up a spot at a roulette wheel, until now occupied by just two other members, and tossed down several coins. Desperate men were capable of desperate things, and there was a thrilling vindication in the reversal of roles they'd been dealt. The fact he'd set aside his quest for his *beloved* missing sister to wager away additional coin he didn't have here was further testament to his depravity . . . and not at all surprising to Calum. But then, the duke was one step away from debtor's prison, and Calum, risen from Newgate and now king of his own empire, was responsible for Bedford's fall. He continued to carefully watch him.

The irony was not lost on Calum. First, in order to feed his family, he had stolen the nobleman's fob. Now that same ruthless bastard willingly handed over coin and vowels for the privilege of sitting at Calum's tables.

How . . . odd. The man came here, never knowing Calum was the same boy he'd turned over to the constable and ordered to hang. Lord Bedford glanced around. His gaze fleetingly touched on Calum and then moved onward.

Or mayhap it was that in his conceit and pomposity, it was simply that he didn't care. Members of the nobility had long demonstrated that their own pleasures and comforts came above all else—including the starving children in the street. Most men, his own brothers included, wouldn't have rested until vengeance had been doled out to the duke. Calum, however, had not built a life on revenge. Rather, he'd found his strength and stability through rising up and taking from that man, and all those like him, in ways that were legal and vindicating. Calum's successes were triumph enough.

Thrusting aside musings about the Duke of Bedford, Calum quit the floors and sought out his offices. Until a replacement was found, the task fell to him. Other than the security on the floors, there was no more important task than overseeing the club's accounting. Reaching his office, Calum pressed the handle and stepped inside. The sun crept over the horizon, spilling orange-red light into his rooms. He fetched himself a brandy from the sideboard and then carried it over to his desk.

Calum blinked.

His eminently neat and tidy desk. Rather, his empty desk.

He blinked again, and yet the sight remained.

What in blazes?

Calum set down his brandy with a hard *thunk*. Liquid splashed over the edge, spilling onto the leather surface. He looked under the broad surface of the oval-shaped piece and, with quick movements, yanked out each drawer, searching. He'd received a knock to the head, but surely he'd remember moving his damned ledgers.

Settling his hands on his hips, he did a sweep of the shelving.

Gone.

Christ in hell . . .

The Hell and Sin had been infiltrated countless times in the past two years. From disloyal staff aiding their rival establishment, the Devil's Den, to their old gang leader Diggory and his wife attempting to bring actual harm to them. *It is happening, still . . .* Calum stomped across the room, thundering for a servant.

A moment later, a young guard ducked his head in the room. "Ya called, Mr. Dabney?"

"MacTavish," he boomed. "I want MacTavish." The last person whom he'd knowledge of being inside Calum's office . . . He froze. And Mrs. Swindell, who'd been cowering one moment and boldly insistent the next.

He pounded his fist into the wall. *Bloody, bloody hell. She's one of Killoran's.*

The door opened a moment later, and MacTavish rushed in. "Ya asked to see me, Mr.—"

"My books," he said brusquely, his voice calm despite the fury pumping through his veins.

The red-haired guard angled his head.

"My books are missing," Calum bit out, sweeping a hand over to the empty place on his desk.

Several creases lined MacTavish's brow, and he scratched at his thick mane of red hair. "Mrs. Swindell has them."

"Mrs. Swindell," he repeated dumbly as the man standing across from him confirmed his worst suspicions.

The burly man nodded. "Took them last evening—"

Calum unleashed a stream of black curses. With the murder and death of their rival gang leaders and a truce reached with the Devil's Den, they'd let their guard down too much.

"And just what did she do with my books?" he asked, straining to keep his temper in check. After all, this fell to him. When he'd stormed off to see to the fight on the club floors, he'd given nothing more than a vague order of what MacTavish was to do with the damned woman.

"Why, she took them to her rooms."

"Her rooms?"

The guard gave another nod, confirming Calum had spoken aloud. "What rooms?" he bellowed.

"The first available one farthest from the gaming"—Calum had already started from the room—"hell floors," MacTavish called after him. "Just like you advised."

Just like I advised?

A stranger had wheedled her way inside his club—inside his office—made off with his books, and even managed to secure a damned room with her ruse. *You bloody fool.*

The maids cleaning the floors hurried out of his path. Calum kept his gaze trained forward, questions whirring in his mind.

Who had sent her? She'd surely come at the bequest of Killoran. Who else, after all, would have want or use of their books and records? Though, previous breaches had shown the peril in failing to see the true enemy lurking.

Reaching the last room on the floor of the main suites, Calum threw the door open hard. The panel bounced loudly off the wood with such velocity that it came springing back. He put his shoulder up to keep it from hitting him in the face. And the second surprise of the day slapped him with another healthy dose of shock. From where she lay sprawled at her desk, Mrs. Swindell shot her head up.

She is still here . . . What in the . . . ?

Those saucer-size eyes, glazed with sleep and confusion, stared into his.

"Mrs. *Swindell*," he greeted coolly, stepping inside the rooms she'd commandeered for herself. Calum drew the door closed behind him and leaned his hip against it.

And waited.

Chapter 6

He knew.

Calum Dabney had determined that Eve was, in fact, the girl who'd once sneaked him food, and then on a night of fear, betrayed him in the worst way . . .

There was no other accounting for the burning fury in his eyes that scorched her skin.

Only—she puzzled her brow—all these years she'd believed he'd been hanged. Her brother Gerald had taunted her with the truth of Calum's death with a regular frequency, until she'd become a master of her emotion and deprived him of the tears that admission had always rung.

Calum winged a chestnut brow.

Blinking back the haze of sleep and confusion, Eve followed his stare to the stacks of books littered about the too-small desk she'd commandeered last evening.

And remembered.

Being turned out.

Stealing his books.

"Oh," she said lamely. "That."

With a languid grace that stirred warring parts warmth and unease inside her, Calum shoved away from the door. He started forward. "That?" he echoed back, his smooth, deep baritone rousing further havoc on her senses. It had the consistency of warmed chocolate but coated with icy steel.

Oh, dear. Eve forced herself to remain still as his long legs easily ate away the short distance between them. She really wished she'd risen on her own and at least had an opportunity to formulate a proper defense of her actions. Though, by the barely restrained glint of fury that sparked in his eyes, not a single explanation would be accepted. Still, Eve forced a smile. "Mr. Dabney." And with all the grace drummed into her by a sea of proper governesses and nursemaids, she climbed to her feet and executed a deferential curtsy.

"By God, I can't sort out whether you're insolent as brass or missing a brain between your ears."

"If I'm forced to choose from solely those two options? The former."

"Do you think this is a matter to jest about?" Calum swept his thick chestnut lashes, and the dark brown of his irises disappeared. Eve's breath caught. And she'd never been one of those breath-catching-type ladies. She was practical and logical, with her life so focused on surviving that she'd not noticed the small, but beautiful details around her—like Calum Dabney's eyelashes. It was a silly thing to note, for any number of reasons. Reason one: with her theft of his books and her setting up a room in his private suites, he could return the cruelty her family had done him and send her off to Newgate. Two: she was one order away from being tossed out, with no place to go . . . but home.

Yet, she'd noticed, and could not stop noticing. The breadth of his shoulders. The sandalwood scent upon his skin. His slightly hooked nose. His . . . twitching, wrinkling nose. "Well?"

Registering her own scent, that noxious blend of berries and vinegar, Eve warmed, struggling to call the question he'd put to her—and remembering. "It wasn't my intention to make light of your worries. I was merely stating that if given just the two options you present . . ." At his ever-cooling gaze, she let her sorry explanation trail off. "Yes, well, I apologize for that," she finished lamely. She couldn't very well go explaining that with the passage of time, with the absolute dearth of friends and family and eventually servants, she'd become rather inept at those casual conversations between two people. *You weren't always that way around this man . . .*

"Who sent you here?" he ordered, taking another step her way.

Unnerved by the steel in his dark-brown eyes, Eve stood and edged away from him. She'd sat beside him for hours upon hours each week over the course of a year. She'd been a child and he a boy on the cusp of manhood. But in that time, he'd never put his hands upon her. Life with Gerald, however, had shown her a decidedly ugly part of man's soul that had taught her enough to be wary. "I—I will gather my references." Eve rushed over to her bag.

"That isn't what I meant," he said tersely, staying her.

What had he meant, then? She fought back her worrying. "I'm here because I'm in need of work, Mr. Dabney," she answered truthfully.

He snorted. "And you expect that lying to my staff, stealing my ledgers, and commandeering my rooms will earn you a rightful post inside my club?"

"I suppose, no, when you say it like that," she demurred. A strand of hair—albeit dyed black and unfamiliar for it—tugged free of her now lopsided chignon. She tucked the piece back behind her ear.

His lips tightened, turning down at the corners. That unique tau-shaped scar drained of color under the strain of his frown. "You have ten minutes to gather your belongings and take yourself off." There was a warning there she'd have to be deaf to not hear. She curled her hands tight, leaving crescent marks upon her palms. Why could she not have been one of those ladies clever with words and ready with a coy smile?

"A guard will see you out and to a hack, madam." With a death knell of finality to his order, he turned on his heel.

"Th-there are errors." Desperation made her voice quaver, and she stiffened, hating that hint of weakness.

Calum abruptly stopped. He didn't turn back, but neither did he leave, so she took heart.

Hurrying to the desk, she shuffled through the books she'd spent all her early-morn hours here sorting through and studying. She grabbed the brown leather book, a volume that contained the current month's expenditures. "If you look here . . ." Eve flipped through the pages, skimming, searching—and then finding. "H—*ah*—" A startled shriek escaped her when she picked her head up. Calum stood a mere hairs-breadth away.

In her surprise, the book slid from her fingers. She cursed and made a grab for the ledger, just as he shot his own hands out, easily catching it.

Their fingers collided, and an explosion of heat passed at that faint meeting of flesh. Her mouth went dry . . . and yet it wasn't fear that held her immobile. It was this perilous, unwanted awareness of him as a man. "Here," she ordered, reaching over and opening the book in his hand, then pointing to the eighteenth column on the page. Her breath emerged with far more steadiness than she believed herself capable of in this moment. "Whoever kept records before was stealing from you."

Calum opened and closed his mouth like a fish tossed ashore. "Let me see that," he demanded, pulling it closer until her hand slipped off it.

Finding normality in this familiar task, she leaned around him and tapped the book again. "There."

"Impossible," he muttered, shock and indignation rolled together.

Unlike her brother Gerald, Eve had never been one to revel in another person's misfortune or humiliation. In this instance, however, desperately needing the role of bookkeeper, she had been excited to discover that the woman to hold the post before was a thief. And being able to show Calum the evidence only served to highlight the beneficial role she could play here. Still, as Calum proceeded to frantically turn the pages, racing his gaze from left to right and then back to the left again, she took heart. "Anyone might have missed it."

"Everyone *did*." He cursed blackly, nearly burning her ears with the wickedness of that inventive phrase about the king's affinity for his mother.

Eve cleared her throat. "Yes, well, I am certainly glad to stay on"— *for three months*—"and assist you."

He leveled her once more with that burning stare that said she was mad and a lackwit, all at once. "Surely you don't think I'd go from employing one woman who deceived me to another who stole my books and rooms."

"I didn't steal your books," she said defensively. "They are all right here." She paused. "And for the most part, now orderly." She'd not had an opportunity to investigate his liquor accounts before exhaustion had weighted her eyes closed. "And I cannot very well steal rooms. At best, I could borrow—" Her words ended on a shuddery gasp as he dropped his brow close to hers.

"For a young woman desperate for a post, Mrs. Swindell, you are surprisingly insolent," he whispered.

If she were more in control of her faculties in this instance, she'd point out that she'd never been the insolent sort. A dearth of family and friends had left her instead with a startling-to-strangers ability to speak her mind. Alas, the hint of honey and coffee on his breath fanned her cheeks a surprisingly heady blend . . . and a surprising one from the harsh owner of a gaming hell.

Fighting to reclaim control of her wits, Eve wet her lips. "It is not my intent to be insolent. I'm d-direct, Mr. Dabney. You require a book-keeper." Hurrying around him, she rushed to retrieve the ledger he'd set down. "I require a post. Why need either of us dance around the mutually beneficial terms of a relationship?" He met her barrage with an imperturbable silence. His harshly angular features a set, stone mask that only showed but glimpses of the boy he'd been. *You have no right being here . . .* Thrusting aside the niggling guilt, she tipped her chin up. "I'm not asking you because I'm desperate." She paused. "Which I am. Rather, I'm urging you to do so because I am capable and qualified, and I'll not fail you." *As I did before . . .*

When moved to emotion, Mrs. Swindell's brown eyes came to life with gold flecks dancing in their irises. Her impassioned self-defense had turned her pale cheeks a becoming shade of red. The swell of Mrs. Swindell's bosom, pressed against the fabric of her silver dress, rose and fell with the force of her emotion.

And when she shed the quavering, terror-filled miss of the prior evening, Calum was left with the stunning, staggering truth— Mrs. Swindell, whom he'd taken for a homely and odorous creature, really was quite . . . *pretty.*

Oh, she still stank of vinegar and a peddler's fruit on the cusp of rot, but there was something intriguing about the slight tilt of her pert nose dusted with freckles and her high, elegant cheekbones.

It was not, however, that surprising appeal that most intrigued him, but rather her fearlessness. Every woman who'd held the post prior had avoided his eyes and only addressed him when spoken to. They certainly didn't prattle and issue tart retorts.

Mrs. Swindell cocked her head, dislodging a limp black strand over her brow. She shoved it behind her ear. "I take it you are considering it, then," she incorrectly surmised, beaming.

He'd been considering something . . . her, to be exact. Mad as that was.

He most certainly hadn't, however, been thinking of granting her the post—until the damned hopeful brightness lit her eyes. "No," he replied more for himself than anything.

The glow in her gaze dimmed.

Bloody hell. "Give me your damned references," he growled.

Mrs. Swindell froze, then sprang to movement. With a speed and grace to her small steps, she darted quickly over to the armoire in the corner of the room. A veritable Queen Mab of those stories his mother had told him, long, long ago. Disquieted with the reminder of the parents he'd not thought of in more years than he could remember, he trained all his attention on Mrs. Swindell. Kneeling beside her valise, she reached inside the gaping bag and drew out the papers. Wordlessly, she carried them over and handed them to him.

Unfolding the handful of velum layered together, Calum scanned the glowing references written on the young woman's behalf. It accounted for four years of Mrs. Swindell's life, and yet what had gotten her to the point that she'd needed to seek out work for a merchant? With her cultured tones and proudly set shoulders, the woman was undoubtedly a lady born. "What became of Mr. Winchester?" he asked, picking his gaze up from the top sheet.

She shook her head.

Calum held the page aloft, bringing her eyes to the sheet.

"He died," she blurted. "Or was dying. He was sick." At her prattling, Calum dipped his eyebrows, and her words faded to nothing. The lady dropped her gaze to her serviceable boots, the leather showing its age and wear. In his years on the street and then time running the Hell and Sin, he'd appreciated that a person rambled when they were nervous, hiding something, or afraid. What was Mrs. Swindell's story? Or was she simply a person with torn and tattered shoes, as desperate as he himself had once been?

Mrs. Swindell looked up and matched his stare. "He was a good employer," she said with a soft solemnity that could only come from a place of truth. "Loyal to his servants. Loving to his family. He treated me with fairness. It didn't matter that I was a woman. He saw me as capable." A shadow passed over her dark-brown irises, and a brief paroxysm of grief contorted her delicate features that not even the most skilled Covent Garden actress could feign. "He became ill, and through it, I oversaw his finances. Then he died and everything fell to . . ." She clasped her hands before her and looked away.

Calum shot a hand out, and with his knuckles forced her focus back to his. It was a bold touch. One he had no right making, and yet the satiny softness of her skin held him momentarily enthralled. Her lips parted, and a shuddery exhalation filtered between them. No doubt with fear. Enduring the torture of *ton* functions for the sake of his two siblings now married into the nobility, he'd become the recipient of nervous glances. Calum swiftly dropped his hand.

Only . . . Mrs. Swindell did not back away, rising in his estimation. "Everything fell to?" he urged, his command gruff to his own ears.

"His son." And just like that, all pain in her revealing brown eyes was lost to the burn of hatred. That seething sentiment Calum knew all too well. It was an emotion that burned deep inside and could be neither extinguished nor faked. "He was . . ." Her lips tightened in the corners. "*Is* cruel." He narrowed his eyes. "And so I left."

From most any other woman, that admission would have been given with tears in her eyes and a plea on her lips as a means to wheedle a post. Mrs. Swindell fixed him with a defiant glare. One that dared him to pity her and promised she'd take him to task should he do so. Another pull of admiration tugged at him, as did a simmering fury for the unspoken gentleman she mentioned. Calum had known his share of cruelty at those ruthless lords' hands. "Did he touch you?" With all the sins he was guilty of, harming a woman was not one he had on his blackened soul, and it was a crime he'd never forgive.

Mrs. Swindell hesitated, then gave her head a terse shake. She lied, and he only knew because he'd become adept at identifying a person who fed him mistruths.

Calum sighed and reexamined those names there, and then he looked over to the books.

The lady required work, and she had suffered at the hands of a cruel employer before.

Such a truth wouldn't have mattered to Ryker, not if the woman posed in any way a threat to those who lived inside the Hell and Sin. But Calum had never been wholly like Ryker.

His lips pulled in an involuntary grimace. Storm's blow to the head last evening must have rattled a few somethings loose in Calum's brain for him to be seriously contemplating allowing the young woman to remain on. It went against everything he believed in: intuition, the value of showing up when one was supposed to for a meeting, and his own good judgment.

So why, why when he'd always let his instincts drive his decisions, did he waver? Why, when the sole time he'd gone against the niggling of warning in his gut, he'd nearly swung for it?

Because you were her. You were terrified and scared. And she's desperate.

"Three women held this post before you," he said gruffly. "One of them was and will remain the best bookkeeper in the whole of England." His sister Helena's mind for math could have rivaled the best scholar in the world.

"And the others?"

Mrs. Swindell wasn't afraid to put questions to him. It was a mark in her favor, even if he'd sooner cut her in as an owner than admit as much. To do so would only show his own proverbial hand. "One you accurately pointed out was stealing from me." A small sum each month that not even Ryker had noted. "And who cowered whenever she was summoned for our meetings. And the other who also left this place in tears."

"I assure you, I'm not a lady given to tears." Spoken in that firm, husky contralto, he could almost believe it. He knew better than to trust too much a stranger fed him.

"Perhaps not," he said instead. By the slight pout of her slightly fuller lower lip, she took umbrage with his doubt. "But neither is this a merchant or gentleman's establishment," Calum bluntly informed her. "This is a gaming hell. It is a place where men get soused and lose their fortunes. It's a place where women fight for the coin and *pleasures* of a nobleman's attentions." Color bloomed fresh on Mrs. Swindell's cheeks, highlighting her innocence. "The man . . . or woman who holds this post isn't going to be coddled."

"I've no interest in being coddled. I take care of myself, Ca . . . Mr. Dabney," she swiftly corrected. If her cheeks turned any redder, she was going to catch them both afire.

Uttering his Christian name would bring this one to blush. Despite the severity of the exchange, he fought to suppress a grin. "It's also a place where a person doesn't go blushing because they use someone's given name." He stared at her pointedly, in large part because he wanted to know the one affixed to the spirited lady before him.

"Eve."

That was it.

One syllable. A name born of temptation and darkness and sin that conjured wicked musings of the slender miss before him.

Eve stared back, a piercing intensity in her thickly veiled eyes, and he forced aside those weakening thoughts.

He cleared his throat. "The responsibilities will include observing the gaming hell floors. Speaking with the guards and other proprietors. Visiting vendors and merchants we deal with on Lambeth." With every item tossed out on his perfunctory list, the color leeched more and more from her cheeks so that only the dusting of freckles along her nose stood out, stark in an otherwise white palette.

When Eve spoke, her threadbare voice revealed the same hesitancy of last evening. "O-observing the gaming hell floors." She captured her lower lip between her teeth and worried the flesh. And damned if he didn't feel a dose of guilt for reducing her to a worried miss. "Wh-where the patrons wager."

Calum looped his arms across his chest. "That is generally where gentlemen conduct their wagering, Mrs. Swindell," he said drily. He'd not spare her sensibilities by sharing that the one-sided glass windows that overlooked the floors would be sufficient for those observations.

Eve expelled her breath slowly through compressed lips. "I see." The lady rocked back and forth on the heels of her feet.

He puzzled at that two-word acknowledgment.

"I will do it," she said at last.

She would . . . ? With determined steps, Eve Swindell marched over to the door, and yanked it open. "If you'll excuse me, Mr. Dabney, I must see to my morning ablutions so I might begin my assignment."

Again, his lips twitched. "I wasn't offering you the post."

He may as well have run her through with the tip of her abandoned black pen for the shock there. "You weren't?"

"I wasn't."

"Oh." The lady leaned against the doorjamb.

Calum dusted a hand over his chin, warring with himself. *Trust your damned instincts. Trust . . . Goddamn it.* "It is yours . . ." The lady's eyes lit bright, and she propelled away from the door. "As an interim post." All the wind went out of her sails.

"Interim?" she repeated back.

"I don't trust people who lie to me, Mrs. Swindell," he informed her flatly. "No matter their reasons. A person capable of lies is capable of any kind of treachery." Their gazes locked in a silent, meaningful battle. The lady glanced away first. "But I believe you." *Against my own judgment.* Her eyes, teeming with surprise, flew back to his. "If you prove yourself loyal and capable, then I'll consider hiring you on permanently."

She fluttered a hand to her chest. "Thank you."

Unnerved by that breathy expression of gratitude, Calum jabbed a finger in her direction. "One misstep and you will be gone. Be warned, if you bring harm to this hell, you will regret ever crossing me. I intend to watch you. And if I see any signs . . . any hint of deceit, I'll make you regret the day you set foot inside this place. Are we clear?"

Did he imagine the brief hesitation and the fear in her eyes before she concealed all and nodded? "We are."

"Your first order of business is to review the club's records." He waved a hand over at the ledgers she'd begun work on. "I'll have the other books brought to your rooms until an office can be readied. You have a week to provide a detailed accounting."

"Three months."

Three months? "I beg your pardon?" Had the same insolent woman who'd maneuvered her way inside his club just put a demand to him?

"A week is hardly enough time to oversee all the accounting for an entire gaming establishment."

By God, she was bolder than any man, woman, or child he'd met in St. Giles. "And yet three months seems arbitrary," he drawled.

The young woman's expression grew instantly shuttered. "Three months," she repeated, firming her mouth.

Ryker would have tossed her out on her arse for that impertinence. Once again, Calum merely demonstrated how bloody different he was from the other man. "I expect the first report readied tomorrow morning, at six o'clock." Calum studied her for a hint of horror at that early hour and found none. "In my office."

"As you wish, Cal . . . Mr. Dabney." It was the second time she'd taken bold possession of his name. And there was something . . . familiar . . . something oddly right about hearing her wrap those two syllables in that husky timbre. Also, something that those instincts he'd been failed by only once told him spoke of danger.

Fighting another wave of disquiet, he started for the door. "Calum." At her puzzled brow, he clarified. "You may call me Calum, and I find, given the unfortunateness of your name, Eve is preferable to Swindell."

A poignant smile graced her lips and dimpled her cheeks. "Calum, then," she murmured in gentling tones, as though familiarizing herself with it.

And as Calum hurried to take his leave, he couldn't shake the damned niggling thought he'd committed a great folly in hiring the enigmatic bookkeeper.

Chapter 7

Eve's back ached, and her eyes hurt. Neither of which were attributed to the miserable spectacles Nurse Mattison had insisted she don.

She was fairly certain with the constant work she'd done on the Hell and Sin's ledgers, she'd be dreaming numbers until she drew her last breath.

But the following morning, winding her way through her new, temporary home, Eve felt a thrill of triumph. She smiled. She'd done it.

Not only had she secured work inside the Hell and Sin—albeit an interim post—but she'd also managed to complete the daunting, near-impossible task set before her less than four and twenty hours ago, by Calum. A task that she was more than certain he designed to see her fail.

As she'd explained to him in their meeting in her temporary chambers, Eve had never been one to crumble under the weight of a challenge. She'd not done it when her father fell ill, and then eventually died. She'd not done it when her brother had at last remembered her existence and sought to force her into an unwanted union. And she'd certainly not falter because of some numbers recorded on a page . . . no matter how important they might be.

Eve reached the end of the hall, squinting through her lenses at the main stairway. Even with her blurred vision she detected the slender, wiry guard positioned there. He gave her a lingering look.

She bowed her head in greeting and then made her way down the servants' stairs. In the privacy of her own company, she yanked off her glasses. Blinking to adjust to the dimly lit, narrow space, she adjusted her steps. The aged wood creaked, and she took note of those given to the loudest protest. As a girl who'd attempted to help Calum Dabney and only earned her brother Gerald's wrath, Eve had grown accustomed to hiding and making a quick escape. Silence was the key to survival. She'd learned that at Gerald's cruel hands. One never knew when one must make a quick escape . . . and this place—*especially* this place—was no exception.

Eve reached the bottom of the stairway and stopped. With all the enthusiasm with which she'd gone into her stern governesses' lectures, she perched her spectacles back on. She sniffed the air, ignoring the still-offensive odor that clung to her now black strands. Then, following the far more pleasant smells of molasses and cinnamon, she found her way to the kitchens. She entered, and the servants scuttling about all seemed to note her arrival at once. The noisy activity came to a jarring halt. "Good morning," she said with a smile. "I am Eve Swindell, the new bookkeeper," she clarified.

Apparently appeased that she wasn't someone come to bring harm, but uninteresting enough to merit further exchange, the men and women of varying ages resumed their work. Eve picked her way over to the pine trestle dining table, filled with dishes and baskets and oddly set with porcelain plates and lapis lazuli candlesticks. How singularly . . . odd . . . and very much out of place. Claiming a spot at the end of the table, she stretched her fingers out to touch the ornate gold vase, better suited to the breakfast room she'd left behind. She touched her blurry stare on the platters and platters of food. So very much of it.

"That's 'er ladyship's," someone hissed, freezing Eve's hand mid-movement. Removing her spectacles, she looked about and found a young girl with thick golden curls and heavily freckled cheeks glaring back. Flummoxed, Eve assessed the tiny slip of a child. She was near in age to the children Eve visited at the Salvation Foundling Hospital. Her plump cheeks were full, and her gown had a soft quality. Yet her language spoke of a child who'd also known strife on the streets. "Something wrong with your 'earing *and* your eyes. This is 'er ladyship's and—"

A boy close in age moved up behind her and nudged her in the side. "Ruby, she's the new bookkeeper," he said on a loud whisper. By the equal shock of golden hair, and handful of inches he had on the child, he was the older brother.

"Indeed, I am." Eve bowed her head. "I'm Mrs. Swindell."

The little girl snorted. "Lousy name for a gaming hell."

She scratched at her brow. Now the second person to point out her name.

The pair exchanged a beleaguered look.

"Ya don't know what that is, do ya?" Ruby accused.

"Alas, I'm afraid I do not." Eve motioned to the empty table. "Perhaps you'd keep me company while I break my fast and enlighten me?"

"It means you're a cheat, by the way." Ruby eyed her suspiciously. "Ya talk funny."

Eve merely stood in patient wait until Ruby and her partner settled into the seats opposite her. Gathering a napkin, Eve carefully unfolded it and then set it on her lap. All the while aware of the children following her every movement.

"Ya weren't born on the streets." The boy shot those words his sister had previously alluded to, in the form of an accusation.

"No," she conceded. She looked pointedly at him.

"Gideon," the girl supplied, earning a glare.

"Given that we're to share the same roof, it makes sense that we share breakfast." It spoke volumes to the lives they'd surely led that they continued to eye her with a healthy dose of skepticism. Carefully, and with deliberate purpose, Eve sliced up the still-warm plum cake and made three plates. Her father had once said, "A person could learn much about another person by the way they treat animals, children, and servants."

"Unless . . ."—she looked between the laconic pair—"the proprietors don't permit you to do so?"

Gideon scrambled forward. "There ain't no better man to work for than Mr. Black." He spoke with a vehemence and passion in his eyes, born of true loyalty. Not the fear her own brother inspired.

"Ya," Ruby piped in, sitting next to her brother. "Gave us a home and work so we didn't 'ave to go to one of those miserable workhouses."

Eve fiddled with her fork and watched her dining companions as they ate. How many lords and ladies failed to help the children suffering in the streets? Rather, they were content to call the constable and have them carted off, without ever sparing them another thought, as Gerald had done. "And what of Mr. Dabney?" she ventured, carefully presenting the question. Ruby and Gideon looked up from their plates. She was more than half-afraid the boy would snap and hiss and withhold any information about the man she'd once called friend.

"Wot about 'im?" Gideon demanded around a mouthful.

The boy reminded her much of the child Calum had once been. Snarling and hissing when she'd discovered him in the mews, he'd threatened to gut her if she didn't run off. Eve had learned long ago how to deal with skittish strangers. She picked up the pitcher and poured two glasses. "Is he as fair as Mr. Black?" she asked, presenting the question as a casual one.

"Not a fairer one," Ruby chimed in. "'e sees we 'ave beds, missus. *Beds*," she said on an awe-soaked whisper. "And food in our bellies."

So that was the manner of man Calum had become. He and the other men who ruled this gaming establishment gave shelter to children. As a girl, knowing nothing more than his first name, she'd been hopelessly enamored of Calum Dabney. He'd spoken to her not as though she were a duke's cherished daughter or a little sister in need of protecting. And he'd grown up to be a man who looked after those in need of nurturing. "I see," she said softly. "He sounds very kind."

"Not a nicer one. He . . ." Little Ruby's words trailed off as her brother stuck an elbow in her side. His faint whisper barely strained the level of audible. The girl rounded her eyes.

Furrowing her brow, Eve followed her gaze, casting a glance over her shoulder. Her heart stilled its beat.

For in the doorway stood Calum. With a newspaper tucked under his arm, he may as well have been any proper gent come to breakfast. That illusion was shattered by the seven hulking, menacing strangers at his back. However, her attention was not on any of those still-smaller, less-broad men, but rather the one she'd called friend. There was nothing, however, friendly, and only anything menacing about the glint in his near-black irises.

"Mrs. *Swindell*," he greeted.

Eve damned her fair skin prone to blushing. *Oh, please, say he didn't hear me quizzing two children about him.* She searched his stoic face. Yes, perhaps he'd not heard any of her discourse with Ruby and Gideon, after all.

Ruby nudged her under the table.

Her flush deepened. "Mr. Dabney," Eve returned belatedly, coming to her feet.

"If you'll meet me in my office. I'll be along shortly."

Well, drat.

She'd been talking about him. Putting questions to Ruby and Gideon, to be precise, which life had proved was invariably dangerous. If one sought information about a person, it was a sign that one needed to sleep with one eye open and a blade in one's hand because danger lurked on the horizon.

And yet why did he stand here appreciating the delicate sway of her generous hips as she made her way to his office? Watching, until she'd disappeared around the corner.

"Well, this is hardly regular morning business talk," Adair drawled in hushed tones, snapping Calum from a fleeting moment of madness.

His neck heated, and he shot his brother a black glare meant to silence.

Alas, this was Adair, and the moment one gave him an inkling that one had fallen to his baiting, he was worse than a starved dog with a bone. "You hired her?" Incredulity underscored that inquiry.

Mindful of the guards seated in the kitchen now taking their breakfast, Calum dropped his voice. "Temporarily." It was a weak defense, merely met with another shocked look. "She found errors in the damned books," he said, giving his collar a tug.

"Oh, it is not the fact that you hired the woman. Rather that you failed to mention the club is, in fact, in possession of a new employee."

Yes, he'd been remiss there. "I intended to speak of it over breakfast," he groused, feeling very much like a boy being scolded by a disapproving parent. And yet, Adair was entitled to the questions in his gaze. For after he'd granted Eve the post, Adair had been deserving of a meeting. Instead, Calum had assigned a guard to watch her rooms and delayed the discourse . . . until now. What he hadn't expected was a lady who rose long before any of the street-hardened men who lived in this club. "I granted the post as an interim one," he felt compelled to add, when Adair continued to scrutinize him. "If she proves herself capable and skilled"—and truthful—"then she can stay on."

Adair cracked his knuckles. "And if not?"

"Then, she'll be turned out." That truth came with a levelheadedness born of placing the club before even the desperation of a lone woman on her own. Calum looked over his shoulder to where Eve Swindell had made her exit a short while ago. "I've a meeting to evaluate the lady's reporting on the accounts. Speak to the men." He glanced to the two children now eating with the guards. "And everyone else inside the club. Let them know there is a new employee. Ask them to be looking for anything amiss or suspicious. If she sneezes even too many times, I'm to know of it," he ordered.

Adair grinned wryly. "You do know the lady merely arrived late for her interview."

Calum dropped his voice. "And secreted off the club books and seized rooms for the night."

"If she intended to gather our information for Killoran or anyone else, she would have made off with the books," Adair rightly pointed out. "Your feeling?"

At that casual question, his hand tightened reflexively on the paper in his hands. He gave a brusque nod. Life had shaped them each in different ways. However, Adair hadn't nearly swung for ignoring his instincts—Calum had. And the lesson had left an indelible mark of his own mortality.

Calum turned to go, when Adair touched his shoulder.

Adair passed a somber gaze over him. "Whatever decision you make, you have my full support," he said, his meaning clear. He trusted Calum implicitly enough to send a small, desperate woman out into the streets, without the security of work.

And this was where he and Adair had been forever different from Niall and Ryker. Their brothers lived their lives with a ruthless edge, where their small street family mattered above anything and everything else. They'd not have thought anything of turning away a woman who'd given them reason for suspicion. Calum, however, hadn't been born to the same life as they had. He'd been a failing merchant's son who'd still known a loving home and devoted parents. He knew desperation in a different way. Struggling to survive to one's suddenly changed circumstances. "Just be listening and watching. Instruct the others," he repeated, and started the trek for his office. He climbed the same servants' stairwell Eve had ascended a short while ago. When he reached his office, he silently opened the well-oiled door. And instantly found her.

The lady sat demurely at the foot of his desk, back squared, hands on her lap, gaze trained forward. The queenlike elegance of her position-ing highlighted the length of her graceful neck. Not for the first time, he wondered about Eve Swindell's story. He'd come to appreciate that people, regardless of station or birthright, all carried their own demons and darkness. It was what one made of it that determined a person's worth, however. He pushed the door closed until it made a near-silent click, lost to the ticking clock. "Eve." Her gasp exploded in the quiet, and she surged to her feet.

"I didn't hear . . . how . . . when . . . ?" She pressed a hand to her chest, and his gaze was involuntarily drawn to her small bosom, modestly constrained. But for the generous flare of her hips, there was nothing overly tempting about the lady. Not in ways he generally pre-ferred in the women he took to his bed. He hooded his eyes. And yet there was an allure of innocence and a hidden beauty that made her somehow . . . intriguing. Much like the sapphire he'd found nestled in the cobblestones outside Covent Garden.

"Please sit." Pausing beside his desk, he tossed his paper down and then made his way to the velvet curtains. Feeling the young woman's eyes on his every movement, he drew the heavy fabric back, letting the morning sun shine through the floor-length windows. A knock sounded at the door. "Enter," he called, fetching himself a brandy from the side-board. "Leave them on my desk," he instructed, not glancing back.

MacTavish's footfalls heavy in the quiet, and then a slight thump as he set the club's books down. A moment later, he'd gone. Glass in hand, Calum claimed his chair.

"How did you do that?" Eve blurted. "You didn't even look at him."

Among the many skills he'd been forced to hone in order to survive had been his uncanny heightened senses. "I'm clear-sighted." She eyed him suspiciously, adorable in her wariness. "There are also the windows," he pointed out on a secretive whisper.

She opened her mouth, no words coming out, and then whipped her gaze over to the crystal panes. Color tinged her cheeks. "Of course." He'd not point out that he also knew the distinct footsteps of each person in his employ. That every footfall was different, defined by a person's size, their shoes, and the rustle of their garments.

Setting aside his drink, he sat and dragged over the ledger on top. "What have you found, Eve?"

She opened her mouth to speak, but froze, her attention fixed on the contents of his desk. At her protracted silence, he followed her stare and frowned. "Eve?"

Jerking her head up, she met his gaze. "Y-your books are not as dire as I'd believed," she said, clearing her throat. Regret coated that admission. "Your previous bookkeeper stole in sum fifty pounds, from the liquor and wheat budget. Her thievery accounted for the mistakes in those records. But for several mathematical errors in the other books, she was largely proficient in her role."

"With the exception of stealing," he pointed out drily.

"With the exception of her stealing," she reiterated. Eve sank back in her seat and studied her clasped hands.

Collecting his glass, Calum leaned back in his chair and studied her from over the rim. "And do you believe I'll send you away for that revelation?"

Eve lifted her shoulders in a slight shrug and looked him squarely in the eye when she spoke. "Given your reservations, I'm not altogether certain what your intentions are for my future here." Where the two previous bookkeepers had been unable to meet his gaze and cowered in his presence, Eve Swindell was unapologetic in her directness.

"One learns to take security when and where one can find it for as long as one has it," he shared. That she didn't yet know that lesson indicated the sheltered life she'd lived before this one. "Worry less about how much time you'll have here, and worry that you are here for now." He raised his glass to take a drink when she spoke, staying him midmovement.

"That is easy for one who has a steady roof and security over his head to say," she said quietly.

"That is easy for one who has lived a life without both of those gifts to say," he corrected without recrimination.

She winced and swiftly darted her eyes from his . . . but not before he detected the guilt there. Feeling like the bastard who'd kicked a stray pup, he took a long drink. "I called you here to review your role and responsibilities, Eve." Not to move her to sadness. It was those damned eyes. Her damned large brown eyes that may as well have been a window into her soul, mind, and thoughts. "You'll oversee the ledgers, expenditures, and books. You'll meet me each Friday to review your work." It was a task they'd all been remiss in with the previous bookkeepers. "In addition, you'll be responsible for conducting meetings and reviewing our shipments with our liquor distributor and suppliers."

"And where do these meetings take place?"

From her question, he tried to make out sense of her thoughts or emotions but found none. "Primarily Lambeth. Chancery Lane."

She gasped, and the spectacles slipped forward, tumbling from her nose.

"Do you have a problem with those streets?" he put to her. Most any lady born to a respectable family would.

"Not at all, Calum."

The sound of his name wrapped in her husky contralto sent a bolt of lust through him. Hers was an unexpectedly deep voice for such a slender, small lady, and it conjured wicked words whispered in bedrooms.

Calum gave thanks for the desk that concealed his burgeoning desire. What manner of employer was he, hungering after a respectable woman newly hired on his staff, no less? He cleared his throat. "You'll have your own offices, separate from your chambers," he added, for himself as much as for her. "Anything you require to fulfill your responsibilities should be put as a request to me, or Mr. Thorne, the other proprietor." She nodded with each enumerated item. "Your payments will be made on the last day of each month." He paused, taking in her brown, striped silk taffeta. The faded garment showed its wear and age. He settled for, "In the form of two one-hundred-pound notes."

Surprise shone in her eyes. "Two hundred pounds? Each month?"

Unnerved by the reverent awe there, Calum shifted. That sum would have seen Calum and his siblings with food in their bellies for months and months. Instead of begging strangers in the street . . . or little girls sneaking around their family's mews. He started. Where had the thought come from? After Little Lena had turned him over to her brother, he'd taken care not to think of her beyond the lesson she'd given him. Uncomfortable with the intrusion of his past in his meeting with the stranger before him, he nodded.

"You'll be expected to spend ten of your hours each day working, but you may set the hour at which you begin. You'll have Sundays free. Do you have any questions?"

"No." Indecision filled her eyes. "Yes."

His lips twitched. Leaning forward, he dropped his elbows on the desk. "Which is it, Eve?"

"Yes. Not a question, as much a favor," she said quickly, her words rolling over one another. "Two of them, really."

"Just two favors?" he drawled.

She either failed to hear or acknowledge his dry mockery. "The first pertains to my funds. The funds you spoke of."

Calum settled his eyebrows into a single line. Surely she wasn't expecting more than he'd offered. He'd upped her wages by one hundred fifty pounds from the previous two who'd held the post. He set his glass down, waiting for her to put forth her *favors*.

"I know I've given you reason for suspicion, and I surely have no right to ask for a favor and expect you'd grant it, but . . ." The lady drew in a slow breath. "Would you be willing to advance me my first month's salary?"

As a rule, no one, unless their familial circumstances were in crisis, merited an advance. Advances made for sloppy workers and encouraged laziness. Time and experience running the Hell and Sin had proved that. When one extended a branch of generosity, invariably it was taken and turned to kindling. So why did he sit here, considering giving an advance to this woman—a stranger more than anything—who'd, as she herself had pointed out, given him leave to doubt?

"You might deduct a percentage from my future wages," Eve ventured. She was astute. Clever enough that she'd sensed his indecision.

She needed the funds. That much was clear in the way she wrung the fabric of her skirts and squirmed under his regard. He'd known Eve Swindell less than two days and already determined she was a woman of resilience . . . and some pride, which was why she hated putting the request to him.

He opened the center middle desk drawer, and Eve followed his every movement as he withdrew a leather folio and pulled out two notes.

Calum slid them across the desk.

Eve wet her lips and looked tentatively from the two hundred pounds lying between them, and then to Calum.

He gave a slight nod, and with almost reverent hands, she collected those notes. She caressed the edges with her long, ink-stained fingers, and by God, if he wasn't pathetic for envying a damned hundred-pound note for those attentions. *Bloody pathetic fool . . . What would your brothers say about you not only advancing a stranger funds but lusting after her?* "I'll not dock your future wages unless you give me reason to do so."

"Why would you do this?" she asked quietly, wonder in her words.

Uncomfortable with the adoration there, he grabbed his glass. "Because it is the right thing to do," He stared at her over the rim. "Unless you prove that it was the wrong thing."

"I won't," she assured him. "You'll find I am t-trustworthy." She stumbled over her words and promptly colored. "I'll serve you loyally while I'm here."

It was an honest pledge. One meant to assure him that he'd done the right thing in trusting her. And yet, in that handful of sentences, just three words gave him pause. The final three, tacked on the end of her promise . . . *while I'm here* . . . It was a statement that was telling.

Calum swirled the contents of his drink. "Are you intending to go somewhere, Eve?"

She froze. "It is an interim position," she said cautiously. "By your own words, I'm here as a temporary member of your staff."

Once again, she proved her quickness and cleverness. She also proved she was hiding . . . *something*. And while all people had their secrets and were entitled to them—every last man, woman, and child inside his club included—there was a layer of intrigue to the spirited Eve Swindell that he wanted to peel back. Secrets that he wished to know for reasons he himself did not understand. "What's the second?" At her perplexed look, he added. "Request you'd put to me."

She sat up straight. "Your kitchens produce a vast amount of food."

His lips twitched. "That is generally the purpose of the kitchens."

"I would ask that you permit me to donate the uneaten foods."

Calum's smile faded at the solemnity of both that request and the words themselves.

"There are *foundling* hospitals," she entreated, turning her hands up. "Children who have empty bellies, and I'd—"

"Fine," he said quietly.

The young woman opposite him parted her lips. "That is all?" she asked, her question heavy with bafflement. "You'd not have me make my case?"

Did she expect him to be a monster incapable of aiding others? But then, you hadn't given a thought to the very favor she'd put to you, until now. "Will the foods be put to use?"

She nodded.

"Then that is the extent of the case you need make." A glimmer lit the young woman's expressive eyes with such warmth, he shifted in his chair—unnerved. Bringing them back to safer talks that didn't involve that awestruck glint, he said, "Later this afternoon, when you're properly settled in your rooms and office, MacTavish will provide you a tour of the club. Tomorrow morn, he'll show you to the club's Observatory for our next meeting. You are free to go."

Her notes in hand, Eve rose with that ever-present grace. "Thank you," she said softly.

Dropping a curtsy, Eve started for the door.

"Oh, and Eve?" he called when she had her fingers on the handle. "Don't ask my staff questions about me." She stiffened. "If you have them, ask me yourself." He couched that rebuke in an unspoken warning.

Eve gave a nod and then left.

Chapter 8

The following morning, Eve stared at the bevel mirror of her temporary chambers. Her wide brown eyes stood stark among her even paler
than usual cheeks. He was looking for her. But one glimpse of that
page yesterday on Calum's desk had revealed that truth—he'd begun
his search for her.

What did you expect? That he wouldn't look for you?

She balled her hands. Gerald was in need of a fortune, and he would
not rest until she was located. And of all the places she could have gone,
she'd unknowingly chosen the home of Calum Dabney—the friend
she'd once brought hurt and suffering to. A man who'd not hesitated
to grant her an advance and who'd also, without any questions asked,
allowed her to coordinate deliveries of food to the foundling hospital.

Weighted by guilt, she briefly closed her eyes. She'd no right being
here. *What choice do I have?*

The truth rang clear—none. Eve had no options. None that were
feasible. With one brother missing and the other a reprobate who'd
sooner see her raped than happy, she was remarkably without help,
outside of that offered her by Calum.

"You don't have any other choice," she whispered aloud, needing to give that fact life. The needless reminder didn't drive back remorse.

Calum had now not only given her work and security but with no questions asked, had given her two hundred pounds.

And she was here on nothing more than a lie. She was the girl who'd betrayed him, and whose family had nearly seen him hanged. Yet here she stood, a recipient of his goodness. For there could be no accounting for why he'd done those things for her . . . a stranger, no less.

But they were also generosities he'd shown many others. Ruby's and Gideon's fine garments and comfortable lifestyle were proof of that. For the cold, painful life he'd lived on the streets, he'd retained his heart, and through it—his goodness. With the work she did in the foundling hospital and her father and Kit now gone to her, she'd begun to lose sight that there were men still capable of that good. Men driven by more than avarice, greed, and their own self-importance.

Eve smoothed her palms over her drab skirts. There was good she could do while she was here. She could keep his books, for the club he so loved, and on which so many depended. Nor would he even miss her services when she eventually left. After all, he'd already stated his intent and willingness to replace her—should she prove herself untrustworthy.

Which she had no intention of doing. She'd not betray his generosity.

"Any more than you already have," she muttered. Sticking her tongue out at her reflection, Eve grabbed the loathsome spectacles, then paused.

The damned spectacles she could not see a blasted thing through. It was really only a matter of time before the too-perceptive Calum noted her conspicuous habit of not wearing them. She studied the wire-frames in her hand. And, it was not as though he'd recognized her to this point. The spectacles were at best a flimsy disguise, ill thought by Nurse Mattison.

Taking care to avoid the hint of sound, she lowered herself to her haunches and settled the frames in the middle of one of the slats. She straightened and then, throwing her arms open to maintain her balance, lifted the heel of her right boot and brought it down on the lens.

Craaack . . .

A sense of satisfaction raised a smile as the shattering of that glass filled her room.

Eve bent and retrieved the pair. Plucking fragments of the lens free, she dropped them into the dustbin, and as she did so, her gaze caught the hanging clock on the opposite wall.

Three minutes to six.

A curse slipped out.

Bloody hell. Given Calum's avowal on the importance of timeliness, the last thing she needed to do on her second day here was arrive late to another meeting. Eve grabbed free the last shard, gasping as it pierced her flesh. The sticky warmth of blood immediately sprang free like that Icelandic geyser Kit had regaled her with tales of on one of his infrequent visits home. Her stomach revolted.

Oh, good God in heaven. Do not look at it . . . Do not look at it . . . Pressing her eyes tightly shut, she stuck the wounded digit in her mouth to stop the flow, gagging slightly.

A knock sounded at the door, forcing her eyes open. "J-just a moment." Her voice emerged a threadbare whisper, which resulted in another knock. "Just a moment," she said again, steadying her voice. Stuffing her spectacles inside her apron with her uninjured hand, Eve grabbed a small journal and a charcoal pencil and rushed to the door. Pulling it open, she stepped out into the hall.

"Mr. Dabney doesn't like to be kept waiting," MacTavish growled in his fierce brogue, by way of greeting. Not bothering to see if she followed, he led the way through the halls.

That ominous threat also provided a distraction—albeit a terror-inducing one—from her earlier injury. Quickening her step to match the guard's longer strides, she hastened after him. He brought them to a stop beside the last door on the floor, with a guarded entrance that led to a set of stairs.

Not bothering with a knock, MacTavish pushed the door open.

Holding her belongings close, Eve gazed about the wide room, immediately noting the large window where a wall should have been. It was not, however, that peculiar window that looked out to a ceiling lit with chandeliers that held her attention, but rather the broad, powerful figure who stood at the front. His legs slightly spread and his arms clasped behind his back, Calum had the look of a Greek god assessing the mere mortals who lay before him.

Her heart quickened with a dangerous awareness. When she, Evelina Pruitt, hadn't ever before noticed a single gentleman before. Not anyone who'd made her feel—

"You are late," he said, immediately quashing her racing thoughts.

"Forgive me." She cringed at the breathless quality to her words, praying Calum had not heard it. Praying that he'd continue in his offish way as head proprietor of his club and—

Calum turned around. Of course, the Lord had proved inordinately busy where Eve's favors were concerned, of late.

Now praying the dim lighting concealed her burning cheeks, she reached trembling fingers inside her apron and fished out her spectacles. "I broke my glasses," she explained lamely.

His gaze went to her extended fingers, and he narrowed his eyes. "You're hurt," he reproached, ripping out a white kerchief. Calum was across the room in three long strides. He snapped the fabric open. "Here," he murmured, gathering her injured hand. Since the day he'd been dragged off by her brother, Eve had been unable to look at a hint of blood without thinking of Calum. Those crimson drops had been reminders of his suffering and her complicity in what she'd believed had been his death. In this instance, there was none of the usual horror. There was simply . . . him. Tending her wound as she'd tended his years earlier. Little tingles radiated from where his larger hand encompassed hers. His grip strong, and yet surprisingly gentle in its tenderness, belied by the nicks and scars on his own.

Her heart turned over as she caught and fixed not on the now crimson-stained fabric he held to her thumb . . . but on one single mark marring his own skin. That faded scar, from a wound he'd received long ago. One she'd tended, in the same way he now returned the favor.

"Who did this to you, Calum?"

"And what will you do? Fight them for me, Duchess?"

As he pressed the embroidered fabric to the slight gash on the pad of her thumb, she stared at his bent head. The deep chestnut hue of his hair was a glorious shade, one she'd secretly envied him for as a girl of nine. Now a woman of nearly six and twenty, nearly seventeen years older, she was filled with a different longing. A longing to slip her fingers through those strands and explore whether they were as silken as they appeared.

He looked up, and their gazes collided.

She braced for him to step away and put a respectable distance between them.

Calum, however, remained rooted to the spot before her, unrepentant in his regard. A man in control of any moment he wished to command.

I should step away. I should remove my hand from his grasp and be the proper duke's daughter I was raised to be. She was wholly incapable where Calum Dabney was concerned. The sandalwood scent that lingered on his skin, wholly masculine, held her spellbound. How very different he was even in that regard from Lord Flynn and Gerald, who doused themselves in floral-scented fragrances.

Calum leaned closer. Eve's lashes fluttered, and she tilted back to receive his kiss. And there was no fear as there'd been with Lord Flynn. Only an aching, pressing need to know Calum in this way—

"There," he said with a matter-of-factness that had the same effect as cold water being tossed upon her head. "I believe it is stopped."

Skin burning at her girlish mooning, she swiftly directed her gaze to the hand still clasped in his.

And then reality intruded in, in a whole new way.

Nausea churned in her belly, and bile climbed her throat at those vivid crimson stains. *Do not be a weak fool . . . he is alive . . .*

Except, her mind cared not for the truth before her. It was grounded instead in thoughts of betrayal and treachery ruthlessly committed by her brother, and unwittingly conducted because of her.

"Eve?"

Calum's gruff baritone came as if down a long hall as she blinked, fighting back the dull humming in her ears. "You're afraid of blood," he said, as though he'd discovered another wonder of the world.

"I'm not afraid of blood, Calum," she managed to get out, past a heavy tongue. For she wasn't. She was horrified by the memories attached to the sticky, warm substance. Altogether different than simply being afraid with groundless reasons. Her fingers searched about for something with which to steady her legs, and she found purchase from the carved oak writing table.

"Sit," Calum spoke in tones suited to a military general. The scrape of wood upon wood indicated he'd dragged the chair closer.

Incapable of words, fighting to still her panic, Eve sank onto the edge. Closing her eyes, she concentrated on the rasp of her breath, inordinately loud in her ears . . . until it calmed, and stilled—and order was restored.

"Drink." Calum set a glass down on the tilted red velvet surface of his desk.

She gave her head a shake. Having witnessed her brother's cruelty after he'd imbibed, Eve despised even looking at a decanter. "I don't . . ."

"I said drink," he said firmly, and with slightly unsteady fingers, this time, Eve complied.

She took a small, experimental sip, grimacing as the aromatic bitterness burned her throat. What rotted stuff. What man in his right mind would ever willingly consume such a potent brew?

"Take another," Calum urged.

"I'm fine," she assured him.

"Take *another* sip," he ordered.

Eve complied, and this time the acrid taste was slightly lessened, so much that she took another. A soothing warmth suffused her chest, blotting out the earlier nightmares and replacing them with a pleasant calm. In control of her thoughts once more, Eve set aside the unfinished drink.

He eyed her with more concern than she deserved from this man, and she braced for questions and worrying that she didn't want. "You summoned me, Mr. Dabney," she reminded, deliberately using his surname in a bid to throw up a wall between them and drive him away from questions she couldn't answer . . . couldn't answer without revealing dangerously too much information.

Having protected himself since he was an orphaned boy of five, living first in a ruthless foundling house and then on the streets, Calum had become a master of diversionary maneuvers.

From picking pockets, to avoiding punishment at the hands of his brutal gang leader, to missing payments on the first hovel he and his siblings called home, Calum had perfected the art of evasion.

It was why he knew from Eve's use of his formal name and choice of language that she sought to deflect questions.

That attempt on her part also spoke to the lady's naïveté in matters of diversion. For with that curt, out-of-character reply, she'd only further stirred his wondering about her . . . and what brought her inside his hell.

I'm not afraid of blood, Calum.

Yet it was that weak pronouncement she'd uttered that whispered around his mind, calling forth memories of long ago, those same words, uttered with that same resolve. God, he'd not thought of the little girl who'd nearly sealed his fate in more years than he could remember. With time, he'd accepted that a child born of the peerage had first allegiance to her family . . . just as Calum did to his kin of the streets. And he'd buried away thoughts of Little Lena.

So, what was it about her that made him want to know more about Eve Swindell . . . for reasons that didn't have to do solely with suspicion? Because she had more pride than most men he knew, and he'd wager she'd sooner pick up a knife and make herself bleed once more before admitting that she'd been so affected by the gash on her finger.

Taking in the slowly restored color to her previously wan cheeks, he backed away from the questions he had for her and brought them around to the reason for their meeting. "Tomorrow, you'll meet with our brandy distributor. I'll accompany you, perform introductions, and allow you to discuss next month's shipment."

She wet her lips. "I—I'm to leave the club, then."

Was she eager to be free of this place? "That's generally how meetings occur," he said in droll tones.

The young woman glanced distractedly about, briefly dropping her stare to the copy of the *Times* resting on his desk, before returning her gaze to his. "And are these *respectable* streets?" she asked hesitantly.

He narrowed his eyes. Eve demonstrated the same reservations as the previous two women to hold the post before her. "Lambeth. If that is a problem, you're free to find another post," he said bluntly. He'd not waste either of their time with an assignment that wouldn't work for either of them.

Eve gave her head a dizzying shake. "No. No," she said quickly. "That is fine. Lambeth Street, you said?" Drawing forth her little journal and a charcoal pencil, Eve made a note in her book. Her fingers faintly trembled; however, when she spoke, her tones were even, and he gave a silent nod to that bid for strength on her part. "What time am I to meet him?" she asked, picking her gaze up.

I. Not *we* or *you.* There was a total ownership of the responsibility laid out, and Eve rose all the more in his estimation. When the former bookkeeper had discovered the less-than-savory location, she'd refused to go, pleading with Ryker to send someone else in her stead. For his earliest reservations in hiring her, it was hard to not acknowledge that she was a woman of strength. "Tomorrow at eleven o'clock. Immediately after, I'll coordinate a meeting between you and our wheat supplier."

Eve merely nodded and scribbled several more notes in her book. Businesslike. Professional. And damned seductive for it.

"Yesterday you mentioned I'd be responsible for visiting the floors." Whereas she'd initially demonstrated unease at the prospect, now she spoke with a calm pragmatism.

Regretting that he'd deliberately set her at unease the day before, he motioned to the windows. "This is the Observatory," he explained. He strode over to the clever glass panels that had been installed at his request and insistence at the inception of the club. "In here, you'll have free opportunity to assess the crowds, as well as the habits and behaviors of our clients." From within the window, he saw her climb reluctantly to her feet and make her way over. She hovered at the edge of his shoulder, that tentativeness at odds with whom she'd proved herself to be. What made Eve Swindell go from fearless challenger one instant to hesitant, silent miss the next? She was a conundrum that he had a dangerous yearning to unravel.

Eve lingered behind him, peeking out at the floors below.

Ah, so that was it. Not unlike the two previous women to come before her, she'd reservations about having any form of dealings with the men who tossed aside their fortunes inside these walls. "In here, you'll be able to observe them; however, those on the floors will be unable to see you," he expanded. "The windows were specially designed so that one side presents as a window and the other a mirror."

An appreciative murmur left her lips. "I've never seen anything like it." Eve drifted closer and pressed her uninjured hand to the glass, almost experimentally. Then, glancing about, she touched her forehead to the surface.

Her eyes formed round pools of wonder as the patrons, guards, and dealers below all carried on with their tasks. None sparing any notice to the two people now watching them.

"How?" she breathed, with the same reverent awe as Calum when the mirror-maker he'd commissioned had managed the feat.

Calum ran his palm over the pane, the surface warm under his touch. "The gaming rooms are brightly lit, and the Observatory is kept largely dark. Those lit rooms mask the reflection."

"Brilliant," she said, stroking her fingers beside his.

He followed the path they traced—the distracted but appreciative stroking that conjured wicked images of her graceful hands moving a like path over him. Desire humming in his veins, Calum forced himself to look out to the patrons mingling below.

"Whoever thought of such a thing?" she asked, angling her head up.

"I had the idea for them and interviewed numerous mirror-makers, many who couldn't understand what I was requesting, many others who said it could never be done, and one who asked for a time frame to have the project completed by."

She eyed him with some surprise. "You are an inventor, then."

He scoffed. "Hardly that."

"You're modest, Calum. Do you know how many items I'm responsible for creating?" With her thumb and forefinger, she formed a round circle. "So, do not diminish your accomplishments merely to circumvent any praise."

His neck heated, and he tugged at his collar. "They're but a handful of ideas, and all for the betterment of the club."

Brow creased, Eve peered out, searchingly. "What are the others?" she pressed, fixing on that first part of his statement.

"The pillars," he clarified, indicating the wide columns throughout the establishment. "There is a hidden handle, and in the event of emergencies on the floor, a person can open the latch and slip down a narrow stairwell."

Eve eyed those unused emergency escapes—his brothers had fought him on constructing them for the cost—with new interest. She wet her lips. "And have you . . . had need for one of those emergency exits?" she ventured.

She'd no place probing, and he had no place sharing with this woman, who was a suspicious stranger come to him just two nights earlier. Calum stuffed his hands inside his jacket pockets and rocked on the balls of his feet. "Not here," he confessed, the admission dragged slowly from him. What accounted for his sharing details with her, details she'd no place knowing?

"But somewhere?" She whispered the words more to herself.

She was astute enough to be dangerous. Her question brought Calum back to another night . . . to the man who'd indelibly marked Calum for his carelessness—the Duke of Bedford. Fiery hatred stung his veins as it always did when he saw or thought of or heard mention of one of their best patrons at the Hell and Sin. Even the satisfaction in earning his coin was insignificant when compared with the fears that powerful peer had left him with.

Eve settled her hand on his sleeve. The warmth of her touch, through the fabric of his garments, penetrated his dark musings. "Somewhere," he said at last, and in a bid to drive away the temptingly dangerous tenderness gleaming in her eyes, he gave her the darkest part of himself. "Newgate."

Her fingers curled reflexively on his arm, and all the color leached from her cheeks. She said nothing. And then it reached him, faint and hoarse with regret. "I am so very sorry."

Only this time, the mere mention of that hellish prison, which usually brought him to a cold sweat, only ushered in a need to assure this almost stranger before him. "I survived and I learned," he said reasonably, not elucidating.

At her silence, he glanced down. A lone tear streaked a path along her cheek, and the unspoken sign of her sadness gutted him. With the pad of his thumb, he automatically caught that drop at the corner of her mouth. "I thought you said you didn't cry," he whispered, lingering his finger near those bow-shaped lips.

"I don't. I haven't. In two years," she clarified, and that telling statement spoke to a period of suffering in her own life.

But God help him, as she spoke, his gaze remained fixed on her unconventional mouth—that thinner upper lip and plump bottom one—

I am lost . . .

With a groan, he covered her mouth with his. For a moment, Eve went tense in his arms, bringing her fists up against his chest, and that penetrated the incomprehensible lust he had for this woman. But then Eve twisted her fingers in his jacket and retained her hold on him. Angling her head, she opened herself up to his kiss.

Emboldened by the breathless rasps spilling past her lips, he explored the fascinating textures of her with first a tenderness and then, increasingly emboldened with a groan, he was set free.

Calum claimed her mouth in a ritual devoid of innocence, one meant to taste, brand, and forever remember. She panted against him, one word—his name—driving his lust to a blinding level. Gathering her buttocks in his hand, he guided Eve against the mirror and thrust his tongue inside to learn the taste of her.

She kissed with the same spirit she'd showed at their first meeting. Tentatively at first, and then she tangled her hands in his hair and angled her head, meeting his tongue in a primal dance.

Their breaths rose and fell in a rapid cadence as he searched his hand over her body, exploring her through the fabric of her wool gown. Wanting to strip it away and feel only her satin-soft skin against his. Calum shifted his attentions from her mouth, and she cried out in protest.

But he only trailed his lips lower, to the corner of her mouth, then over to the delicate lobe of her right ear. He captured the flesh and gently suckled, ringing a gasp from her kiss-swollen lips. Thrilling at the way her hips began to undulate against him, his shaft sprang even harder to life, and he continued his exploration by touching his lips to her neck, to that place where her pulse pounded.

"Calum." His name emerged as a keening plea, heavy with desire, and fueled his ardor.

"Who are you, Eve Swindell?" he whispered, his breath coming in a deep, panting rasp as he shifted his focus to her modest décolletage. Who was she that she'd make him forget his every principle on trusting his instincts, letting her in his club and his life?

Her only reply was a whimpering moan as she thrashed her head noisily against the window, clasping his head and holding him against the swell of her breasts.

Footsteps sounded in the hall, cutting across this stolen moment of madness.

He wrenched away from Eve. She immediately slumped against the wall. Legs slightly splayed, her gown disheveled, and her limp curls mussed, there could be no disputing just what they'd been doing. "What . . . ?" she rasped, befuddlement in her desire-hazed eyes.

Quickly guiding her about to face the hell, he hurriedly moved himself into position at the writing desk, presenting his back to the front of the room.

An instant later, the door opened.

He stole a glance at the window just as Adair stepped in. "A note's arrived from . . ." His brother's words immediately trailed off. And

Calum didn't even have to glance back, or look in the mirror, to note his brother's clever eyes assessing a still slightly slumped and flushed Eve Swindell. "Helena," Adair finished, stalking over. He placed the page down on the damningly empty surface of Calum's desk.

His skin pricked under Adair's piercing scrutiny. "That will be all, Mrs. Swindell," Calum said. Eyes averted, the lady tripped over herself in her haste to leave.

When she'd closed the door behind her, Calum's neck went hot, and that embarrassed heat climbed to his cheeks. By God, who'd have imagined he, Calum Dabney, guttersnipe turned pickpocket and gaming hell owner, was still capable of blushing? "What?" he groused, as with Eve's departure and Adair's recriminating stare, guilt settled hard like a stone in his belly.

"I didn't say anything," Adair pointed out, holding his palms up.

"You didn't have to," he muttered, grabbing the note from his sister, grateful for the diversion. Calum had kissed a woman in his employ. Not just any woman . . . a respectable lady whose kiss spoke to her innocence. And he'd backed her against the wall and wanted to drag her skirts to her waist, lose himself inside her. Breaking the seal, he skimmed the missive from Helena. All the while Adair's accusatory eyes remained fixed on him. As they should be. Calum wasn't a man given to forcing his attentions on an employee, and he certainly wasn't one to forget all logic and reason with a stranger he'd known but a handful of days.

Focusing all his energies on Helena's letter, Calum refolded it. "I'll need you to escort Mrs. Swindell to Lambeth. Coordinate her introductions with Carter and Bowen."

The window reflected Adair's casual stance as he tapped his index fingers together, studying Calum over the top. "And does this abrupt change of plans in your escorting the lady have anything to do with Mrs. Swindell's wrinkled dress and blushing cheeks?"

I'll be damned if I answer that.

When Calum said nothing, he smirked. "I thought so."

Ignoring his brother's attempt to needle, Calum held out Helena's missive. "Write Helena. Let her know I'll be 'round to visit Sunday morn." Notoriously the quietest times at the club, after gentlemen slept off a night of their depravity and maintained at least an artificial sense of civility and decency.

Adair stuffed the page inside his jacket. "Seems stronger than the two prior bookkeepers," he ventured searchingly.

He grunted, refusing to feed his brother's encouragement or curiosity. "She's a stranger." One he'd had against the glass windows, kissing senseless, moments ago.

"We were once strangers, too. Eventually we became family."

Calum didn't need him to point out tales of the bonds strangers could form. Having found his street family at a young age, he himself knew the strength that could be found in those connections . . . but also the peril. And there could be no doubting that with her inextricable pull, Eve Swindell was more dangerous than walking with one's pockets turned out through the streets of St. Giles. For his brother's seeming ability to make light of Calum's inexplicable draw toward the clever-witted lady, the fact remained there was nothing amusing about the entire situation involving Eve.

"See to the letter," he said, steeling that order with a finality meant to tamp out any probing. "Oh, and Adair," he called when Adair turned to take his leave, "let me know if the lady gives you any leave for suspicion."

Because even desiring her as he did, he'd be a fool to not be wary of a person new to their midst.

Calum dragged a hand through his hair. In the handful of days he'd known her, Eve had shown mettle that no other woman had ever demonstrated in his presence. Yes, she'd wavered and shown deserved fear at moments, as any sensible lady would . . . and yet she'd not backed down. She'd not been reduced to a blubbering mess of tears, as the last two bookkeepers had. Even the prostitutes, turned servants and serving girls, demonstrated a propensity for histrionics. Of course, it was natural that a woman of Eve Swindell's strength would have this maddening hold on his senses.

The truth still remained—lusting after a lady in his employ went against his every moral fiber. Acting on that hungering marked him the worst sort of scoundrel.

Regardless of this inexplicable awareness of Eve Swindell, she was a worker on his staff, and outside of that there could be nothing else with the lady. He steeled his jaw. He'd do well to remember that.

Chapter 9

Indiscreet servants could less than discreetly destroy a lady. It was a foolish adage her stiffly proper governess had ingrained into Eve's head early on . . . a reminder to always be cautious and on guard.

Now Eve saw that old saying in an altogether different light. One that reminded her a lady could learn much by simply listening to the men and women who knew the inner workings of a household. Or in her would-be case now—a gaming hell.

It was how Eve knew Calum had a meeting planned with his sister, the Duchess of Somerset, and when and where that meeting would take place. She'd even gleaned some of the speculation of what brother and sister would discuss.

Eve, however, had been far less interested in the personal discourse shared by a brother and sister than in the duration of said meeting.

From the elegant chambers she now called home, Eve stared out her small, lone window into the streets below. Just as she'd been staring for the better part of an hour. Calum was to visit his sister in Mayfair, which in and of itself was remarkable. One of her brothers, though loving and devoted when he was around, had spent the majority of his life traveling for the Home Office. Her other sibling hadn't had a use for her over the years, until their father had died and he'd seen the value in a match she might make. Calum, however, paid visits to his own sibling, and by the whispers of the servants, did so to discuss the overall health and business of the club. Her own father had never allowed her to touch a ledger or so much as discuss their estates or holdings . . . until he'd fallen ill, and Gerald had only turned the task over to her because he was too indolent to waste his time with anything that wasn't liquor, wagering, or whoring. Calum not only entrusted those meaningful tasks to a woman but also, by his servants' whisperings, valued and appreciated his sister's business acumen.

Then, that fit so very perfectly with the boy she'd known long ago. He'd not cared that she was years younger or an underfoot girl—as Gerald used to complain. Rather, he'd spoken freely the way he might speak to any boy or peer, and as a little girl she'd been hopelessly in love with him for it.

It was no less heady for her as a woman grown, still invisible in society because she'd been born a female. Her heart did a little somersault inside her chest, and she briefly closed her eyes. This appreciation and awareness for the man Calum had become was perilous. For nothing could ever come of them—not any relationship. Not even a true friendship. Nothing but lies had brought her here, and every day she remained in his hell, she perpetuated further falsehoods. A man who valued honor and respectability as he did could never—nay, would never—forgive those transgressions. Particularly not from the woman whose family had nearly seen him hanged.

No, had he gleaned her identity, he'd have more than likely tossed her out on her buttocks than kiss her as he had.

A kiss that had been the height of magic, wonder, and beauty. One that she'd secretly dreamed of one day knowing, while all the while giving up on hopes for that passion. Men were not attracted to a barely five-foot lady with a freckled nose and crooked teeth.

Calum had disproved something she'd taken as fact. He'd made her feel—for the first time in the whole of her life—beautiful. And he welcomed her opinions on his business and ledgers. She groaned and knocked her forehead against the windowpane. "You are a fool," she muttered as a litany, over and over. She'd not come here to lust and long after the proprietor of a gaming hell. Even a towering, broad, perfect specimen of masculinity like Calum Dabney. She'd come for shelter and safety, and she'd do well to remember that. Eve gave her head a hard shake and, thrusting thoughts of him back, opened her eyes.

And froze.

Calum collected the reins of his mount from a waiting servant.

Gasping, she jumped back and let the curtain fall promptly into place. She stood frozen, heart hammering wildly. Had he seen her? As soon as the thought slid in, she groaned. *I am rot at this subterfuge business.* It hardly mattered whether he'd seen her staring out into the streets. Why should he assume she was waiting on him to leave? Edging over to the window once more, she pulled the curtain back and glanced down.

Calum stood, his back to her perusal, and surveyed the streets. Periodically the liveried servant nodded. A moment later, Calum pulled himself astride and guided his mount onward down the street. She followed him until he'd disappeared from vision. *He is gone.*

It was what she'd been waiting nearly an hour for—the proprietor to take himself off for his visit so she might leave. Her stomach lurched, and she stared blankly out at the streets of St. Giles. "Go," she whispered, willing herself to move. And yet, for all her resolve to get to the foundling hospital and see Nurse Mattison, she could not bring her legs around to form a single, simple step. Instead, words splashed upon the front page of one of the *Times* swirled around her head.

. . . *the brokenhearted Duke of Bedford vowed he will not rest until she is returned to him . . .*

Eve pressed quaking palms to her face. *Do not let him control you in this . . .* He'd too much power over her. In the end, thoughts of that beloved nurse and the children at that hospital propelled her into movement.

Before her courage deserted her, she rushed to retrieve her cloak.

Shrugging into the garment, she drew her hood up and grabbed her reticule. With purposeful steps, she hurried to the door and let herself out. Taking care to use the servants' entrance, she made her way into the belly of the house. Every step taken sent her pulse racing and frayed her nerves. She held her breath, all but waiting for someone to jump out and demand to know where she was slinking off to.

Except, as she reached the lowest level of the club, passing servants engrossed in their tasks didn't even bother with a spared look. Clutching her reticule close, she used the side entrance. The guard, MacTavish, spared her a brief look, and she favored him with a forced smile. Wordlessly, he pulled the door open and stepped aside.

All the while, he eyed her with a flinty stare. Her cheeks warmed. Did she truly expect any other reaction from the guard she'd also deceived into showing her rooms and borrowing the club's books? "MacTavish," she said with a jaunty wave, feeling his eyes follow her as she picked her way outside.

Ignoring her greeting, he shut the door behind her.

She grimaced, imagining that her wave had probably been nothing close to jaunty. She'd never been one of those casual, demure ladies. Such skill, as her governess had called it, always eluded Eve.

Once she reached the end of the alley, she paused. The peril in being out here gripped her with a staggering hold. The hunted . . . that was what Gerald had made her, for in those copies of the *Times* she'd taken to reading, he'd the whole of London looking for the poor, cherished sister. Her gaze caught on a smartly dressed dandy strolling to the entrance of the Hell and Sin, and unwittingly, she drew her hood closer and huddled inside the worn wool fabric. Anytime she stepped outside the club, she risked being discovered by her brother. If she was discovered . . .

Her palms moistened, and drawing in a steadying breath, Eve borrowed support from the stucco wall. A brother who sent a friend to rape his sister, who buried that sister's head in a bucket of freezing water, was capable of evil and ruthlessness that her mind could never understand or anticipate. The terror and helplessness as water flooded her nostrils, choking off airflow.

And not for the first time since she'd talked herself into leaving the club and visiting the foundling hospital, fear, ushered in by her own cowardice, held her immobile. For having credited Gerald with being brainless in all ways that mattered, the truth remained that he was clever in the ways that could destroy a person. It was dangerous to visit the foundling hospital. Given everything her brother knew about her devotion to that place, and the likelihood that he'd think to search for her there, it was the last place she should go. *Go back inside . . . Nurse Mattison will understand when you return . . .*

Eve cast a long look over her shoulder, logic warring with her sense of right. *If you do not do this, you are as shameful and weak and wrong as you were all those years ago to Calum . . .* That taunting, niggling, and bloody accurate whispering in her mind slammed into her. Silently cursing, she whipped her head forward and scanned the streets for a sign of a hackney. Finding one stopped on the opposite side of the road, nearly twenty paces from where she now hid, Eve abandoned the safety of her hiding place and marched determinedly toward that conveyance.

She didn't know what she expected as she made an endless-feeling walk. For cries to go up at a sighting of the missing heiress? Instead, she reached the carriage without incident. From atop his perch, the balding driver flicked a dismissive glance over her brown cloak.

Reaching inside her reticule, Eve fished out a coin. "The Salvation Foundling Hospital on Lambeth," she said in regal tones that immediately sent the man scrambling to the ground.

"Aye, miss," he said, quickly stuffing the coin inside his jacket. He pulled the door open and helped her inside.

Moments later the door closed, the conveyance dipped, and they were rumbling on, and only then did Eve allow herself to sink back on the uncomfortable squabs. She dropped her head against the wall. Yes, it was folly visiting Nurse Mattison. Eve, however, was remarkably without choice. Eve's visits to that institution had been as regular as a ticking clock, and the monetary contributions she'd been able to make were vital. It was not just the nurse who relied on Eve's assistance with the record keeping and overall running of the fast-crumbling institution, but all the children who were unfortunate enough to find themselves alone in the world.

Just as Calum had been.

Her throat pulsed as she considered the snarling, starving boy he'd been. Taking scraps from her and shelter in her family's stables, he could have so easily died in the streets. Instead, he'd risen up and created an empire that provided work to men, women, and children. She absently rubbed her fingertips over her reticule where the two hundred-pound notes rested. How was it possible for a place to provide security and stability for some, but then destitution and hopelessness as it had for women such as Eve? Women who, by a chance of fate, found themselves dependent upon husbands, fathers, and sons for security and stability. And when those same gentlemen cared not for preserving those gifts, all that remained was fear and uncertainty.

This is what Calum's life had been like . . . As a girl, she'd witnessed his suffering and ached for his sorry state. As a woman, who'd been marred by her brother's failings and evil, she now understood just what Calum's existence had been like. The tangible fear. The helplessness. The sense of shame and regret in needing the gracious help of others in order to survive.

The carriage rolled to a slow stop, and she looked out the window. She'd arrived.

"We're 'ere, miss," the driver said, pulling the door open.

Before her courage deserted her, and reason won out, she accepted a hand down. "Please, see that you wait. There will be more," she promised, handing over another precious coin. She took a step and then froze. Her skin pricked with the feeling of being . . . watched. Huddling inside her cloak, she stole a look around, grateful for even the slim concealment of the garment. *Do not be silly . . . it is your fear causing you to see monsters in the shadows . . .* And with a courage she did not feel, Eve hastened across the street, climbed the steps of the foundling hospital, and slipped inside.

"Well?"

It took nothing more than his sister Helena's single-syllable greeting to determine that Calum's company had been motivated more by business than any polite, familial social visit.

Smiling wryly, Calum settled his large frame into the chair opposite her spool-turned desk. "Generally, visits usually begin with a *hello* or *good morning*," he drawled, stretching his legs out and hooking them at the ankles.

His sister removed her spectacles and set them down. "You've hired a bookkeeper."

"Unless you're you," he said drily. "Then, that is how a morning visit begins."

Rolling her eyes, Helena scooted forward. "Well?" she demanded again.

The former bookkeeper, she'd overseen the ledgers with a skill no one else had proved capable of and a meticulousness that was nearly unmatched. Having grown up in the streets, she'd had a sharp mathematical mind that had helped their family rise from the rubble and establish greatness.

"Well . . . I've hired a bookkeeper." He paused. "Again," he added for good measure, because it really did bear mentioning that since she'd gone and married the Duke of Somerset two years earlier, they'd been wholly incapable of replacing her.

Eve, as she'd been jabbing a finger in challenge at one of those erroneous columns, flashed to his mind. Or they had been unable to find a suitable replacement.

The scrape of Helena's chair as she dragged it forward slashed into his musings. She peered at him with a stoic intensity she'd always been in possession of. *What would she think and say should she discover that you had the new bookkeeper in your employ against a wall, and your mouth on hers?* Calum forced himself to go absolutely still.

After an interminable stretch, his sister reclined in her chair. "Who?"

He provided a brief detailing of the previous bookkeeper's flight and theft, and the subsequent hiring of Eve. Calum took specific care to dance around the details. When he'd finished, Helena drummed her fingertips along the immaculate surface of the desk.

"You were fleeced."

He sighed. Of course, she'd focus on that. As she should.

"We were fleeced," he pointed out. All their siblings were shareholders of the hell and in equal ways affected.

"Even worse," Helena chided, and he winced, realizing too late he'd stepped neatly into her trap. "If you require help, ask for it, Calum." She steepled her fingers under her chin and looked over the interlocked digits. "I expected as much from Ryker, not you." Yes, because Ryker had been the one of their loyal lot to shut everyone out from what he was thinking and worries he did or did not carry. Though he'd been a changed man since he'd married, Ryker was still proud as the London night sky was black.

And with his own loyalty, he'd not point out that Ryker had also missed the important details caught by Eve Swindell. "Regardless," he said uncomfortably. "I've since hired a competent"—if suspicious—"bookkeeper, and she is putting the records to rights."

"And you've checked her work?"

As much as he despised those books, he had. Countless times when the lady slept at night. "I have." He grinned. "I might even say she's more skilled than you," he teased.

His sister swatted his hand. "I'm not so arrogant and proud as a man who'd rather think he's the best, and not truly hire the best." No, she hadn't been. She'd been coolly logical and levelheaded. A perfect businessperson whose freedom had been deliberately sheltered away from the world by her blood brother, Ryker, which Calum, as well as Adair and Niall, had also agreed to, in what they'd felt was her best interest.

And then there was a woman such as Eve Swindell, on her own and making her way without the benefit of anyone to look after her, who'd proved herself wholly capable. Not for the first time, questions stirred about the woman who found herself inside his club.

"You never did explain how you came to find your Mrs. Swindell," Helena observed, then immediately grimaced. "A horrid name—"

"For someone inside a gaming hell," he interrupted. "Yes. I pointed that out to her."

His sister dusted a hand over her scarred cheek. "You told the young woman that."

He shifted in his seat. Calum had spent but five years in a respectable family and the majority of his life among men and women who spoke freely, without fear of offending. He wasn't one of those fancy gentlemen capable of pretty words and pleasantries. "For what it is worth, she was unfamiliar with the word as it pertains to gambling."

Surprise lit Helena's eyes. "So, she is respectable."

He opened his mouth to counter that supposition. And then closed it. Calum tried again, but no words were forthcoming. For—he frowned—given the opinion drawn, he was forced to acknowledge that by Eve's cultured tones and aversion to the gaming hell floors, she'd likely been of a respectable family. Having by her admission been employed by those powerful peers stood as proof of that. Yet, that was vastly different from being a member of the peerage. "She worked . . ." For some bounder. And whatever threat the man had posed had surely been a great one for Eve to seek out a post inside a gaming hell.

Helena quirked an eyebrow. "She worked . . . ?"

"On the record keeping of a nobleman prior to coming to the Hell and Sin," he settled for. There was something . . . wrong in sharing those pieces Eve had shared with another—even if it was his sister. It was illogical to let a handful of days knowing one woman in his employ supersede the lifetime he shared with the sister across from him.

"You trust her?" Helena put to him, the meaning clear in her words and in her eyes. If Calum vouched for the woman, then Helena trusted her as well.

His mouth went dry, and he tried to force the words out. Over the years, he'd prided himself on his cautiousness. That sense of wariness was one that had only truly come to him after the Duke of Bedford had seen him thrown into Newgate. Such a misstep was enough to make a man question every decision he made thereafter. However, then, his mistake in trusting a small girl of the peerage would have only cost Calum his life. Mistakes that would have repercussions and consequences on the men and women he called kin were far more perilous.

"Should I take that as a no?" Helena asked drily, and yet that question contained a hard edge that reflected her life on the streets and not her existence in these new exalted walls.

Calum cracked his knuckles. "You should take that to mean I've known the woman but a handful of days," he sidestepped. "And I'd hardly give anyone my full trust after such a brief time."

A knock sounded at the door, and they looked as one. The old, weathered butler appeared in the doorway with a silver tray and a note.

He came forward with his burden extended. Helena reached out, but the servant held the tray under Calum's nose.

He frowned and accepted the page. Skimming his gaze over Adair's familiar scrawl, he slid his finger under the red wax seal and unfolded the note.

As he read the brief contents, his frown deepened.

> You asked to be made aware of whether the young woman sneezed wrong. MacTavish discovered her taking a hired hack and followed her to—

Lambeth Street? What in blazes was Eve Swindell doing there now? "What is it?" Helena asked, bringing his head snapping up.

Schooling his features, Calum carefully folded the page and tucked it inside his jacket. "There is a matter of business that calls me away," he said, climbing quickly to his feet.

Helena instantly jumped up, revealing a belly rounded with child. "I want to meet her."

There could be no doubt as to the *her* in question. Her, as in Eve Swindell, who even now by Adair's note was hiring hacks and sneaking about Lambeth Street.

"You will," he promised, and turned on his heel. That vow was far less certain, given the suspicions roused this day by the young woman. Calum rushed through Helena's impressive Grosvenor Square residence and found his way quickly outside. One of the liveried servants stood in wait, with Calum's horse, Tau, already saddled.

With a word of thanks, he climbed astride and urged the black mount down the alley and out into the fashionable end of London. Cursing the crowds of bustling passersby, lords, and ladies, he carefully navigated the thoroughfare. As he rode, Calum focused on the steady clip of Tau's hooves striking the cobbles to keep control of the unease roiling around his chest.

Of course, he'd allowed Eve her Sundays. There was nothing untoward in her going out, and taking a hack no less. Except as he rode, and the fashionable ends of London gave way to the unsavory, seedy streets Eve sought out, something more than suspicion gripped him—it was fear.

Battling back the sea of panic, he urged Tau onward, faster through the streets, until the familiar ones of Lambeth pulled into focus. Calum frantically searched the less-crowded end, where MacTavish had followed the lady to. He did a search and instantly found the tall, burly guard. Cap down, head trained on the building in front of him, Calum swiftly dismounted. Reins in hand, he marched over.

"What is it?" he asked, as soon as he reached the other man's side.

"You asked if the woman gave me any reason to be suspicious," MacTavish said in low, gravelly tones. "Seemed suspicious, Mr. Dabney. Looking around. Jumpy. Found her sneaking down the alley. Went there." MacTavish lifted his chin toward the building across the street.

Calum followed his stare and frowned. A foundling hospital? He faltered. What business did Eve have inside that establishment? It did not present as an ideal locale for a nefarious meeting. A recent request she'd put to him echoed around his mind: *I would ask that you permit me to donate the uneaten foods.* Wordlessly, he turned over the reins of his mount to his guard.

"Went down to the side entrance," MacTavish murmured, gesturing to that portion of the building.

Eyes trained forward, Calum marched with purposeful strides to the white structure. He reached the side door of the building and, stealing a glance about, pressed the handle and slipped inside.

Drawing the door silently shut, Calum trained his ears on the sounds around him. The bustling activity in the kitchens, broken by an occasional order from the cook and intermittent laughter from the servants, showed that the staff remained focused on their tasks. Using the same skills of silence he'd mastered as a boy in the Dials, Calum crept along the hall leading away from the kitchen. He paused as he passed each closed door, listening for the muffled whisper of voices. Continuing on, he reached a stairwell.

Stealing another furtive glance about to verify there was no one lurking in the shadows, he started a slow climb. When he arrived on the main floors of the hospital, an eerie quiet rang within the sterile building.

He furrowed his brow. Mayhap MacTavish had been wrong. Mayhap he'd not seen the building she'd sneaked off to. After all, what business could Eve have here?

Distant voices reached his ears, followed by the sharp wail of a babe. Drawn to those sounds, Calum crept down the hall. He pressed his ear against each door he passed until Eve's soft, lilting tones—better suited to a lady of the peerage—met his ears. Her words were periodically followed or interrupted by the quiet, somber ones of an unfamiliar woman.

". . . you should not be here . . ."

". . . I needed to be here . . ." Eve's muffled replies moved in and out of focus.

The voices engaged in a frantic discourse that dissolved to a barely discernible whisper that he strained to hear.

". . . I cannot come back as much as I once . . ." Eve was saying. ". . . but Mr. Dabney granted permission to make donations of food, and I need to work through the details . . ."

". . . You cannot come back *at all* . . ."

"You need to hear this, Nurse Mattison," Eve spoke in strident tones. "The children are to be protected at all costs. All costs. Do you understand what I'm saying? If their safety is at risk . . . you must think of them before anyone and everyone else . . ."

Calum damned the heavy oak panel that swallowed the remainder of Eve's cryptic request. What promises did she make, and what obligations did she have here?

"Are ya spying?"

That loud, indignant voice piped across the quiet, echoing damningly off the halls. Calum swung about, and bloody hell in this humiliating moment of discovery did it feel a good deal similar to the day a child's carelessness had seen him hurled into Newgate.

A tiny child stared back, with a street-aged wariness better suited to a grown man than a boy of four or five. The shuffle of footsteps sounded on the other side of that door, and for a frantic moment built on embarrassment, Calum contemplated escape.

The door opened, and he looked past the tall nurse in white skirts to the young woman with ink-black hair, sitting, a babe on her lap and horror in her eyes. It was not, however, the fear and shock that held him riveted. Rather, it was the sight of the plump baby bouncing up and down on her lap. The child with thick gold curls and impossibly round eyes had the look of a cherub, and there was something . . . so very beautiful in the protective hold Eve had upon him. Hers was a tender embrace, fierce and gentle all at the same time. A thousand questions sprang, with all the answers only coming back to one obvious conclusion. *It is her child . . .* Was this boy the product of that scoundrel she'd only briefly alluded to?

The tiny boy's cooing, incoherent babbling—at odds with the thick tension blanketing the room—brought Calum reeling back.

"M-may I help you?" the nurse stammered, and in a remarkable show of bravery placed herself directly between Calum and Eve.

"A moment alone with Mrs. Swindell."

"Mrs. . . . ?"

He glanced to the older woman in time to detect the brief flash of confusion and then slow understanding.

Calum narrowed his eyes. She'd no idea who Mrs. Swindell was.

He held Eve's gaze. "Mrs. *Swindell*," he said by way of greeting, strolling uninvited past the befuddled nursemaid and deeper inside the room.

Chapter 10

Oh, God. He is here. Why is he here?

"Mr. Dabney," she greeted. How was her voice so steady when inside her panic mounted? He was a wall of immovable granite, unyielding, revealing not a hint of thought, emotion, or that he'd so much as even heard Eve. At the protracted silence, her heart threatened to beat a path right outside her chest.

"A moment alone, Mrs. Swindell."

The baby in Eve's arms squealed and yanked hard on her hair. Lightening her hold, she made soothing words meant to assure both of them.

Nurse Mattison wrung her wrinkled hands together. "That would not be appropriate. I . . ."

He quelled the woman with the flinty stare that had terrified Eve as a girl. Until she'd come upon him whispering to her horse, Night, one day and seen past the gruff facade to the gentle, kind young man underneath. Oh, how she adored that life had not left him that often-unsmiling, snarling boy.

"It is fine, Nurse Mattison," she said calmly. In her accounting of where she'd been, and why she'd not be able to return with her usual frequency, she'd also taken great pains to ignore mention of the Hell and Sin and the head proprietor who, with a mere look, could reduce her to a bevy of wild fluttering.

The nurse hesitated and gave her a meaningful look. One that asked questions and promised safety all at the same time. It spoke volumes of the woman who'd stand in opposition to one as fierce-looking as Calum Dabney. "Very well," she said tightly, and then she came forward, gathering Jamie.

The little boy immediately kicked and howled, reaching for Eve. Her arms felt empty with the loss of his familiar weight. Nurse Mattison lingered in the doorway a moment more, then pulled the door closed behind her, leaving Eve and Calum—alone.

As soon as the faint click echoed around the room, she stood and planted her hands on her hips. "You followed me," she charged, leveling that accusation at him. Dealing with her unpredictable brother over the years had demonstrated the advantages of taking the offensive. It unsettled and unnerved one's opponent.

Then, Calum Dabney was cut of an entirely different fabric than her wastrel brother. The powerfully built proprietor folded his arms at his chest and scrutinized her through those impossibly thick, long chestnut lashes. "I don't trust you," he said with such bluntness she flinched.

Hearing him voice that admission aloud ripped at her, and even as she wanted to rail at him for the unfair opinion he'd drawn, he was right to doubt her. It was hard to say whom she hated more: him for having judged her, or herself for the lie she lived in the name of her own security.

"Nothing to say to that?" he challenged.

"What would you have me say?" She set her chin. "I cannot demand your trust. I can only seek to earn it."

"Which you'll not do by sneaking off and—"

"Is this not the day you gave me?" she cried, hating that guilt lent a high-pitched timbre to her retort. "Do you make it a habit of following the other members of your staff about? Or am I the only one whom you chase around London?"

"I did not chase you," he said tightly, a dull flush staining his cheeks. "Furthermore, I've known you but a handful of days."

Eleven months, Eve thought. *You knew me for eleven months.*

He stalked over, and she quickly backed away. "And that is only after you failed to appear for your interview, then stole my books and commandeered rooms for yourself."

Her back bumped against the wall, forcing a halt to her retreat. That abrupt movement knocked loose a limp strand of still vile-smelling hair. She blew the bothersome tendril back. "I did not steal your books," she mumbled. Did she imagine the ghost of a smile hovering at the edges of his hard lips? Then a somber mask fell, driving back all hint of lightness.

"Is he your son?" he asked quietly.

As she was just an inch over five feet, most men, women, and some children towered over Eve. For the whole of her life, she had despaired over and despised her small frame. Until now. Now she gave silent thanks for the great disparity that brought her eyes into focus on his chest and spared her the intense scrutiny of his probing eyes.

Is he my son . . . ? Her mind tumbled to a slow stop as she fought to sort through that question. She widened her eyes. He believed Jamie was, in fact, her son.

"That is why you're desperate for employment, and why you needed the funds," he murmured, his voice a low, quiet rumble.

How neatly he'd assembled that puzzle. Only those were not the pieces of her life. She troubled the inside of her cheek. He'd crafted a neat story that explained away everything, from her seeking a post in the Hell and Sin to why she would periodically visit the Salvation Founding Hospital. *Yet . . . I cannot give him this lie.* There were already enough she'd perpetuated between them, all in the name of her security.

"He is not my son," she finally said, glancing down at her hands.

She looked up and found his focus trained on her. He didn't demand answers, or order an explanation from her lips, as her brother had been wont to do. Instead, Calum allowed her to disclose the truth of her own volition.

Needing some distance to order her thoughts, Eve stepped around him and made her way to the chipped and scarred desk. "Jamie is not my child," she repeated. "I've come here . . ." Since her father had died and she'd come to London. A pang struck. "For a number of months," she quietly settled for. "I visit with the children, and"—she gestured to the stack of ledgers—"help with their bookkeeping."

His eyes fell to the leather folders and folios. Joining her at the desk, Calum picked one up, as easily in command of this room as he was his own club. He flipped through the pages, working his gaze quickly over the columns and numbers. "The two hundred pounds wasn't for you?" He paused in his perusal and glanced up to meet her stare.

"No." She shook her head. "They . . . the hospital is in dire straits, and—" He snapped the book closed and set it aside. "And they needed the funds."

"So, you gave your own . . ."

Unnerved by the intensity of his gaze, she focused on stacking her books. How to explain why a woman in need of funds and employment had given up an entire month's wages? And yet, even if she did not have a fortune awaiting her in three months' time, she would still have offered over those monies to Nurse Mattison. Calum brushed his knuckles over her jaw, forcing her chin up. She gasped and abandoned her task.

"What manner of woman would give up all for the course of a month?" he asked, in an echo of her very thoughts. His was an alluring, husky baritone capable of pulling a lady's secret from her lips.

She lifted her shoulders in a shrug. "They needed it more than I. You've provided me employment. A roof over my head. Food to eat. I'm not so very selfish that I'd not in turn give that to those who would otherwise go without." *No, I'm just selfish enough to lie to the man my brother nearly ended.* "A person doesn't need more than the air to breathe, food in their belly, and—" His breath caught on an audible inhalation, and Eve curled her toes hard into the soles of her boots. Those words he'd given her long ago when she'd read to him from a child's book came forth too easily. Damningly. Wringing her hands in her skirts, she braced for the moment recognition settled in.

"Why?"

She frowned, meeting his gaze squarely. "I already told—"

"Why do you come here?"

His question brought her up short. What to say when *he* was the reason she'd found this place? That because of the pain she'd brought to him, and her need to see children spared from a life of begging in the streets, she'd sought out the foundling hospital? She pressed her fingers hard upon the table, draining the blood from their tips until they turned white. Someday, when she left him, when she was free of fear from her brother, and in possession of her fortune, she'd offer him up the truth. She would reveal who she was and give him the belated apology that would change nothing and could never right the wrongs committed by her family against him. Now she offered up the closest she could. "There was once a . . . boy I knew. I saw how he suffered and railed at the unfairness that he had been born to his lot and I mine." How fate, that fickle, capricious lady, must now laugh at their reversed circumstances.

"What became of him?" he asked quietly.

He became powerful and successful and wealthy beyond all measure.

"He died," she said hollowly, handing him the lie she'd believed all these years. "And I vowed that someday, when I was able . . . if I were able," she amended, "I would see that I helped others like him."

Calum said nothing for a long while. It was that contemplative silence she'd come to appreciate from him. How many lords and ladies filled voids of quiet with senseless ramblings? She far preferred Calum's thoughtfulness. He weighed his words like the finest coins, and he handed them over as though they were just as precious. "Those are your secrets, then, Eve."

She'd have to be deafer than a post to fail to hear the warning there. The unspoken question asked her to lay out the secrets she'd carried into his home and hell. Her tongue felt heavy in her mouth, and she tried to get out a proper reply. "They are." *Among others that would earn nothing but hatred from you . . .*

He caught her wrist in his hand, a touch surprisingly tender and gentle for the sheer size and strength of him. And given the brief time she'd known him long ago and the handful of days he'd been back in her life, she'd wager away the entire fortune awaiting her that this was not a man who'd ever lift his hand in violence against a woman. Unlike her eldest brother and the soulless reprobates he called friends.

"The life I've lived, Eve," he said quietly, "has made me cautious. I've learned to trust my instinct and to be wary of all that give me reason to be wary."

Me. He's speaking accurately of me.

"That is the reason why I followed you here."

The breath lodged painfully in her lungs, until her chest ached from the excruciating weight of it. He was explaining himself. Trying to make her understand. "Stop," she said in a rush as he made to speak. "Please, stop. You do not need to explain anything to me, Calum." He owed her nothing. She owed him everything, and yet had nothing with which to pay that could ever make anything right between them. "Truly," she beseeched when he made to speak again.

"Very well."

Very well. Surely it was not that . . . easy? She followed his movements as he dragged over a chair and claimed a place at her makeshift desk. His long fingers laid possession of one of those complicated ledgers, and she shook her head. What was he doing?

"What are you . . . ?"

"They need help. I expect it will be vastly easier with the both of us going through their books."

Eve clasped a hand at her throat as he turned his attentions to the book before him. His gaze made quick work of the page, and then he grabbed a pen. The scratch of that tip punched a steady beat inside that ledger.

After her mother's death, Eve had been largely invisible, with her father truly failing to see her until he was sick and wasting away, confined to his bed with no choice but to see her. Kit had been studying and then traveling, and ultimately gone to her. As cruel as Gerald had always been, she was better off that he'd failed to acknowledge her existence until just recently. Even though she'd been born to a family of once great wealth and still great power, through most of her life, she'd been largely alone. She'd relied upon herself and depended upon no one. And now Calum, who knew her as nothing more than a stranger, would give of his time to help not only her but also all those dependent upon the Salvation Foundling Hospital? A wad of emotion lodged in her throat.

"You'd give of your own time." He, a man who owned one of the most successful gaming hells in London, would take time from his own affairs for this?

Calum paused, glancing up from his work. "I'm not so very selfish that I'd not in turn give help to those who'd otherwise need it." He followed that earlier echo of her words with a slow wink.

A little laugh bubbled from her lips. As a child, she'd loved Calum for the friendship to her, a then-little girl who'd been so very lonely. And in this instance, a large piece of her heart chipped away and fell into his hands for the man he'd become. Smiling, Eve claimed the miserably stiff cane back chair opposite him, collected a book, and began to work.

Eve devoted her time to a foundling hospital.

She neither knew a child inside these halls nor had a familial connection to anyone else who worked or lived here, and yet she visited and sought to make better the lives of the children who called the sterile place home.

Calum stared blankly down at the columns.

I was one of those children . . . Only there had been no kind-eyed, protective nurses who watched over that institution, but rather merciless men and women who'd beaten children until they'd screamed themselves raw. As Calum had. The day he'd crept out of the miserable dwelling and into the streets of St. Giles, he'd vowed to never again set foot inside another foundling hospital. And he hadn't.

Until Eve. Until Eve had reminded him there were boys and girls who, by a cruel twist of fate, found themselves alone.

His stomach lurched, and he forced his hand to move as he went through the rote calculations. Except, guilt had crept in along with the past, and there was no escaping it.

When his parents had both fallen ill and died within two months of one another, Calum had found himself alone, without a single relative or familial friend to care for him. He'd fallen into the mercy of the streets, which even in his then-innocent and tender years, he'd quickly learned were ruthless ones that destroyed the weak.

So, he'd stolen to put food in his belly, and he'd killed for the right to draw another breath, and he'd all but bartered his soul to the Devil in order to live. Through it, there had never been a person who'd cared. Lords and ladies had kicked him out of the way and spit on him for coming too close. He'd learned in short order that no one cared about him. Certainly not the people of those exalted stations with their fancy speech. Instead, he'd found a new family . . . people who did care, but people who cared because they lived a shared experience. And in those streets, he, Ryker, Adair, Niall, and Helena had formed a bond greater than any connection he'd shared—even with his own parents. Lords and ladies of the peerage, wealthy merchants, members of the gentry—none of them had acknowledged Calum's existence.

You cannot die . . . You have the mark of life . . .

That child's voice of long ago whispered fresh around his memory. The pen slipped from his fingers.

"Calum?"

Blinking, he looked up at the woman hard at work across from him. Concern wreathed her features.

He'd not allowed himself to think of Bedford's sister, who'd betrayed him and nearly cost him his life. Mayhap it was the frequency with which that missing woman's name was mentioned now in the scandal sheets. But for the first time, he wondered after her. Whom had she become?

"Fine," he said succinctly. Unnerved by the intensity in Eve's brown eyes, he fixed his attention on the ledger. It was surely being in this place that had forced to the surface memories he preferred dead and properly buried. Only a man bent on madness and a life in Bedlam chose to focus on the darkest time in one's life. And with every sin Calum had committed and every struggle he'd endured, the time he'd spent in Newgate was greater than the flames of hell undoubtedly awaiting him. But for a brief time, there had been a member of those lofty ranks of nobles who had helped him. Who'd brought him food and read books to him, reminding him of his—until her, forgotten—love of literature. He'd not allowed himself to think of Little Lena Duchess.

"Who was he?"

It was harder to say who was more surprised by the question that left him.

Startled from her task, Eve picked her head up. "Who?"

Setting aside his pen, he rolled his shoulders. "You mentioned you began coming here because there'd once been a boy you knew?" he clarified. Muscles fatigued from the cramped position they'd been in for the better part of two hours, he stretched his right arm out before him, and then the left.

Eve's expression grew shuttered. "He was . . ." She glanced quickly about the room, putting him in mind of the wild cats who crept around the back of the Hell and Sin, wary of all who came near. "He was a friend," she said at last, laying her own black pen on the table before her. With fingers that shook, Eve fiddled with that slender instrument, adjusting it into a flawless horizontal line. "I'd been a lonely girl, invisible in my own household."

"No siblings?" he asked, filled with an urge to know more about the woman seated across from him. A woman who so fearlessly made her way in the world.

She held two fingers up. "Two brothers."

He scowled. "Miserable bastards?" he ventured, hoping she'd contradict his drawn opinion. Already knowing by her earlier admission that he was unerringly on the mark.

"One is," she said tightly. Her gaze took on a far-off quality, distant with so much pain he hated himself for having asked even a single question with his selfishness to learn more. She cleared her throat. "The other is gone."

Gone.

So much agony underscored those four words, his gut clenched. And yet, as she'd vowed at their first meeting, not a tear was shed. She jutted her chin out at a mutinous angle, daring him to offer empty words of condolence. Calum, however, had learned firsthand the value of knowing when to allow a person one's secrets.

Eve coughed into her hand. "Yes, as I was saying, through that loneliness there was a friend. One day he was just . . ." She turned one hand up. "There. It didn't matter to him that I was a bothersome girl, underfoot. It didn't matter that we were of different stations." There it was. The first statement confirming what Helena had predicted and

Calum had suspected, that Eve Swindell had been born to a respectable family. "He spoke to me as though we were equal in every way."

He'd known her but a handful of days, but with her clever wit, spirit, and determination, she was unlike any other he'd known before. Prior to meeting Eve, Calum would have said there was no braver, stronger woman than his sister, Helena. Even Helena had not survived without help of her kin. They'd all depended equally on one another in different ways. Eve, however, had carved out an existence of her own. It may not have been in the streets, and instead in the comfort of some fancy lord or lady's home, but Eve had no one else to rely upon. "I'd wager you're equal to none and superior to most."

Her lips formed a little moue, and such adoration spilled from her eyes, he shifted in his seat, uncomfortable with that show of emotion. Mayhap she'd ignore that statement that had spilled forth. Mayhap—

"You hardly know me. You . . . you followed me here because you don't even trust me."

Then, Eve was not one of those women who danced around her word choice and suppressed a question. He rested his elbows on the desk. "I'm an excellent read of character . . . but cautious, anyway," he said, lightening the sudden intensity of their exchange with a wink.

They shared a smile, and just like that, the casualness of her earlier telling was restored.

Calum and Eve fell once more back into a companionable silence, working away at their respective ledgers, when something she'd said crept in. He paused. "You have a brother."

Blinking, she glanced up. "Beg pardon?"

"You indicated that one brother *is* miserable."

Eve shook her head slowly. "No. I . . . I—you misheard me," she said quickly. Too quickly. Then, darting her gaze about, she retrained her attention on her work.

Her head bent over her desk, she gave every indication of being engrossed in her task. Only, he took in the tense set to her shoulders, the quiver of her hand as she splashed ink upon the otherwise immaculate page.

The same warning bells that had gone off countless times in his life, saving him from certain disaster, rang clear at the back of his mind.

He leaned back in his chair. "Eve?"

Her tightfisted grip on the pen drained the blood from her knuckles. "If someone intends you harm—a brother . . . a father . . . a husband . . ." He put that last, loathsome possibility out, hating the taste of the word on his mouth and hating more the idea there might be someone to whom she was bound.

She cleared her throat. "I assure you, there is no husband."

Some of the tension slid from his frame. "I would not send you away," he said quietly. "My family is a powerful one, and I could help you. If you need it." He held her gaze squarely. "If you trust me."

Eve stretched a hand out, covering his with her smaller one. He glanced down at her fingers, stained with ink, callused. They were the hands of a woman who'd been forced to work with her hands. Another mark of her strength and skill. "There is no one, Calum." She spoke in such even tones, with such a matter-of-factness, he may as well have imagined her earlier reaction. For a moment, it looked as though she might say more. To let him in on the secrets she kept. But then she picked up her pen and resumed her calculations. And for everything Eve had revealed to him this day, more questions lingered about the new bookkeeper.

Chapter 11

It had been a week.

Seven days had passed since Calum had followed her to the foundling hospital and sat down beside her to work on Nurse Mattison's worrisome books and records. In that time, he'd not only accompanied her back each day but also continued to assist her. And somehow, even with the impending threat of doom that hovered and the breathless fear of discovery, when she was with Calum, there was no terror or worrying about being found or harmed.

As such, given how Eve now worked tirelessly on the accounts for two establishments, she should be exhausted.

And yet, late that evening, with the early-morn hours looming and her work for the Hell and Sin waiting, Eve lay abed, restless, unable to sleep.

Her forearm draped atop her forehead, she stared overhead at the naughty mural painted in vibrant jewel tones. In the past, where she'd been riveted by the wickedness of that tableau playing out, now her mind ran amok.

"I'm going to hell," she said. Even spoken in quiet tones, those four words echoed around the room. Having given them life, however, did not make her feel any better. "Nor do you deserve to feel better," she muttered, flipping onto her belly. Dragging the thick feather pillow from its spot against the rococo rosewood headboard, Eve punched her fist against the satin pillowcase.

That soft, fine fabric was smooth against her palm, only highlighting just how generous Calum had been with her in every way. Groaning, Eve buried her head into her pillow.

Must he be so . . . so perfect?

A proprietor who not only hired women but also held them to the same high standards he kept his male employees to. Who would devote his time to overseeing the books of a foundling hospital, sacrificing his own time at the Hell and Sin? What manner of man did that? *Any* of it? Her father had been loving and kind while he'd been living, but neither had he given anything more than the occasional donation to local charities. And he certainly wouldn't have sacrificed time spent on his own business matters to benefit anyone else.

It is why Calum deserves the truth . . .

Restless, Eve turned onto her side and propped her head on her elbow. Staring out the lone window of her chambers, she considered the offer he'd made her that Sunday inside the foundling hospital. To his thinking, he'd known her but four days and vowed to help her should she require it.

He'll not be so generous when he discovers you're Bedford's sister. "If," she mumbled. For the kindness Calum had demonstrated to her and those at the foundling hospital, she could not be naive enough, trusting enough, to believe that he'd forgive both her connection to Gerald and her complicity that day long ago in the mews.

Eve rolled onto her back once more and stared overhead. No, the truth remained: with all the lies between them, the last thing Calum should or would offer Eve for that duplicity was help. This time she accepted the guilt washing over her.

Giving up on all hope of rest, Eve swung her legs over the edge of the bed and stood. The hardwood floor cool under her feet, Eve rushed over to the deep, carved Normandy armoire. She shed her nightshift, shivering as gooseflesh dotted her skin. Eve grabbed a chemise and hurriedly yanked it on. Then she collected another drab muslin gown. She pulled it overhead until it settled noisily at her ankles. She made to close the door but stopped suddenly as her gaze snagged on the inlaid mirror, the reflection that stared back more a stranger than the figure who'd fled Mayfair. The odor of her hair had faded slightly, but the strands remained as black as midnight. Her skirts revealed their age and wear.

It was no wonder Calum had not gleaned her identity. Not only had she been a child when last they'd met, but she'd also been an elegantly attired one, clad in only the finest silks and satins. Eve gathered her plaited strands and stared at that unfamiliar shade of hair against her white palm. How far a person fell. Yet, Calum stood as proof of how one who struggled might also rise up. And Calum, unlike the pompous nobles who wagered away their money on the floors below, had made his own fortune. Eve pulled on her slippers and, quitting her rooms, made her way to the offices Calum had set up for her—directly alongside his.

Nor did she believe that placement a mere coincidence. The fact that he'd followed her through the streets of Lambeth and his earlier admissions at the foundling hospital were proof that he'd misgivings about her as a person and her being here. He was right in those reservations, just not in the way he believed. She wished no ill upon his club—even if he and his fellow proprietors owned a large portion of her family's fortune. Gerald was to blame for those losses. Her only secrets were meant to preserve her own safety and security.

As she padded by Calum's office, the rumble of Calum's and his brother's voices from within carried out to the hall, bringing her to a slow stop.

"Attendance is still down . . ."

What Calum discussed with his brother did not involve her. She'd no place standing here listening at keyholes. So why could she not make her feet move? Eve strained to make out the remainder of Mr. Thorne's words.

". . . Profits are also d . . ."

Whatever Calum's reply was, however, was lost to the heavy wood panel. *His club is . . . suffering?* She furrowed her brow, contemplating those books she'd attended during her time here. The club's earnings from the month alone were enough to feed a small village for that period. Those facts stood in direct contradiction to the somber, rapid-fire discussion between Calum and his brother. Tiptoeing past his office to the next door, she quietly pressed the handle. Her eyes struggled to adjust to the dimly lit space. She collected an unlit candle from a silver candelabra and carried it to the hall.

Borrowing the flame from a lit sconce, she returned to her office. Eve went about the room, touching the tip of her candle to the candelabra. Replacing the white wax to its previous position, she picked up the fine silver piece and carried it closer to her desk, to where Calum's books now rested.

Eve snapped open the first book and set to work. Periodically, the loud rumble of Calum's baritone as he spoke with Mr. Thorne penetrated the wall.

". . . it is becoming increasingly clear we have a problem . . ." Mr. Thorne shouted, and Eve jumped.

She picked her head up briefly from her task, and when the voices on the other side of that wall dissolved to hushed, muted murmurs, she resumed working. Where certain people were born with an effortless skill, and tabulating columns and comparing monthly and annual reports came effortlessly, anything mathematical had always been a chore to Eve. It had been something she'd despised in the schoolroom. Her proficiency had been born of necessity. When her late father had taken ill and the Pruitts' accounting had shifted to her, Eve's entire life had become those records and books. Alone in the country when most women were making their Come Outs, she'd instead spent the hours she wasn't attending her father focused on the ledgers. They'd given her purpose and proved a distraction from the agony of watching her father deteriorating from his wasting illness.

However, just as they'd provided a diversion, she'd also detested those books. From the moment Gerald had thrust those responsibilities onto her shoulders, every other pleasure and joy she'd taken in life had become nothing more than an afterthought. Her love of literature. Those great Greek works. Astronomy. All of it had become nothing more than a frivolity not permitted for a woman on the cusp of financial ruin. For even with her brother's evil, and as much as Gerald deserved nothing but misery, just as men and women relied upon Calum and his club, so too did they depend upon the Pruitts.

". . . You need to send word to Ryker . . . explain we are in troub—"

Mr. Thorne's sharp tone brought her head back up.

We are in trouble . . .

She peered at the open pages, running her gaze back and forth over the columns. Surely things were not so dire . . .

"Focus," she muttered under her breath. *It's not your place to listen in on their exchange.* What Calum intends for you to know about the financial details surrounding the club are for him to decide. Except . . . Chewing at her lower lip, she stole a little peek at the wall dividing her and Calum's offices—it was hardly her fault that she'd picked up pieces of their discussion. The same curiosity her nursemaids had lamented would bring her trouble propelled Eve to her feet. Setting her pen down, she picked her way carefully over to the adjoining wall. She fiddled with the latch at the window and pushed it open. The hinges, in desperate need of oiling, creaked loudly in the silent room, and she abruptly stopped.

With the window hanging partially agape, Eve stood motionless, breath held. Distant shouts and the clatter of horses' hooves echoed outside. She focused on counting the beats of the clock atop her mantel, and when there were no fiery accusations from the room next door, Eve leaned her head out.

We are in trouble.

There it was. At last stated aloud by one of the proprietors of the Hell and Sin. It was a fact Calum had first feared and then known for too long. Now, with Adair having given those words life, it made them true in a way that sent terror knocking around Calum's chest.

We are in trouble. Acknowledging that they'd gone from all-powerful to even slightly vulnerable brought Calum back more than five and twenty years to the darkest moments in his life. Back to a time when he'd been a hungry boy in the streets, sleeping in back alleys and willing to trade his soul for shelter from the snow. How quickly he'd gone from being the beloved, well-cared-for son of a merchant to a street urchin, begging on the streets and eventually picking pockets. He'd learned firsthand how very fickle fate was, as evidenced by his rapid fall and then rise. The gentlemen who'd lost their fortunes and properties at this very club demonstrated that fact daily.

"You don't deny it," Adair accurately pointed out, pouring himself a brandy. He paused, then filled his glass to the rim.

"Why would I deny it?" Calum's gaze slid over to last year's ledgers stacked on his desk. "Not acknowledging the changes that have occurred will not make them go away. The Devil's Den has been bleeding our membership—"

"This is not all Broderick Killoran," Adair cut in.

Calum went silent. No, Adair was correct on that. While the other man seated across from him sipped his brandy, Calum contemplated that statement. They *had* been in trouble for a long time now. It had only *begun* with Broderick Killoran taking ownership of the Devil's

Den and slowly building up that club into an empire to challenge, then rival, and now surpass, the Hell and Sin. But even then, the Hell and Sin might have remained largely unscathed. There were enough wastrel lords for the two clubs to share.

"It might get better," he lied.

Adair paused, glass midway to his mouth. "It's gotten worse."

Yes, the nobility might freely visit a gaming hell run by former street ruffians. There were many crimes and sins those reprobates could forgive. What they'd not tolerate nor accept were the proprietors of the hell bedding and then wedding members of their noble ranks. Oh, when Ryker had inadvertently ruined and been forced to wed Lady Penelope, that had been a *crime* the lords had overlooked. Having been born the bastard of a duke, and then titled for an act of bravery, Ryker had—whether he liked it or not—ascended to their ranks.

To the *ton*, men such as Calum, Niall, and Adair were altogether different. It wouldn't matter to the peerage that Calum's parents had been married and his father a failed merchant. The world would forever see them in a like light: bastards risen from the darkest streets of London. Baseborn thugs and thieves turned club owners would never be welcomed within their midst. Niall's recent marriage to the Duke of Wilkinson's daughter was proof of that. Many of their once loyal patrons turned faster than the swiftest pickpocket making off with a fat purse. For with that union, the Hell and Sin proprietors had crossed an egregious line that could not be uncrossed—one of theirs had believed himself an equal and dared touch one of theirs.

And the worst of it was . . . Calum had no idea how to set this to rights. Calling Ryker back when his wife was due with their first child wouldn't solve their dire circumstances. Societal disapproval was not something that could simply be overcome. They'd worked countless years to establish their reputation and set themselves apart from the Whites, Brookes, and even the Devil's Dens of the world.

"Reinstating prostitution might—"

"Employing whores will not solve the problems we are having," Calum snapped out. At best, it would bring in one revenue and cost them another. "If anything, it will only hurt our numbers." After all, with Ryker's wife, a viscountess, living inside a gaming hell, and Niall's wife, when they'd returned from their travels, also calling this club home, the Hell and Sin would only earn society's further censure.

Grabbing a cheroot from his pocket, Calum stood and touched it to the sconce. He took a long pull, letting the smoke flood his lungs. Only, this time it failed to calm him.

Adair hooked his ankle across his knee and leaned back. "Given the increasingly dire situation facing us, you've allowed the bookkeeper an inordinate amount of time free of her responsibilities." A sharp rebuke hung on the end of that statement.

Calum's neck went hot, and he took another draw. He let the air slowly out, forming perfectly rounded circles. "Is that a question?"

His brother shook his head. "It's an observation. You were placed in charge—"

"Because I'm the second greatest shareholder," he reminded him. They'd all been skilled pickpockets, but Calum's speed and deftness had surpassed all his siblings. Had the purses he'd filched been fatter, he'd have found himself head of the club. As it was, that had never mattered to Calum. It had only mattered that they had their security.

"You're still answerable to all." Abandoning his negligent pose, Adair set his glass down hard on the corner of Calum's desk. "Ryker's gone, Niall's gone, and you"—he slashed a hand over in his direction—"are now sneaking about with Mrs. Swindell, the *bookkeeper*."

A muscle pulsed at the corner of his mouth. "I'm not sneaking about," he bit out.

"Fine, then visiting a foundling hospital with the woman." Adair spoke that as an indictment more than anything.

So, his brother had been monitoring his actions. But then, was that truly unexpected? Each proprietor, as Adair rightly pointed out, was accountable to one another. One's actions had direct consequences on not only the siblings who'd found each other all those years ago but also the employees who relied upon them. Calum tipped his ashes into the crystal tray and, bringing his cheroot to his lips, sucked in a long puff. He exhaled through the side of his mouth. "Given our own origins, I hardly took you as one who'd disapprove of our club helping children suffering a like fate."

"*Pfft*, this isn't about approving or disapproving." Adair swiped his drink off the desk. "And you *know* it isn't," he said, jabbing a finger at him. "There's just two of us here, now." He held out a second digit. "And everything, until they return, falls to us. *Everything.*" Adair held his gaze. "Who you spend your time with"—*Eve*—"and how you spend it is your business." His mouth hardened. "Except when that goes on during our business. Tell the bookkeeper her Sundays are her own, but until our numbers are righted and our reputation restored, then her obligations are to us." *As are yours.* The glint in Adair's eyes lent voice to those unspoken words. Then, some of the fight drained out of his usually affable brother's frame. "We should send word to Ryker."

"He knows." No good could come in calling Ryker away from the country where he and Penelope awaited the birth of their child. "Him returning will right nothing."

"Then send word to Somerset." Their sister and her duke of a husband were newly returned from the country. "Our reputation is being smeared about town by the *ton*. We need their influence to quell those whispers."

"Is that what you want? For our brother-in-law, the duke, to drum up business?"

Adair flinched.

Frenetic energy hummed in Calum's veins. Coming to his feet, he stalked over to the window and stared out at the cloud-filled night sky. He scraped his gaze over the cobbles below, to the pair of dandies now stumbling up their steps. This is what their life had become. They'd gone from the most powerful hell in the kingdom . . . to this: proprietors dependent upon fancy lords to vouch for them. He steeled his jaw. "I'm not . . ." *Creeeak.* The unoiled hinges squealed loudly and then abruptly stopped. When they'd taken over ownership of the former bordello, and architects and servants had come in to see to the transformation, at Calum's insistence, with the exception of their offices, the doors and windows were to go unoiled. It had been a calculated barrier thrown up between them and the men, women, and former children wishing them harm. "We're not contacting Ryker, and we are *not* begging Somerset to come speak on our behalf. Are we clear?"

From the crystal windowpane, Adair's visage reflected back. But for the ticking vein at the corner of his left eye, he gave no outward indication that he heard. Without another word, his brother stalked out of the room and closed the door quietly behind him.

By God, this was a bloody disaster. He took another long pull from his cheroot. Who could have figured that the greatest peril and danger to visit their club came not from any of the street toughs and gang leaders in St. Giles . . . but because of their growing connection to the nobility? Ryker's rule inside the club had been at a time when there'd been no connections to the nobility complicating their circumstances. Calum and Adair, however, had been left with the mess of setting it all to rights.

Creeeak.

He sighed. Well, it was certain that the woman next door wrestling with a too-loud window was not one of the nefarious sorts sent as the eyes and ears for Killoran or anyone else.

With his spare hand, Calum unlatched the hook and pushed his oiled window open. Dropping his elbows on the slate windowsill, he leaned out. "Mrs. Swindell," he drawled.

The young woman cried out. Swiftly jerking herself back, she disappeared behind her smaller, narrower window. Given the ominous discussion he'd had moments ago with his brother, there called for solemnity and careful thought. One more misstep and their club was on the cusp of ruin.

Yet, at Eve Swindell's rather poor attempt at furtiveness, his lips twitched. He took another pull from his cheroot. He slowly exhaled a small plume. "If you're determined to listen in, you'd be better served putting your ear to the plastered wall than hoping to hear over the noises of St. Giles." Silence met his reply. And here he'd taken Eve for being far more courageous than that. "Mayhap listening out windows in Mayfair and Grosvenor is more conducive, but you're in St. Giles now," he said drily, deliberately baiting.

From the room next door, a flurry of unladylike curses and ramblings met his ears. He grinned as she damned one of the Devil's body parts. Then . . . the bookish miss ducked her head out. "Mr. Dabney," she greeted with such feigned surprise, his grin widened. "Good evening."

"Morning," he pointed out. At nearly thirty minutes past one o'clock, the club was bustling and the respectable sorts were sleeping. Except, it would seem, for his new bookkeeper.

She glanced out to the half-moon buried behind thick gray clouds that muted all hint and hope of a glow. "Yes, I suppose it is morning," her voice rang loudly in the courtyards below.

Dixon, the guard on duty, strode into the middle of the courtyard. The younger man with steel in his eyes that had earned him the post two years earlier, raised his pistol. Eve gasped and retreated behind her window.

"It's all right, Dixon," he called out.

"You're certain, sir?" Dixon looked pointedly at Eve's window.

"I'm certain." The clever miss now silent next door couldn't manage duplicity if her life were dependent upon it.

Tucking his gun back inside his waistband, Dixon nodded and took himself back to his post.

Calum took a final draw from his dwindling cheroot, then stamped it out on the windowsill. "Never had a gun trained on you?"

"Indeed, not." Eve's voice emerged muffled and muted from where she now hid. She dipped her head out once more. "I'll have you know—"

"You'll also have young Dixon know, too, if you speak in that volume."

The clouds shifted overhead, exposing the moon, and the glow splashed light upon her face. It revealed a becoming blush. "I'll have you know," she started, then dropped her voice to a barely there whisper. "I'll have you know," she repeated a third time, "I was not spying. I simply required fresh air—"

"It smells like rotten fish in St. Giles."

"And prefer gazing at the stars," she continued over his interruption.

"Are there so many stars visible?"

Eve glanced out to the cloud-shrouded sky. "Oh, yes," she said with a solemn nod. They shared a grin, and he dropped his smoked cheroot to the grounds below. Eve's smile dipped. "Is everything"—she glanced briefly to the mews—"all right?" And just like that, she quashed the too-brief interlude of pretend he'd allowed himself.

Cursing, he scanned the area. Even breathing a hint of a problem facing the hell was enough to do in their reputation with not only their noble patrons but also the men and women on staff. Oftentimes a person was only as powerful as his or her perception. Calum drew back and quickly closed the window. Determinedly, he found his way to Eve's office. Without sparing a knock, he pushed the door open.

Standing on the tips of her slippers, Eve leaned dangerously far out the window. "Calum?" she whispered, rousing another grin. Short, slender, and yet in possession of notably rounded buttocks now pleasingly outlined by the fabric taut from her efforts, she was an unlikely carnal delight. Silently, he stalked over. "Cal—" He caught her about the waist, hauling her back in.

"You lean out any farther, you're going to tumble out," he said through tight lips.

She gasped and angled her head back. Her voice emerged on a breathless whisper. "I didn't hear you."

No, she wouldn't have. Growing up in the streets, that stealth had saved his life and become a way of his existence. "But everyone heard you," he countered. Calum gave her waist a light squeeze. "Rule one, don't publicly discuss matters of business, Eve," he ordered, and the enormity of what she'd nearly done sent tension coiling inside.

Color suffused her face. "I didn't think . . . I didn't realize . . ." She worried her lower lip—her full lower lip. He lingered his gaze on that lush flesh and swallowed hard. A woman by the name of Eve could only ever have such a mouth that conjured thoughts of sin and wicked delights.

"Now you know," he said hoarsely. Reluctantly, he set her free, his hands bereft at the sudden loss of her. He took a quick step away from her. "I want a report drawn up by tomorrow evening. A detailed accounting comparing the past three years of profit earnings and cost expenditures across all ends."

And before he did something mad, like forget the dire situation Adair had insisted they confront openly and again kiss Eve Swindell, he marched from the room.

Chapter 12

For a long, never-ending moment built on wanton hope, Eve had believed Calum was going to again kiss her.

And having been caught leaning out the window and listening in on his personal discussion like a naughty child, she should be awash in proper humiliation. Except, everything had gone right out of her head—including logic, order, and reason—the moment he'd sneaked into her office and taken her about the waist. Then he'd looked at her mouth in a way that made her believe he was about to kiss her—again. And how she ached to know the feeling of being in his arms, with the heat of his solid body pouring off his muscled frame and burning her from the inside out.

Instead . . . he'd *left*. Not before he'd issued a heap of work for her to complete by tomorrow night.

The door opened, and she wheeled around.

MacTavish entered, his arms near overflowing with books. Favoring her with the same glower he had since she'd deceived him and then set up residence here, he emptied his burden onto her desk. They fell with a noisy *thunk* and scattered about the surface.

Folding her hands primly before her, she offered him her most winning smile. "Mr. MacTavish, thank you so much for—"

"Oi don't want your thanks," he snapped, giving her more words than he had since their first meeting. "Ya made me look bad before Dabney and Thorne and every other guard here. Ya nearly cost me my assignment."

In her selfishness to secure her own safety, she'd put her well-being above everyone else. Regret pebbled in her belly. She'd not thought how her bold commandeering of Calum's books and rooms might impact the guard MacTavish, who'd handed over the club's ledgers. "Forgive me," she said softly, turning her palms up.

His scowl deepened. "And Oi certainly don't want your apologies." He wagged a finger at her. "Oi don't trust ya. Oi don't care how ya are with the club's numbers, no woman who sneaks inside the way you did can be up to any good." MacTavish touched that same scarred digit to the corner of his eye. "And Oi'm watching you." With that he stomped out and slammed the door so hard it shook the frame.

She winced. "Well." This day had become a veritable disaster. She'd been caught listening in on something she'd had no place listening to. Calum couldn't have been clearer in the perfunctory list he'd given her that she'd shattered the peace between them. "You fool," she mumbled, returning to her now cluttered desk. "Gazing at stars. Smelling the St. Giles air. *Gah.*" Eve grimaced. Where most ladies of the *ton* were demure misses capable of prevarication, Eve had always been *hopeless.* She'd never been one to possess a distracting smile. Instead, there'd long been a bluntness to her words and actions that earned stiff recriminations from her governesses. When Calum had challenged her, she'd owed him the truth. She had been listening in.

And it was how she now knew his club was in dire straits. Eve tapped her index finger against her bottom lip. One would never know as much, given the impressive profits the Hell and Sin had yielded these past three months. She, however, had failed to remember a lesson she'd first gleaned after taking over her father's accounts. How one's business fared in the past against how it fared in the present was an even more important mark of its success.

Determined to sort through Calum's finances, she pulled out her chair and slid into the comfortable leather folds. Skimming her gaze along the gold etchings on the spines, she set to work organizing the books into neat, corresponding piles. Each month filed with each like month until there were twelve rows, with three ledgers in each. Next, she withdrew a sheet of parchment from inside her center drawer, as well as a pen. "Let us begin," she murmured, and gathered the most recent dates. Beginning with the oldest, she proceeded to read. Periodically, she made notes on the page, the rhythmic tap-tap of her pen soothing. Now, just like when her father had been ill and she was left to right the family's books, it served as a slight distraction. It was far easier to focus on that light beat than the misery of one's own circumstances.

Moments turned into hours, and Eve worked with a frantic diligence until the numbers and annotations blurred before her eyes. She worked tirelessly on book after book, creating a detailed chart with her information.

Her fingers cramped, and she gasped. The pen slipped through her fingers, scattering ink upon an otherwise flawless page. She sighed and flexed her sore digits. Stretching her palm over, she shook it in a small circle to bring blood flowing back to the appendage. Eve took in the large stack completed, and the even larger one awaiting her attention.

Groaning, she dropped her head atop the desk. If he'd been attempting to punish her for listening in on business that wasn't her own, Calum couldn't have found a more miserable, fitting one. God, how she missed being able to simply read a book . . . with words. Fictional ones that didn't pertain to failing crops and dwindling coffers and now declining club profits. Those tales of great Greek gods and goddesses now read so long ago, she may as well have imagined poring over them. Yet, losing herself in those pages didn't dull the reality that was life. It hadn't solved her own miserable circumstances, and it wouldn't help Calum and his club.

That discourse she'd overheard between Calum and his brother whispered forward. Aside from finding a refuge from her brother's machinations, Eve hadn't truly given thought to the Hell and Sin. It had merely represented a shelter until she reached her majority and at last found her freedom. Since the day Nurse Mattison had insisted on this course for her, she'd always known and embraced the fact that her position as bookkeeper was to be not only a temporary one—but also a brief one. She'd come here to fulfill the responsibilities of a book-keeper, but whether Calum's business thrived or died hadn't really been a consideration—until now. Remorse settled like a stone in her belly.

With the sun peeking out past thick gray storm clouds, she shoved to her feet. She yawned, burying that sound of fatigue in her ink-stained hand. In a noiseless whir of skirts, she returned to the window where she'd earned Calum's annoyance. Eve tugged the curtains back. And then, as though she'd conjured him with her musings, he was there. She pressed her eyes briefly closed. Or mayhap she'd worked her eyes to the point she now saw him everywhere. Yet, he remained.

Calum stood exchanging words with the guard who'd pointed a pistol at her last evening. She cocked her head. How in absolute control he was of every exchange. The guard gave intermittent nods, and then he stalked off.

After he'd gone, Calum lingered.

She should quit her spot at the window. She should seek out her rooms and steal at least an hour of sleep before she resumed her onerous task. Having been discovered a short while ago should have taught her the peril of watching from windows. Except, she remained transfixed.

Calum withdrew the gold chain tucked inside his jacket and consulted the timepiece, and that glitter of gold harkened her back to another fine piece . . . and another mews. Her family's. And her brother's watch fob. The horror of that day came rolling over her in waves. Eve's throat worked spasmodically. How many years had she believed him dead? How many years had she thought that her careless-ness in summoning Gerald had found him swinging from a rope—as Gerald used to taunt her with?

An errant ray from the sun played off his face, highlighting his strong, unyielding jawline and sharp cheeks. With his height, power, and strength, he embodied that statue of the Greek god Helios once erected in her family's Kent estate. Only, where that marble masterpiece and the Colossus of Rhodes had both fallen, Calum Dabney could never be toppled. Gerald's attempt to destroy him all those years ago was proof of that. And Calum had become not only wealthier with the passage of time—he'd also become more powerful.

Except that wasn't altogether true. Unbidden, her gaze traveled back to those piles of ledgers. All was not perfect in the Hell and Sin world. Then, wasn't that life for all people, regardless of station? Eve let the curtain fall back into place. Abandoning her offices, she found her way from the room and down the corridors, where servants awake for the day bustled back and forth. She skirted a bevy of maids carrying buckets of steaming water. Eve reached the end of the hall and made her way down the servants' stairs. She stopped at the doorway leading out to the mews. An unfamiliar guard with hard eyes and a scarred right cheek gave her the once-over.

"If you'll excuse me?" she murmured, and he jerked his chin.

Eve grabbed the door handle and let herself out. The early-morn air, cool and invigorating, drove back the fatigue that had driven her from her assignment. She strode down the alley, heading for the mews.

How very different life within this new, temporary home was. She'd left a world where, even with the Pruitts' failing finances, servants had always been plenty, and those meticulous servants had always rushed to open her doors. Those same men and women had anticipated what she needed and when she needed it, and through their devotion, she'd been denied the simple acts of walking freely inside a house and opening her own door without questions raised or sneaking involved.

Eve reached the center of the mews and glanced around.

"Do you ever rest, Mrs. Swindell?"

Heart racing, she jumped. Pulled forward by that husky, familiar baritone, Eve came to a stop at the edge of an open stable door.

Time stopped, with the earth ceasing its perpetual movement.

Calum stood beside a magnificent black mount. The horse's face clasped in his hands, he'd the look of that boy she'd first come upon all those years ago inside her father's once prized stalls. Only, then Calum had been a belligerent boy who'd threatened her life if she raised a hue and a cry. Instead, she'd remained, and an unlikely friendship had been born—until with one reckless request put to Gerald, she'd killed that precious bond.

They'd been reunited, inside a different mews, alongside a different horse, and with only Eve knowing about their shared history. Numb, she followed his movements as he gave that enormous creature a final scratch between the eyes and fetched a currycomb. Silently, he scrubbed those bristles over the stallion's body. Calum's large hands revealed a power and strength that could easily fell a man or effortlessly inflict pain. And yet, unlike her brother, who'd buried her head in a bucket of freezing water and threatened her very life, there was tenderness to Calum's measured strokes. He was a man who, despite his own club's precarious circumstances, gave of his time anyway to a foundling hospital with a woman he barely knew, actions that spoke to the strength of his honor and character. He'd never descend to the evil Gerald or Lord Flynn was capable of. She'd bet her very life Calum wouldn't even put his self-interests before those dependent upon him. Unlike Eve's brother Kit had.

"I *was* listening in," she said softly. He briefly paused, looking over from his task. Their gazes locked. "I *should* clarify that I do have an appreciation for the night air and starlit skies." For it was important he know she'd spoken some truth. Those were details he'd known long ago. She'd shared them with him early on in their friendship. If he knew, remembered, or ever thought of that girl he'd called Little Lena Duchess, he gave no hint of it. Eve sucked in a slow breath and glanced around the elaborately appointed stall. "But it was not my place to interfere in your discussion with Mr. Thorne. Forgive me." When he still said nothing, just resumed looking after his mount, she fiddled with her skirts. She turned to go.

"Here," he called out, staying her. He set aside the comb and walked over to the fine equipment hanging up. Calum grabbed a hard-bristled brush and held it out.

Why do they need so many damned brushes . . . ?

Eve came over without hesitation and accepted that offering. She automatically stroked the horse in the direction of his hair-coat growth.

"You've experience with horses."

His was an observation more than anything. Nonetheless, she nodded anyway. Her hand ceased its strokes as the past trickled forward. *Here, let me show you, Calum . . . you stroke him this way . . .* Her lips ached with the struggle of keeping the truth in. To keep from telling him that she'd, in fact, been the small girl who'd shown him how to hold a comb and care for a horse.

"Here," he murmured in an eerie echo of that memory. Calum settled his hand over hers, and a thrill burned through her, like running barefoot across the carpets and feeling that sharp charge. He merely guided her hand back into the forward strokes. The horse stomped his rear right leg in equine approval.

Eve continued brushing Calum's mount. "He's magnificent," she murmured. The creature whinnied his approval. "Aww, but then, you know that, don't you, you arrogant thing." She touched her nose to his, softening the gentle rebuke.

Feeling Calum's eyes on her, she briefly paused. Her cheeks warmed. With the exception of that fleeting time when she'd found Calum, Eve had never had friends. She'd developed a tendency to speak to herself and the horses in her family's stables. Embarrassed, she swiftly resumed brushing his horse.

"Ah, but you are correct. Isn't she, Tau?" Calum directed that question to his mount, and the evidence of his bond with the magnificent creature and that he either did or pretended to speak to his own horses, sent heat blossoming in her chest. Then . . . she froze. She dimly registered Calum gathering the brush from her fingers and returning it to its proper place on the wall alongside the other fine equipment.

Surely, she'd misheard. *You have the mark of life . . . it means . . .* "Tau."

Calum moved beside the horse's—Tau's—right shoulder. Angling his back toward the massive stallion, Calum bent his knees. "Tau," he confirmed. He ran his long, calloused fingers down the horse's right leg. Instantly complying, Tau lifted the limb. Calum examined the right hoof. "It is Greek for—"

"Immortal," she finished on a whisper.

He glanced up from his task, something akin to surprise in his brown eyes.

Eve went motionless, her gaze stubbornly, of its own volition, drawn to the jagged *Tau*-shaped scar near his mouth. *You are immortal, Calum . . .* Did he recall their long-ago exchange? That bold, girlish request to test the jagged edges of that mark.

"You're familiar with it?" he asked, releasing Tau's limb. The horse immediately stamped his foot in the hay.

Of course, he wouldn't remember her. Except, in a way—*he had.* That long-ago exchange between them had meant something to him that he'd named his beloved mount after it. Surely, if he'd despised everything about the girl he'd called Little Lena Duchess, he would have stripped all hint of her from his life.

"I am," she began hesitantly. "How did you come to name him that?" It was a bold question pulled forth by an inherent need to know just why he had all these years retained hold of that part of their now distant meeting. For a long moment, she thought he might not answer and despaired of his silence. And then, when he spoke, she wished he never had.

"I nearly died." He spoke casually, the way one did about the quality of the soup or the stretch of fine weather they'd enjoyed, and yet even with that nonchalance, her heart ached still. "Picked the wrong pocket and found myself thrown in Newgate for it," he explained, fetching a heavy leather brush. Returning to Tau's side, he proceeded to pull it gently through Tau's mane.

The air stuck in Eve's lungs, choking off the ability to properly breathe. She fisted her hands into tight balls.

He continued, his actions remarkably mundane while tumult raged within her. "I made the mistake of trusting a person I'd no place trusting, and for it nearly swung. I chose Tau's name as a reminder of what those missteps can cost a person."

Eve bit the inside of her cheek hard, and she, who'd insisted she was not the crying sort, was proved a liar once more. Tears pricked behind her lashes, blurring her vision. Thunder rumbled in the distance, an ominous laugh of the gods.

She forced her gaze out the stable door, to the courtyard where servants rushed about their daily tasks. Eve blinked frantically trying to dispel the useless drops. For the name he'd chosen hadn't a thing to do with tender remembrance of their friendship . . . but rather he'd selected it so his own folly and her greatest crime could live on. That fleeting friendship that marked the happiest moments of her solitary existence was nothing more than a regret for Calum. She rubbed the dull ache in her chest. To no avail. "I should go," she said hoarsely, taking a step toward that door. "The report—"

"You've worked all morning, Eve," he called out, staying her. "I'm not a cruel employer who'd not allow you your rest." He paused. "Unless you care to go, in which case, I'll not keep you here."

She whipped back. "No," she said on a rush. "It is not that. It is . . ."

Calum held up the brush in a silent challenge.

Eve warred with herself.

His gaze worked a path over her face—searching, questioning. Those fathomless brown eyes possessed an intensity that hinted at a man who could see a person's darkest secrets and pull them out for his own. Eve shivered, hugging her arms close. What would he say if he discovered the girl he'd spent years hating for her treachery stood before him now?

He let his arm fall back to his side. "What is it, Eve?" he asked, worry creasing his brow.

Tell him. Tell him so he knows and you can be done with the deception and he can be done with you . . . And then what? Do you think he'll issue aid to the girl responsible for his misery at Newgate? "It is not that I don't want to be with you," she said softly. It was entirely the opposite. There was no one she'd ever wanted more in her life, then as a friend . . . and now as a man who valued her cleverness and gave of his time to help the foundling hospital.

"Then stay," he whispered, like temptation itself.

I want to stay here . . . with him . . . in this stable . . . in his home . . . Oh, God. I'm falling in love with him. Terror clutched at her insides, and she briefly shut her eyes.

Calum held that brush out, and now she knew the hold the Devil had when he'd dangled that forbidden fruit. Drawn like one of those hopeless moths to a flame, she wandered closer. To give her fingers something to do, she accepted the brush and studied the thick bristles.

He brushed his knuckles along her jawline, forcing her gaze up to his. "What is it?" His deep baritone washed over her. Those strong, sure tones that made a lady want to reveal all.

"I . . ." *Tell him.* "It is your club," she finished lamely, proving that she was a coward to her very core. "Your club is in trouble."

Chapter 13

She'd never gone to bed.

The dark circles under her bloodshot eyes and the rumpled garments she'd been wearing hours earlier marked her exhaustion.

When he'd taken leave of her, he'd meant to refocus her on her task inside this club. She was here to serve in the capacity of bookkeeper: oversee the ledgers, provide reports, meet with vendors, and that was it—matters strictly pertaining to business.

Leaning out a window and teasing the lady while she teased back went counter to every purpose she served. It recalled Adair's thinly veiled accusations and roused Calum's own inherent guilt. Now he stood there, talking of his past and learning her interests, and with every exchange his existence became more and more muddled.

"You should be resting," he finally said, removing the brush from her long, ink-stained fingers. They were the hands of a woman unafraid of real work. Callused digits that served as a window into the life she lived.

She leaned into the stable wall. "Are you being deliberately evasive?"

Actually, he wasn't. And the fact that she'd doubt his concern grated. "Eve, I put you in charge of my books detailing my club's finances. It's my expectation that you'd eventually ascertain the shift in our numbers, and if you didn't . . ."

"You'd sack me?" she finished for him with a small smile.

Yes. That was the practical reply. If she was incapable of adequately gathering every last detail from the hell, then she'd no place being here, and he should have no hesitancy tossing her out. Calum scratched his horse between the eyes. "It doesn't matter what I would or would not do," he added, *this* time evasive. "A woman with your cleverness would have always accurately sorted through the club's business."

She cocked her head, and that slight movement sent her loose chignon toppling back. The ink-black arrangement hung loose at the nape of her neck, those strands desperately hanging on to propriety. Hanging on when Calum wanted nothing more than to pull the pins free of her hair and let it tumble around her shoulders. And because in this instance it was vastly safer speaking about the Hell and Sin's changed circumstances than this hungering to lay claim to her mouth again, he explained, "Our numbers are down, as is our patronage. We've seen a steady decline." *Since Niall had wed the Duke of Wilkinson's daughter,* he thought. "In recent months," he said aloud.

"Your profits are still staggering."

He patted Tau on the withers and tossed the brush in the corner. "If one focuses on a given month and not an overall trend, then one's certain to find oneself wondering in little time what happened and where it all went."

"So, you can trace it, then," she persisted, and his skin pricked with the feel of her gaze on his movements around the stall. "You've already identified that the change has been several months ago."

"It goes back before that," he said tersely. She was too clever. Calum sighed and swiped a hand over the day's growth on his face. As a rule, neither he nor his siblings had let strangers inside their world. The one time Calum had, he'd been burned by life. It had been the last he'd ever committed that folly. So, what was it about Eve Swindell, a woman he'd known less than a fortnight, that made him want to share the burdens that had been weighing on him when he'd not even wanted to speak to Adair, Ryker, or Niall? "There's a rival club—the Devil's Den," he began slowly. "For nearly two years, they've been attempting"—he grimaced—"and succeeding in stealing our patrons."

"There aren't enough to go around?" she asked with a pragmatism not shown in either of the two cowering bookkeepers to come before her.

He snorted. Given the number of reprobate lords? "One would suspect there should be. There were a series . . . of recent events that have earned society's disapproval." An increasingly familiar panic simmered under the surface. He began to pace, at last airing the frustration and worry he'd silently and secretly battled. "This club has been my home for eleven years. I've found security here. My family's found security, and there are workers dependent upon us, where we're the only thing between starving on the streets and—"

Eve pushed away from the stable wall and drifted closer. The whispery hint of lemon that clung to her skin wafted about his senses, more intoxicating than any spirits served and consumed inside this hell.

Wordless, he stared on as she gathered his hand in hers, joining their fingers together. Her palm was smaller, softer, and more delicate against his, and yet they went together in a perfect pairing. *Pull away* . . . This gesture of comfort and solace was as unfamiliar to him as when he'd been forced to suffer through Helena's ball. Long ago he'd known the gentle touch of a mother and the kind words of a father . . . but all that had died along with them. In the new family he'd made for himself, of his siblings on the street, there were no shows of affection. Those living inside the Hell and Sin had become masters of their emotions. He made to pull back, but Eve tightened her grip in a surprisingly strong hold for one of her diminutive size.

"I know"—she dropped her gaze to their joined palms—"some of what you speak to." Eve whipped her head up. "Not in the same way, at all. But in others. I know what it is to worry that your work will decide if families eat or starve or whether there will be funds to repair roofs." It didn't escape his notice that she didn't herself speak to knowing those struggles.

Then, her cultured tones and flawless English were proof that she, too, had been born to higher beginnings.

"And that is all you do now," he said more to himself, as the pieces to this woman began to fall into place. "You oversee the records and books of others." Calum turned her hand over in his, and trailed the pad of his thumb over the intersecting lines upon her palm. "What else do you do?"

Eve's breath caught in a noisy inhalation, the sound explosive in the cramped quarters of the stall. "What do I do?" she whispered.

"When you're not overseeing your responsibilities, where do you find your pleasure?" It was the wrong thing to say. A question sprung of a genuine need to know more of Eve Swindell, but as soon as it escaped him, dangerously wicked imaginings surged forward.

Eve toed the hay, marking a perfect circle with a distractedness that doused his ardor. "I used to . . ." Her mouth scrunched up.

Did she seek to stifle that admission? His intrigue redoubled. Time, however, had taught him not to press another person. That whatever secrets Eve chose to share with him were hers and hers alone to decide when to unveil.

"I read." Past tense.

She drew her hands from his and folded them neatly before her. Shoulders erect, chin back, and bearing regal, she'd the look of the proper governesses and tutors they'd first brought in to work with Calum's family.

Tau nuzzled his shoulder hard, and he favored the loyal creature with several strokes, all the while trying to imagine Eve bent over a book. What words would hold her riveted? "Mathematical and scientific journals?" he ventured.

An inelegant snort escaped her. "Because I'm a bookkeeper?" She gave her head a shake and wandered around the opposite side of Tau's muzzle. "My work with numbers is a necessity. It's something I'm accomplished at." She spoke as a matter-of-factness, absent of conceit. "But it's never been something I've either loved or enjoyed. It's simply something I . . . do."

That eerie echo of his very own thoughts on those miserable responsibilities cemented an ever-expanding awareness of Eve. It deepened their connection as a man and woman more alike than he ever would have credited after her arrival eleven days earlier. "And yet, even with that, you became so proficient in mathematics that you found yourself numerous posts using that very skill?"

She strolled over to Tau and captured his enormous midnight-black face between her hands. "When I was a girl, my father would tell me of the great Greek stories contained in the night sky." She directed that quiet admission to the middle of his mount's eyes.

Greek stories . . . for a second time . . . A memory danced around the farthest corners of his mind.

"Nothing is more useful than silence."

"That's your favorite saying, Calum . . . " That indignant child's voice of the girl who'd betrayed him rang as clear now as it had been when he and Little Lena Duchess had lain in another stable, looking over one of her many books.

"That is the reason you know the meaning of Tau?" he asked, thrusting aside those remembrances of Bedford's sister.

She nodded.

A wistful smile pulled at Eve's lips. "Every tale, every constellation mentioned, I was . . . riveted. I wanted to know everything about the stars and their stories contained within. When the household slept, I would sneak outside, gaze up at the stars, and trace them with my fingertip." She pointed her index finger to the stable roof. "My mother despaired of me ever learning anything except astronomy, and my father vowed I'd never be a woman with singular interests."

When his own parents had died, he'd still been just a boy, with a rudimentary understanding of his letters and words. Now the well-guarded gates of his memories opened up, and in flooded thoughts of his loving parents: the booming laugh of a man, pointing at pages while he read to Calum. He started. It had been so long since he'd thought of either of the Dabneys. The day they'd died, Calum's whole existence had gone with them. Disquieted by the intrusion of his past twice now, he broke the thick silence. "Your father limited your studies?"

She glanced up. "No. Rather, he expanded them." At his puzzled brow, she explained. "He insisted if I appreciated the stories in the stars, then I must know the men responsible for creating those stories. So, he opened my mind to Thales, Pythagoras, Plato." She lifted her shoulders in a little shrug. "And through that, I discovered math."

And despite her great love for the stories contained within the stars, as she'd said, instead she remained shut away in an office righting books and ledgers. Did she dream of those long-ago pleasures? Or had she, like Calum, with the passage of time put aside that past and followed along the path of a practical future?

Thunder rumbled in the distance, and with it, reality intruded. As one, they looked to the entranceway. He stared out. The club never rested. There were always fights to break up, records to keep, shipments to order.

"You should return," he said. And given Adair's earlier suspicions, it wouldn't do well for them to return together.

"Yes," she murmured. She lingered. Did she wish to remain as much as he wished her to stay here and share more of those fleeting details about herself? She turned to go.

"Have the morning off," he called after her.

The lady glanced back. "It is not Sunday." There was a challenge there, as they were instantly restored to employer and bookkeeper. At the fiery glint in her eyes, his admiration for Eve Swindell grew all the more. But for his siblings, not a single employee would reject that offer of rest. "And your reports—"

"You've two more days to complete them," he allowed. *Would you have made those concessions for another member of your staff?* Adair's previous accusations reared in his mind.

His spirited bookkeeper propped her hands on her hips and gave a determined thrust of her chin. "I don't need two more days. You'd not make that concession for a man on your staff." How in hell did their thoughts move in a like harmony? He'd not have made that concession for anyone on his staff—except her.

"I do not treat you any differently," he said tightly, lying to the both of them. He had. On numerous scores. Even hiring her when he'd have thrown any other man or woman out on their arse for infiltrating his club.

"Then, if you'll excuse me?" Eve started forward. "I have reports to see to." With a queen's regal grace, she swept out of the stables so all that lingered was the citrusy lemon scent of her.

Calum remained staring after Eve, long after she'd gone.

For the past eleven years, the Hell and Sin had earned his every thought, effort, and emotion. There'd been no place for anything else. Prior to that he'd been solely fixed on surviving. He'd not truly thought of the children alone on the streets, with the only thing between death and survival their own wits. Yet Eve, even as she'd taken on the responsibilities of employment, still thought of those less fortunate—and more, gave her time to assist where she could. She might spend her time reading those works she spoke of with a nostalgic melancholy, and yet she chose to help others. He was both awed by her selflessness and shamed by his own selfishness.

Surely that explained this quixotic hold she had over him?

Reason said allow Eve her role inside the club and confine their dealings to only business matters.

The impractical side he could not explain wanted to drive back the wistful smile she'd worn a short while ago and replace it with a sincerity that matched her eyes.

He swiped a hand over his face.

By God, she'd utterly upended him.

Chapter 14

"Mr. Dabney wants ya in the Observatory."

Engrossed in her work with the month's liquor expenditures, Eve glanced up. The surly guard MacTavish glared back . . . just as he'd been glaring since she'd secured the post with some trickery fourteen days earlier. After she sat for countless hours in the same position, her neck muscles screamed in protest. She winced and rubbed the tight tendons at the base of her skull. "I'll be but a moment," she promised, and resumed tabulations in one of her final columns.

"'e said now."

When she'd first arrived, MacTavish's pronouncement would have set off warning bells of terror that she'd been found out and that Calum intended to toss her out. But that had been before. In the time since she'd been here, she'd come to appreciate that not all meetings represented impending doom. Rather, he summoned her regularly to discuss the club's business and share parts of the inner workings of his establishment. "He also advised me to complete a report for the liquor accounts," she directed to her book. "Given that, I expect he'll be forgiving if I'm a moment late." Which she wouldn't be if MacTavish ceased arguing and let her complete the final tallying.

"Look at ya," he said on a mocking jeer, "presuming to know what Mr. Dabney needs."

At his suggestive tone, her cheeks warmed. "I've been here just two weeks, and I've already gathered that he'd far rather I deal with his reports than your jibes."

MacTavish opened and closed his mouth several times. *Good. Let him be silent. The miserable curmudgeon.* She'd found over the years that most people—men and women of every station—didn't know what to do with a direct woman who spoke her mind. Though, that wasn't altogether true. In their every exchange, she and Calum conversed freely, and he didn't eye her like she'd two heads all because she had opinions.

Task completed, Eve set her pen down. After opening the crystal container, she dipped her fingers in and sprinkled drying powder upon the last page. She blew lightly on the document, then set it aside and gathered the previously completed pages in their proper order. Adding the still slightly wet sheet to the top, she gathered them in her arms and stood.

Report in hand, she swept past the flummoxed guard and marched down the hall. When she reached the middle of the corridor, she stopped, then tiptoed the remaining distance to the Observatory. With a triumphant grin, she adjusted her burden to one arm and raised a hand to knock.

"Enter," he boomed from the other side of the panel.

She sighed and let herself in. He always did that . . . anticipated her moves and presence before she even revealed herself.

"How do you always know when I'm coming, Calum?"

"Come, closer." Widening her eyes, Eve leaned closer. He tweaked her nose. "'Tis a secret."

'Twas a secret he'd never explained, but one that a woman more aware of the injustices of the world would have realized came from the basic need to survive on the streets.

"It was quieter this time," he called from his position at the wide window out to the club. *It*, as in her approach.

Maneuvering around her papers, she pulled the door shut behind her. "It's my boots." Eve stuck out the tip of one of her hideous work boots. "There's nothing else for it."

From the glass panel, his grinning visage stared back. "Only partly."

The trace of that smile, so full of mirth and stripped of the cynicism he was by rights entitled to, sent butterflies dancing in her belly. For all the strife her family had wrought on his existence and the suffering he'd known as a hungry boy visiting her stables, he'd retained a gentle kindness. Theirs had become a game of sorts begun with their earliest meetings—a game she'd inadvertently started as a silent test to see if she could take him by surprise, and always to no avail. Calum had ears like a cat.

He glanced back, and his gaze immediately went to her papers. "The report?"

The report? Eve briefly glanced at the items in her possession. Calum's sudden and abrupt shift from teasing, charming friend to brusque, no-nonsense employer brought her up short. It jerked her back from romantic musings far too dangerous to have for a man who'd hate her if he knew the truth of her identity. Eve joined him at the window. "I've just completed it." She held them out, grateful when he relieved her of the sheets.

As Calum skimmed the top page, she cleared her throat. "It is slightly damp, still. As such, I've placed it on top. The rest of the items are all in proper order." Absently, she rubbed at the tender portion of her arm where her elbow met her forearm. She bit her lower lip at the strain there.

Calum glanced over, his clever eyes lingering on her distracted massage. She swiftly let her arm fall, and as he returned his focus to her reports, she stared out. Other than the previous exchange when he'd shared his clever design contributions to the hell, this was the sole time she'd stepped inside this room . . . or observed the gaming floors. "It is quite impressive," she murmured. The swell of guests was at odds with the increasing worries faced by the club and Calum.

He grunted. Setting aside that damp page, he perused the first item in the report. "It used to be more so."

She flared her eyebrows and surveyed the hell. With the crush of bodies, the air was surely sparse on the floor. The raucous laughter and din of discussion carried up to the Observatory, those robust sounds at odds with the reserved, staid gentlemen who attended balls and soirees and formal affairs. "But it is filled to overflowing."

"There." He touched a fingertip to the window, and she followed his point.

Eve frowned. "There are two vacant places."

He moved his fingertip slightly to the left, to another table. Two more.

Calum held the work she'd spent nearly an entire day completing aloft. "There was a time when there wasn't a place to be had at these tables. Where guests would wait outside until space had opened up inside."

Yes, the three years she'd evaluated of his club's business transactions stood as testament to that fact. And yet . . . "Your club is still healthy," she said gently. Having watched creditors cart off her family's finest possessions and heirlooms, Eve had lived in a rapid financial decline that would result in nothing but ruin.

Unlike the last time she'd raised the topic of his hell's difficulties, he didn't attempt to redirect the discussion. "A business is only as healthy as its trends." He sighed and carried that work over to the mahogany stand at the center of the room. Pulling out the drawer, he tucked the sheets inside.

She frowned. "I can go over the details with you." Attending his books and ledgers, and indicating areas where he might improve upon his profits, had not erased her guilt . . . but it had made her feel that even with her duplicity she was offering Calum something of value.

"Join me, Mrs. Swindell." He started for the door.

Mrs. Swindell. How she hated that name and his use of it. It served as a reminder of the falsehoods she fed him. She'd also come to find it was how he referred to her when he doled out new responsibilities or assigned certain tasks. It was how she'd come to distinguish when they were employer and bookkeeper . . . and . . . whatever else they'd become in the short time they'd known one another.

Calum paused in the doorway and glanced back questioningly. Springing to movement, she bustled over to the door. He guided them from the Observatory and down the opposite end of the hall back toward the main living suites. He brought them to a stop beside a doorway. Pressing the handle, he motioned her forward.

Curious, Eve glanced up at him, then peered into the room. A handful of sconces cast a soft glow upon the otherwise darkened space. She took a step and froze as her gaze collided with the walls. Drawn forward, she entered the room and continued walking over to the floor-length shelving units. She stopped a pace away and, pressing her hands close to her heart, rocked on her heels. Only the wealthiest families were in possession of a library. There had been a time when the Pruitts had been one of those fortunate families. "I once had a library," she whispered, her voice echoing off the soaring ceiling. She had vowed as a young girl to read every item contained within that grand space. Her father had laughed, patted her head, and promised to fill the room with twice the amount when she accomplished such a feat.

It had been an impossibility—the idea that even with the whole of her life, she could have ever read all those volumes. In the end, she'd not even managed to read a quarter of them before life had intruded and responsibilities had erased frivolous pleasures . . . and then they'd all been sold off.

Calum pushed the door closed behind him. "It used to be a storage room." His deep baritone boomed about the space, and she looked over to him. "My sister-in-law insisted it be converted to a library. Saw to the undertaking herself."

This was the library she'd heard servants occasionally whispering of. Given the work that commanded her schedule both here and at the foundling hospital, this was the first time she'd ever found herself inside this precious space. She followed Calum's long-legged, sleek steps as he approached the third shelving unit.

"She carried around a journal and pencil, speaking to all the staff inside the hell. Compiled a list of everyone's interests and what books they might enjoy."

"She sounds like a remarkable woman."

"She is."

A tendril of shameful, wicked jealousy fanned inside for the lady who'd earned his appreciation.

Calum ran his fingertip back and forth searchingly, and Eve followed his every movement, intrigued. "And did you offer a suggestion for the lady?" she ventured.

"I did."

Just that. Two words. And again, there it was: that green-eyed, ugly monster rearing itself that so much of whom Calum had been and become should remain a mystery to Eve while another woman knew his interests.

"Ah"—he plucked a book from the shelf—"here." He set the large leather book down on a rose-inlaid mahogany side table.

Intrigue stirred, and she joined him. Her breath caught. Eve skimmed her fingertips over the gold leaf lettering on the black tome. *A Celestial Atlas* by Alexander Jamieson. While she turned through the pages, he propped his hip on the edge of the table. "You . . . picked this."

Calum chuckled. "Surprised a boy from the streets would have a shared appreciation for your Greek stars, Eve?" he asked without reproach.

Pfft, stars . . . a person can barely see them in London.

"No," she said softly, moving her palm over the constellation Lynx. Even when he'd scoffed at the books she'd carried each time into the stables, he'd stared on, riveted, while she'd quietly read. He'd always been a boy who'd enjoyed learning, but he would have sooner starved than admit as much. Her throat worked. "I just did not believe . . ." Those exchanges had mattered as much to him. After learning he'd named Tau after her treachery, she'd believed that was the extent of his remembrances of her.

"I'd once heard a quote." *You'll appreciate this one. Trust me, Calum . . . Oh, fine . . . read it.*

Ptolemy.

As his deep baritone filled the quiet of the library, the words she'd memorized long ago blended with his recitation. "Mortal as I am, I know that I am born for a day, but when I follow the serried multitude of the stars in their circular course, my feet no longer touch the earth; I ascend to Zeus himself to feast me on ambrosia, the food of the gods."

Her heart swelled, straining at her chest. He remembered her . . . and not solely in hate.

"This is why you called me here?" Her voice emerged thick and garbled with emotion. Picking her head up, she met his gaze. "To share this with me?"

He hesitated, then nodded. "You do nothing but work—"

"Because that is my role here."

Closing the book, Eve wandered over to him.

"When we at last put our life on the streets behind us and called this place home, I vowed to never go without again. I'd know the finest furnishings and attire. I'd never have an empty stomach." He cupped her cheek in his large palm, and at the searing warmth, she leaned into that gentle caress. "And yet, three days earlier when we spoke in the stables, it occurred to me."

She shook her head.

"That you still are living the life I once lived."

Eve made a sound of protest and stepped out of his arms. She held her hands up warningly. It was not a like comparison. "No," she said vehemently. "You've endured far more, far worse than I ever have." It would be the height of wrongness to let him believe that her struggles had ever been what his were. For even with her darkest days and with Gerald's vile cruelties, Calum had known a lifetime of horrors.

Dropping his palms on the table, he leaned back, eyeing her contemplatively. "Just because your suffering was different than mine, doesn't make it any less important."

Her suffering. She bit the inside of her cheek. No doubt, if he'd the truth that a duke's sister stood before him, he'd not be of such an opinion. The world tended to see ladies of the peerage as women unaffected by hardships—people who were cherished and pampered and venerated.

Calum pushed away from the table, gathered Jamieson's work, and handed it over. "I'll not have you only live for your work. Not as long as you are here."

Three months. I've but three months. When Nurse Mattison had presented the terms and length of her tenure inside the Hell and Sin, that time had sounded fleeting. After just a fortnight with this man, she acknowledged that when she left, her heart would forever dwell inside this club with Calum as its keeper. Bereft, emotion clogged her. "Why would you do this?" she asked, voice hoarse. Why would he show this kindness and regard for a woman he'd but recently met?

A ruddy flush stained his cheeks. The evidence of his discomfort with her praise was endearing and earned another sliver of her heart. "I've not done anything," he said gruffly, yanking at his cravat.

He had. He'd given her the gift of security and safety, even if he could not know as much.

"I—"

Eve went up on tiptoe and pressed her lips to his.

Calum stiffened, and with a groan he caught her to him, claiming her mouth in a hard-taking. Moaning, Eve melted against him and, tangling her hands about his neck, drew herself up to know more of him.

Later there would be an appropriate time for shame at having flung herself at him. For now there was only this, and when she left this place, she wanted every memory with him that she could take.

She gasped as Calum caught her under her buttocks and lifted her up onto the table. Tilting her head back, she better received him in an embrace that turned her hot from the inside out. Nearly six and twenty, and referred to by the staff and society on the whole as the Ugly Heiress, Eve had long accepted that she was not, nor would ever be, a beauty of any sorts. There'd never been village boys attempting to steal a kiss or eager suitors in the one Season she'd known overcome with passion. Now, as she parted her lips and Calum slipped his tongue inside, she reveled in the thrill of her own femininity. For in this instance, Calum's strong hands worked a path over her body as though she were a cherished treasure he sought to memorize.

His fingers worked the ties free at the back of her gown, and then, reaching between them, he shoved the fabric down. Her chemise followed suit. The cool air slapped at her burning skin; the two warring sensations wrung a gasp from her lips. Never breaking contact with her mouth, he palmed her right breast, toying with the swollen tip. Moaning, she angled her head, fueled by his touch and kiss combined.

"You have bewitched me," he rasped, dragging his lips in a fiery trail from the corner of her mouth, lower, to where her pulse beat at the sensitive skin of her neck.

He suckled and teased and nipped at that flesh. Eve whimpered, and her head fell back as she opened herself to his ministrations. Hot, wet nectar pooled at her aching center, and she bit her lip. Needing something. Needing more . . .

Relentless in his passionate exploration, Calum shifted lower, ever lower.

A hiss slipped forth on a noisy exhalation as he caressed her right breast in his hand, then closed his mouth over the until-now-neglected other swell. He suckled at the sensitive tip, worshipping that flesh, flicking his tongue back and forth.

"Calum." Her voice emerged a keening entreaty that only fueled his attention. She splayed her legs wide. Her muslin skirts crunched noisily, and the wanton sounds of that fabric mixed with his wild suckling intensified the dull throb between her thighs.

Her hips took on a life of their own, and she undulated, needing something, needing him—only him. Calum drew back. She cried out at the loss of him and grabbed at his lapels, dragging him forward. *No.*

"Tell me to stop," he implored, his words breathless against her lips. "Call me a bastard. Tell me this is wrong."

"Why would I ever tell you that when I want this?" she panted.

His eyes slid closed, and the beautifully scarred planes of his face tensed with the weight of his struggle. Gathering his hand, she gave it a hard squeeze. "I'm a woman capable of making my own decisions." She guided his long fingers back to her right breast; the weight of his calloused palm against the soft flesh brought her eyes briefly closed. "I want you, Calum," she whispered. The column of his throat moved. Eve came up and lightly brushed her mouth over his in a quick meeting.

"I am going to hell," he groaned.

If he was going to hell, she would join him, and gladly burn to know this moment in his arms.

He swept her up and carried her around the table. Against her ear, his heart pounded in a wild, unbridled pattern that matched her own. Gently laying her down on the leather button sofa, he stepped back.

Eve shoved up onto her elbows and stared at him through heavy lashes. He was allowing her to change her mind. He wanted her to end this exchange. She stood, her limbs trembling with the force of her own desire. Not taking her gaze from his, she slid her gown past her hips, so she stood there in nothing but her chemise.

Eyes revealing nothing, Calum stood motionless while the mantel clock ticked away the passing seconds. And the longer she stood there exposed before him, reality intruded . . . and worse, his hesitancy. Cheeks ablaze, she struggled to right her chemise. "I—I'm sorry," she stammered, humiliation making her words run together. "I . . ." Eve bit her lower lip. Had she repulsed him with her brazenness?

Calum clasped her upper right arm, his grip firm and yet tender. For the first time relishing the height difference that saw her eyes fixed on his chest instead of his face, Eve studiously avoided him.

"Look at me, Eve."

She hesitated, and then she reluctantly picked her gaze up.

Desire—hot, real, and unapologetic—filled his hard eyes. "Never apologize. I want you," he confessed hoarsely. "And I know it goes against everything I should want, but God help me for being the street bastard society takes me for . . . I want you anyway." He covered her mouth with his, slanting his lips over hers again and again. And all her reservations melted away. Releasing the fabric of her chemise, she turned herself over to this man.

Calum shoved the garment lower, lower, and in a whispery soft rustle of fabric, it fell away, exposing her to him now in every way.

Yanking off his cravat, he tossed it aside. His jacket and fine lawn shirt followed, revealing the rippling, corded muscles of his olive-hued skin. Her mouth went dry. In her studies of those Greek sculptures, she'd appreciated the marble strength those great artists had captured of those chiseled gods. None of those figures immortalized in stone could compare to the unyielding power of the man before her. Entranced by the light matting of curls, she slid her fingers hesitantly through them. Testing their softness.

Calum's breath caught on a loud hiss, and she looked up. Immobile, with his eyes pressed tightly shut, he'd the look of one in pain. Tentatively, she continued her exploration, running her fingertips over the hard, flat plains of his belly, over—she stopped. Her hand trembled as she took in the jagged scar at his right side. "Oh, Calum," she whispered, as all the terror of that long-ago day intruded. His suffering, his pleas, and her inability to help him. Kneeling on the sofa, she angled her head and caressed that puckered white mark with her lips.

"Eve," he moaned, and his hands settled atop the crown of her head. The pins slipped free, and her hair tumbled about them. She gasped as he dragged her to the vee of his thighs. His shaft thrust hard against her belly. Then he reached between them and slipped a finger inside her wet center. "You are so beautiful," he said on an agonized groan.

Her legs buckled, and she cried out. "I'm not." Her head lolled against his shoulder as he slid that long digit forward and out, mercilessly teasing the swollen nub. "B-but when I'm in your arms, I feel as though I am."

"There is no one like you," he countered, and slipped another finger inside her tight channel.

Eve bit her lower lip and arched into his expert caress. Their bodies moved in a harmonious rhythm until logic and reason ceased to exist and there was only feeling. A steady pressure built at her center, and she quickened her own thrusts. "Calum?" she asked, his name a shaky plea. She was so close. So incredibly close to some magical precipice. Then he withdrew his fingers.

Her legs buckled, and she cried out at the gaping loss left.

Calum tugged free his boots and then, shoving his breeches down, stood before her in all his naked splendor. The sight of him would surely shame a proper lady, but instead the length of his throbbing shaft, pressed hard against his flat belly, liquefied her.

She held her arms open, and with a groan he covered her body with his own. His lips came down over hers again and again, and he lay between her legs. The feel of his manhood against her downy curls fueled her ardor. "Please," she begged, not knowing what she needed, only knowing she'd been so close before and needed to make that climb again.

Calum responded by slipping inside her honeyed channel.

A long, shuddery, unending moan spilled from her lips as in a dual torture, he toyed with her swollen nub. She lifted her hips, needing more of what he promised. "I've never felt anything like this," she rasped.

"Eve," he begged, "I'm trying to go slow. I don't want to hurt you." He slid in another inch.

With fingers that shook, she brushed back an errant brown curl from his damp brow. "You could never hurt me."

He captured her wrist and dragged it to his mouth, kissing the sensitive inseam where her palm met her arm. Little shivers of warmth radiated at the point of contact and raced a path up her arm. "Forgive me." He swallowed her sharp cry with a kiss.

Pain burned where there'd previously only been numbing pleasure. She went absolutely still, afraid to move. His shaft, impossibly long and hard, throbbed. Well, drat. He'd been correct. Clenching her eyes shut, she concentrated on breathing. "Th-that d-did not feel as good as th-the other preceding parts," she managed on a shuddery smile.

"Oh, Eve," he whispered. He touched his lips to her brow, and the tenderness of that caress brought her eyes closed. Calum slipped his hand between them and found her once more.

Eve gasped as he teased her nub, and a forgotten hungering stirred to life. Her breath came in shallow spurts, and all her senses became attuned to that back-and-forth glide of his fingers.

Then he began to move. Eve stiffened, braced for the agony of when he'd thrust inside. Only—a low moan filtered past her lips—a searing pleasure remained. He filled her, the slow drag of him inside her sheath, teasing. Tempting. Eve lifted her hips, matching his thrusts, and as he quickened, all pain fled. She closed her eyes and gave herself completely over to him.

Lifting her hips in wild abandon, Eve wrapped her legs about Calum, urging him on. "Calum," she pleaded as he brought her up again, higher and higher. The sound of his name seemed to fuel him. His movements increased with a franticness that had them panting.

Perspiration glistened on his brow as he deepened his thrusts. "Eve," he groaned. "Come for me, love." He captured her mouth. Desire swarmed her senses as she pressed herself close, scorched by the feel of his bare skin against hers.

He plunged once more, and with a piercing scream, she exploded in a burst of white light. Calum's hoarse shout mingled with hers, and he stiffened, then came inside her in long, rippling waves. Then, on a primal groan, he collapsed atop her.

Eve's heart pounded loudly in her ears, and she held him, not wanting to lose the feel of him in her arms. She struggled to draw air into her lungs. Even if it was a struggle to breathe.

"Forgive me, love," he murmured against her temple.

Calum rolled them over so she lay draped atop him in a tangle of limbs. Then he began smoothing his palm in small circles over her back. Her lashes fluttered, and she burrowed against him. *"Mmm."*

"You are a siren, Eve," he whispered, moving his hands lower.

"Do you know sirens are—"

"Dangerous creatures?" he interrupted, his eyes closed, those beautifully thick, dark lashes concealing his eyes. "I do."

Her heart had slowed to its natural beat, but now it picked up a cadence, and she propped her chin on her hands. "You are so familiar with the sirens?"

Pfft, I'd never be foolish enough to be lured by a woman that I'd smash myself against rocks . . .

His cocksure voice of long ago whispered forward. He remembered.

"I know enough to know that they were tempting creatures who made a man forget logic," he supplied, and she bit the inside of her cheek to keep from asking him more, from seeking answers about the time they'd shared together and whether it had mattered to him as it had her.

"And is that what I've done?" she asked, searching her eyes over the relaxed planes of his scarred face. "Made you forget logic?"

His lips broadened in an endearing, boyish grin that wrought havoc on her heart and senses. "Not enough to forget the appointments we have tomorrow with our vendors." He softened that with a gentle kiss.

She laughed and laid her cheek against his chest, so she might hear that steady beat of his heart. "Are you attempting to talk business with me, Calum?"

He leaned his head up. "Unpardonable?"

"Hardly." For in this moment, they were more than just lovers . . . they were again friends and partners, and after years of being alone, joy filled her. And while he discussed their plans for the coming week, she smiled.

Chapter 15

Eve should have been thinking about her upcoming meetings on Lambeth Street. She should have been filled with a deserved terror at being outside the Hell and Sin. The only news now written in the newspapers pertained to the Missing Heiress. The tale of a devoted brother, a powerful duke, doing all within his power to locate his cherished sister, had fed the *ton*'s need for gossip. According to those columns, Gerald had also taken to hiring Bow Street Runners to have her found.

And yet, the following morning, seated on the bench of Calum's well-sprigged coach, Eve sat in breathless anticipation thinking of only Calum Dabney.

As a young girl, she'd had a reverent awe for Calum. He'd been fierce and unafraid, despite the peril he faced every day, but he'd never treated her with unkindness for her birthright. He'd treated her with more kindness than even Gerald, her own brother, had ever shown her. More, he'd treated her not as a duke's daughter, not a wealthy heiress . . . just a girl. And for it, he'd captured a sliver of her heart.

Years later, Calum Dabney held her in thrall for altogether different reasons: for the future he'd built himself and for so many others who found employment at the Hell and Sin, for giving her and other women the opportunity to take on honest work, when most men of *any* station were content to relegate ladies to the role of dutiful wife and broodmare.

To Calum, she was not simply the Ugly Heiress, valuable only because of the fortune her father had attached to her. Instead, she was a woman he'd found capable, whose judgment he trusted enough to have her visit the men whom he conducted business with. Yet, unlike her ruthless brother and late father, he didn't see her strictly as the keeper of his books. He asked about her interests and her past, as one who seemed to genuinely care about the person she was and had been.

And he desires me . . .

She touched gloved fingertips to lips that tingled with the remembrance of Calum's embrace. His kisses. His arms wrapped about her.

Eve slid her eyes closed. Perhaps she had traces of Gerald's wickedness in her soul, after all.

The click of the door latch filled the carriage. Heart thudding, she looked over in breathless anticipation. Disappointment assailed her. "Oh," she blurted as Mr. Thorne's tall, slender frame filled the entrance. *You nitwit with your loose, runaway tongue.*

Mr. Thorne gave her a long look.

"Good afternoon," she said quickly as he hauled himself inside. Perhaps he'd not heard her overall disappointment at finding Calum's company unexpectedly replaced.

Calum's partner settled himself onto the opposite bench and recoiled. He sniffed the air before settling his gaze on her. But not before she detected the manner in which he wrinkled his nose.

She sighed. Having applied some of the mixture she'd made late last evening, she had her noxious odor back.

"Did you expect someone else, Mrs. Swindell?" He shot a hand up, and the carriage rolled onward.

If it were possible to die by blushing, the heat scorching Eve's entire being was sure to swallow her up. "Yes. *No.* No," she repeated more calmly. "Forgive me. I was merely"—*disappointed*—"surprised. I thought Cal . . . *Mr. Dabney,*" she hurried to correct, but not before she saw the astute glint in his eyes, "might accompany me." *Stop. Talking.* She curled her toes into the soles of her boots. What indication had Calum given that he'd join her? *You simply expected it—hoped for it.*

Unnerved by Adair's probing stare, but grateful he didn't pursue her erroneously drawn conclusion, Eve shifted her focus to the slight crack in the curtains. She took in the passing streets—dangerous ones that would send her father rolling in his final resting place if he'd seen just where Eve had ended up. Yet, how much greater the danger was for her in Grosvenor Square than this end of London that Calum had, and still did, call home. Despite logic and reason battling for control, her attention was drawn back to the proprietor unapologetically eyeing her in silence.

"Have you known Mr. Dabney long?" What was the story of their connection? Had he been a loyal friend in every sense, when Eve had failed him?

"A person asking questions is a soign of danger," Adair retorted, slipping into a coarse Cockney that revealed the truth of his roots.

"Only if the person asking them intends harm." Which she didn't. Long ago, she'd brought Calum pain, and coward that she was, she feared ever learning the details about what had happened to him after Gerald's interference. Her solemn rejoinder froze the proprietor on his seat.

"'e's my brother," he finally said, reluctantly, in graveled tones.

She scrambled forward on the bench. "His brother?" As a boy he'd spoken of kin, but never given her any specifics. Now she knew that had been a wise bid to protect them.

"Met on the streets," he clarified. "*Became* family." His eyes dared her to question that connection.

Eve fiddled with the faded satin strings of her Swedish bonnet. "Blood does not family make," she said softly. Kit had spent more time away than with her. Gerald would have sold her to Satan for thirty pieces of silver if it suited him in a given moment. She was not one who'd ever question familial bonds.

Silence fell between them, with the distant shouts of street vendors and the rumbling wheels filling the otherwise quiet. Capturing her chin in hand, Eve reshifted her attention to the narrow crack in the red velvet curtains.

"'e's loyal."

She stilled.

"Not a more loyal person in the whole of England. Most men and women become jaded and broken from doing the things Calum did, and seeing what he saw . . ." *Newgate.* A spasm racked her chest, squeezing the muscles in a vise. ". . . but 'e's never been bitter. Still manages to smile and care. And Oi'll not see him hurt because of that kindness."

"He is fortunate to have you." She spoke around a ball of emotion clogging her throat.

"We're fortunate to 'ave one another," he said gruffly, shifting on his bench.

The carriage drew to a stop as they arrived at their destination on Lambeth. With the words and warnings shared by Calum's brother ringing in her head, her books held in one arm, she allowed him to help her down. No doubt, were he to learn the truth of her identity, he'd gladly leave her on the streets of Lambeth without another glance. And with good reason. Her family had wronged Calum, and having enlisted Gerald's help against Calum's protestations that day, Eve was very much guilty of those crimes.

"Mr. Bowen is a mean bastard," he shared as they started along the pavement. They moved through throngs of passersby, while raucous calls filtered around the busy streets. "Wouldn't give a pence off a shipment if the king ordered it."

"Why would you remain with him?" she puzzled aloud, comfortable with this safe talk away from mention of Calum and into matters of business.

"Because his brew is the best, and we've had two others before him sending us broken shipments, paid off by our rival."

Ahh. "So, it's made you wary to trust another merchant," she pieced together.

From the corner of her eye, she saw Mr. Thorne frown. "Sometimes familiarity is safe."

"And sometimes it's costly." As it had, according to the records she'd reviewed of past and present liquor suppliers used by the club, proved to be. Given the current state of their finances, every penny mattered.

They arrived at a small establishment sandwiched between two taller shops. The carved wood sign featured gold lettering of far greater quality than any of the others on the street. It was a telling mark of the proprietor's self-importance—and his success. Mr. Thorne reached past and pressed the handle, admitting Eve ahead of him.

He closed the door with a soft click behind her. Tugging off her gloves, Eve glanced around, taking in her surroundings. The tidy inside with its neatly arranged desks and seating served as evidence of Mr. Bowen's wealth.

A graying gentleman, elegantly attired in sapphire breeches and a fawn jacket, entered through the back of the shop. "Mr. Thorne," he welcomed; his slight singsong tones spoke of his Welsh origins. "How very good to see you, sir."

Returning the greeting, Calum's brother motioned to Eve. "May I present our new bookkeeper, Mrs. Swindell."

The slight tensing of the shopkeeper's mouth indicated precisely what he thought of dealing with a female on matters of business. Another wave of appreciation for Calum, who freely hired women on his staff, filled her. Bringing her shoulders back, Eve drew on every lesson handed her as a duke's daughter. "Mr. Thorne, if you'll excuse us while we meet?" She leveled a hard stare on Mr. Bowen. "Given my review of the books, and your exorbitant rates, I expect we have much to discuss."

The liquor distributor scowled and looked to the man just beyond her shoulder. "What's this about, Thorne?"

Eve slapped her worn leather gloves together, answering for him. "This is about your escalating prices, without consideration for the value of our business, and a lack of any noticeable benefits."

The graying man sputtered, "I provide some of the finest brandy in England, and you'd come here and question my product?"

She took a step closer. "By your own words . . . *some of the finest*. Not *the* finest," she pointed out with her most winning smile. "Therefore, there is room for negotiation."

Her bold rebuttal was met with silence from the two men.

If Calum's brother countered her here, he'd cut off her legs with which to negotiate.

After several moments, Adair tipped his hat. "I believe I'll leave you to Mrs. Swindell, then." With that, he claimed a spot over by the door, his meaning powerfully clear—Eve was in charge.

"Well, Mrs. Swindell"—the shopkeeper folded his arms at his chest—"what do you want?" he asked, all earlier traces of good humor and politeness now gone.

Eve stalked over to a nearby desk and, uninvited, took a seat. From too many precarious dealings with Gerald, she'd come to appreciate the need to lay command to a situation where you can. "I'll keep this brief." She set her gloves down and drew out her journal. Opening the leather volume, she flipped through her notes. "Your rates have increased on an average of five pounds each month."

"Depends on what Mr. Black orders," he sputtered, stomping around the other side and sitting down hard.

"Then why, with last month's shipment reduced by five cases, did the rate remain the same?" she demanded, turning her notes around for his perusal.

Cheeks flushed, he didn't even glance at it. "What do you want?" he repeated in whiny tones.

She dropped her elbows on the edge of the table. "I want a set delivery rate on a contracted basis for the year, subject to our breaking the agreement without penalty. All the additional payments from the months you've overcharged the club will go toward future bills." She paused. "And I want reduced rates made on purchase orders over fifty cases."

The proprietor seethed. Fury and outrage burning bright in his eyes. "Who do you think you are, setting out to change the terms laid out by Mr. Dabney and Mr. Black? If they've been content, then I'll not answer to changes laid out by"—he paused and scraped an icy stare over her—"*you*."

She tipped her lips up in an aloof smile. "Ah, but you see, Mr. Bowen. I've been placed in charge of the liquor expenditures, and unlike the proprietors, I am a new member of the staff with no allegiance to you. I doubt I shall have any problems finding another liquor producer willing to meet my terms." On that, she grabbed her things and shoved to her feet.

She made it no farther than five feet.

"Wait," he called in beleaguered tones. "Fine," he gritted out. "But not every fifty cases. Every fifty-fifth."

"Forty-five," she countered.

"But that is not the way negotiating works, Mrs. Swindell," he cried.

Eve favored him with another grin. "Ah, but that is because this is not truly a negotiation, Mr. Bowen."

"Fine, fine," he said when she reached Mr. Thorne's side. "I'll agree to your blasted terms."

"Splendid." Filled with an excited sense of triumph, she marched through the door held open by Calum's brother. Over the years, she'd grown accustomed to men who either didn't want to deal with her or didn't take seriously any appointments with her. Never once had Calum and his brother shown that small-mindedness. Their family rose all the more in her esteem.

As soon as they stepped outside, a sharp gust of wind slapped at them, whipping their cloaks together. "Brava, Mrs. Swindell. Brava," Mr. Thorne said with reluctant appreciation.

Not breaking stride, Eve sketched a smart curtsy. A gust of wind wrenched her bonnet back, and she caught the corners to set it to rights. "Why, thank you."

Adair pointed ahead. "Our next appointment? Everett." He brought them to a stop outside another establishment. "Stingier than Bowen. Meaner."

At his caveat, she cast him a wry grin. "I assure you, Mr. Thorne, I know mean. I can certainly—" Her gaze collided with a tall figure winding his way through the streets. Elegantly attired, blond hair so pale it was nearly white.

Lord Flynn . . .

She froze. With one glance in her direction, he'd find her—and her fate and future would be sealed. A life as Lord Flynn's wife. Nor was there a doubt that if she returned home, either of her free will or against her volition, Gerald's friend would finish what he'd begun, and this time, he would succeed in raping her.

Her teeth chattered, knocking together loudly, as her senses flooded with the remembered horror of his attack—and intentions. *Oh, God.* He was here. Panic and terror made her tongue heavy in her mouth. *Whether you want it or not, I'm going to swive you . . .*

A stinging drop of rain pinged her nose. Followed by another and another. Until the sky opened in a torrent of stinging rain. She blinked slowly. Rain. It was raining. *Rain.* Jerked back to the present, Eve fought the wind for control of her bonnet. At last managing to grab that scrap, she jammed it promptly into place.

Lord Flynn forgotten for a new, more pressing, danger, Eve stole a peek down at her hands. Her ink-stained hands. *Oh, God.* Stomach lurching, she yanked her gaze up to gauge whether he'd seen anything out of place.

Calum's brother reached past her and opened the door.

Eve stumbled ahead of him.

"Mrs. Swindell?" Calum's brother asked questioningly.

"Please perform the necessary introductions," she requested in crisp tones, "and permit me to handle this as you did the last." How was her voice so steady?

Mr. Thorne eyed her a long moment and nodded.

And as introductions were made and Eve commenced her meeting with the nasty Mr. Everett, reality intruded. Her time with Calum was temporary, and until she reached her majority, she was in peril. And there was no one to rely on—most especially not Calum Dabney.

Chapter 16

He'd wanted to accompany Eve on her appointments. Calum's wish to join her had nothing to do with overseeing those meetings and certainly was not because he questioned her judgment.

He'd simply . . . wanted to be with her. Instead, at this given moment, he stood precisely where he should—just not where he wished to be.

Calum assessed the crowd at the Hell and Sin.

This was for the best. He rolled his shoulders. It had been wise to not accompany her. Distance between them was safe for the both of them. She would be free to focus solely on the club's business, which is what she'd been hired to do, and he wouldn't be tempted to abandon his morals again, just for the feel and taste of her.

He tamped down a groan and, not for the first time since she'd entered the Hell and Sin, cursed himself for this growing attraction. Only this was a need that moved beyond the physical. Rather, it came from an even more dangerous place than mere lust. It had to do with who she was as a woman: resourceful, clever, fearless.

Calum continued perusing the guests assembled at the tables, and then he stilled.

A burning at the nape of his neck—that sense of being watched, studied—held him motionless. It was a familiar feeling that came from living in the streets, where that uncanny awareness had the power to save lives.

With feigned nonchalance, he skimmed an intent gaze around the hell and found him.

The Duke of Bedford's brown eyes locked on Calum's. An air of ducal arrogance clung to the ruthless bastard. Time, however, hadn't been kind to the duke. Softer around the middle, and his cheeks given to fleshiness, he wore the evidence of his dissoluteness on his person, the way any reprobate did. Where a man of his power would have roused terror, now Calum stared boldly back, unremorseful. The duke was the first to look away, his attention called back to another losing hand.

Giving up his focus on Lord Bedford, Calum gave another cursory search of the floors and frowned. Adair wound through the club, moving with a determined step in his direction. He'd returned, which meant—

Calum registered the grim set to his brother's mouth, and something unfamiliar, something unwanted, scraped along his spine. Fear.

Calum was already moving. "What is it?" he demanded, meeting Adair. That question emerged rusty and steeped in panic.

"I'd speak with you," Adair said quietly.

Goddamn it. Calum opened his mouth to pepper the other man with questions, but Adair tipped his head. "Let's not discuss business here." The patrons. That was what should matter most. But it didn't. Not in this instance. Unexpected meetings heralded danger and were always call for alarm. Rushing through the dark corridors, he reached the back door.

No sooner had they reached the back of the club and entryway to the private suites than Calum gripped his brother by a shoulder. "Eve?" Terror made him careless, and he didn't give a bloody damn on Sunday about it.

"She's fine," Adair said with a calmness that drove back the cloying dread.

"She is fine," Calum repeated, more for himself. Calum instantly released him.

He gave a meaningful look in the direction of the stationed guard. That silent street language had them both climbing the stairs without another word exchanged. Calum used the brief reprieve to calm his frantically pounding heart. *She is fine. She is fine . . .* It was a litany inside his head. Only, the Hell and Sin for nearly two years now had faced threats from within and without.

First, there'd been an attempt on Helena's life, and then, Ryker's bride had suffered a knifing in the street. Then, Niall's wife . . . Those were chilling reminders of how perilous it was for Eve to be here. She should not be here.

They reached Calum's office. He closed the door behind them. "What is it?"

"It is your Mrs. Swindell."

"She's not my . . . What is it?" Because whatever had Adair's face set in this somber mask merited more worry than how he referred to Eve. As his previous anxiety dissipated, logic was restored. "Did she handle herself poorly?" Doubts crept in. *How well do you truly know the lady, after all . . . ?*

Adair's frown deepened. "No. It isn't that. Not at all. In fact, she handled herself quite admirably. Saved us a small fortune on future brandy shipments, and told Mr. Everett where he could go with his wheat prices."

Despite his unease, Calum found himself grinning. Yes, a woman who'd wheedle her way inside his club and lay claim to his books was certainly not one who'd tiptoe in fear around the always-nasty merchant. *Except . . .* His smile slipped. "What is it?"

Adair lifted his hands up. "I don't know. Something happened during one of her meetings."

Frustration roiled in his chest, and he clamped his lips tight to keep from snapping at his brother to spit out his damned story. "Something with Mrs. Swindell?" he asked slowly, taking care to use her surname.

Adair nodded. "After we fled Diggory . . ." Calum's muscles coiled tight at the mention of the former gang leader who'd controlled their childhoods and shattered their souls. ". . . and we'd see him again in chance meetings on the street. That was the look she had. Her skin went pale, and she looked like she'd seen the Devil at dawn."

Calum's earlier apprehension stirred to life once more.

His brother dusted a hand over his mouth. "And yet," he said slowly, "she handled the meeting with Everett immediately after as though nothing had happened."

Then, when one's demons resurfaced, one had those fleeting slips from the present . . . until one wrestled the monsters back into place. Knowing Eve suffered a hint of that darkness stuck like a blade in his chest. "Where is she?"

"Didn't say a word the whole carriage ride home. Silent as the grave, and then when we returned, she sought out her rooms."

Her rooms.

Not her office.

He frowned. "I'll speak to her," he said quietly.

Everything that day had been nearly perfect.

In fact, Eve would have otherwise said her meetings with Calum's vendors and her discourse with his brother had been faultless. She'd secured Adair's trust enough that he'd allowed her to handle the appointments without intervention or interference. Eve had secured concessions from both Mr. Bowen and Mr. Everett that would see more coin in Calum's pockets and help somewhat defray the decline in club profits.

And then between those two meetings, it had begun to rain.

Standing before the dresser mirror, Eve remained motionless. Just as she'd been since her flight from the carriage and through the servants' entrance to these borrowed rooms. Afraid to breathe. Afraid to move.

Mayhap she'd merely imagined the inky black on her fingers. Of course, she spent the better part of her days working on Calum's ledgers and books, so she was forever using her hands and ink and . . .

Yet she knew. Because she'd only applied a fresh paste of that horrid concoction to her hair last evening, and invariably nothing went according to plan where Eve Pruitt's life was concerned. Nor, given her deception, should she expect fate to kindly intervene on her behalf. Quite the opposite, rather.

Fingers numb from equal parts cold from the rain and dread, she loosened the strings of the beloved, and now drenched, bonnet. Carefully untying the satin ribbons, she closed her eyes.

Just take it off.

What was the likelihood that a brief dousing of London rainwater would wash away the concoction she'd applied last evening? Except, the recipe required the head to remain dry for three days' time. "Enough." She spoke into the quiet. Eve glowered at the pale, trembling lady who stared back. "It is not as bad as all that." She yanked the bonnet off. "It is . . ." Her stomach lurched. "Worse," she whispered.

Oh, blast, double blast, and bloody hell on a Sunday.

Horror wound a path through her, shuttering her thoughts.

Unfastening her cloak, Eve tossed it aside. The garment landed in a wet, noisy heap. She took a step closer to the mahogany dresser, and then another. "No," she whispered. "*No. No. No.*" The litany echoed around her chambers. Yanking out her pins, she dropped them to the floor. Those little pings sounded in time to the rain striking her lone window. She gave her head a shake. Drops of water struck the mirror and marred that perfect glass. Frantically, she dragged her hands through the tangled mess, then stuck her face close.

Her heart sank to her toes.

When her brother Kit had returned from one of his many travels around the globe, he'd carried back a book from America that contained pages upon pages of creatures native to that land. One had been a fascinating rodent said to emit a noxious odor that possessed perfect stripes upon its back. From Eve's previously odorous hair to these great streaks now exposing her brown tresses, she was very much like that American skunk.

Eve slapped her hands over her face and gasped.

She dropped her arms back to her sides. The damage, however, had already been done. Faint traces of black marred her pale cheeks. There could be no concealing this. Eve slid to the floor and, drawing her legs close to her chest, looped her arms about those limbs. What could she possibly say to explain *this*? Her mind raced with lies upon possibilities upon excuses. Of course, she could share the truth with him: that she was a woman hiding from her brother whose nefarious plans were better suited for those gothic novels than reality. She could omit those careful details about their shared past and her own identity. Go on working as his bookkeeper until the three months passed and she attained those funds.

That was assuming Calum would even want her to stay on in her post if he knew she'd deceived him and intended to soon leave.

We're not vastly different from a starving dog in the street. If one listens to one's instincts, one is invariably proved correct.

Eve laid her cheek upon the damp fabric of her skirts. No, he'd never let any person who'd deceived him stay on. She thought of everything that had come to pass: their work together at the foundling hospital, their stolen interludes talking over Greek works, and the night she'd spent in his arms.

A battle waged within between her own selfish needs . . . and what was right.

In the mirror, Eve's gaze locked on her stained cheek. Regret threatened to choke her.

I have to tell him all. I have to tell him that I'm the girl who nearly cost him his life. The one responsible for him landing in Newgate. "The woman he despises," she said softly. Everything. When he discovered the truth, the beautiful bond that had sprung once more would wither and die. And yet, with regret there was also . . . a calming peace. She didn't want to have this or any lie between them. She didn't want to accept his every kindness while withholding from him the most important truth. Calum deserved more. He always had . . . in every way.

A knock sounded at the door. That solid thump was not the faint scratching or hesitant raps used by a servant. *He's here.* "Mrs. Swindell?"

How fitting that he should call forth the false name she'd given. She drew in a shaky breath. It had been but a matter of time. For Eve's earlier resolve, fear made her tongue heavy. Only it was not fear of being turned out and having no choice but to return home to Gerald, but rather, the animosity that would spark to life in Calum's eyes.

Another loud bang shook that oak panel. "Eve?"

At the concern that stretched through the barrier and reached her, tears sprang to her eyes. "You'll lie even about not crying," she whispered, furiously blinking back those drops.

"What was that?"

A shuddery half laugh, half sob bubbled past her lips. Of course, he heard everything. He always had. Back when she was a child, he'd heard her approach through the mews. A life of power, wealth, and strength hadn't dulled those senses. He anticipated her steps, all these years later, a woman grown. "Just a moment," she requested, her voice steady. Using the edge of the mahogany dresser, Eve pulled herself to a stand. She paused to assess her damning countenance.

Streaked hair. Smudged cheeks. Rumpled and wet.

He'd be mad to let her stay.

With a sigh, she pinched color back into her wan complexion. Then, clasping her hands at her back to hide their tremble, she called out, "Enter."

The door opened, and Calum's tall, formidable frame filled the doorway. "Eve, is everything . . . ?" He ceased midquestion, and even as his words trailed off to silence, he pushed the door quietly shut, closing them in. His astute gaze missed nothing. It touched on the rumpled cloak, her beloved and now hopelessly destroyed bonnet, and then the most damning piece of all—her hair.

Eve darted her tongue out, tracing the seam of her lips. "I would speak to you." *I would speak to you?* That was what she'd say? Suddenly, as the course she'd settled on entered into a territory of the real, she wished she'd put proper thought into just what she'd say. How she'd say it.

Calum met her pronouncement with a stoic silence. "What happened?"

She caught the inside of her cheek hard. Couldn't he have come in here, making demands related to her post? Or pepper her with deservedly accusatory questions about her abrupt flight abovestairs and rapidly fading disguise? Instead, this was what he'd ask her. Then, why should this be easy for her?

"Eve," he urged gruffly, taking a step closer.

"Stop." She held a palm up, and he instantly complied.

And waited.

Eve briefly closed her eyes, searching for strength. It was time to tell him all. She forced herself to meet his probing stare. "I . . . have not been . . ." She grimaced. "Entirely truthful with you." He'd been right to mistrust her from the start.

His biceps tightened the sleeve of his black jacket. He folded his arms at his chest and leaned back against the door. The tension pouring from his frame belied that casual repose. "Are you married?"

"No," she said quickly. Eve wrung the fabric of her damp skirts, and then realizing what she did, stopped. Flexing her palms, she laid them flat along the front of her gown. "You asked if I were in trouble," she said quietly, because mayhap he might at least understand. "And I am. It is the only reason I ever came here . . . for the post." The reason she'd been in desperate need of that assignment. Unlike the day he'd discovered her at the foundling hospital and worry had filled his eyes when they'd spoken of her past, now he was a blank mask, revealing nothing. Unable to meet his piercing gaze, she studied her interlocked fingers. "I am not telling you this because I expect sympathy." She deserved none. "I'm telling you so you might . . . understand." But certainly not forgive. At his silence, she forced her eyes back to his.

He tipped his head in a demand for her to continue.

"I have kept books. However, I've not been employed to do so . . . until now."

A muscle leapt at the corner of his eye. "Whose records did you keep?" Those five words, coated in steel, turned her cold. How odd that of all the questions he might ask, he should unerringly settle for the most damning and correct one.

"They were . . . *are* . . . my family's," she evaded, a coward still. She spoke on a rush, needing the story told and all her lies laid out before him. "A number of years ago, my father fell ill. One of my brothers was gone. The other"—she hardened her mouth—"was uninterested in the family's finances." *Or anything except his own pleasures.* "I handled the record keeping. When my father died, I learned he settled a sum upon me. Funds that would be turned over to my husband—should I wed."

Calum stilled, and then a dawning horror registered in his eyes.

"Settled funds upon you?" he seethed.

Unnerved by the volatile fury humming under the surface as he was transformed to the rightfully wary stranger who'd stormed these very rooms almost a fortnight ago, Eve backed slowly away, positioning the wide four-poster bed as additional space between them. "A dowry," she confirmed.

Calum's entire body jerked. "You are a lady . . . of the peerage." His voice emerged hoarse with horror and desperation.

Eve might have laughed if the situation wasn't so dire. For years, the only interest gentlemen extended her was due to her connection to a duke, and now that same connection was causing Calum to eye her as he might a poisonous spider. "Answer me," he demanded, surging forward so the mattress remained the only physical barrier between them.

Eve gave a wobbly nod.

He scraped a gaze up and down her person. "Who are you?" he gritted out.

Folding her arms about her waist, she sucked in a steadying breath. "My name is Evelina Pruitt . . . and my brother is the Duke of Bedford."

Chapter 17

For all the horrors he'd witnessed and taken part of in the streets of St. Giles and all the darkness he'd known, there had been but two moments in his life when Calum had been so wholly lost—at sea.

The first being when his parents had died and he'd found himself inside a cold, lonely foundling hospital. The other when he'd been carted off to Newgate and slated to die.

Calum stared emptily at the small woman across from him. The slightly crooked teeth worrying her lower lip. The dusting of freckles along the bridge of her nose.

"When I was a girl, my father would tell me of the great Greek stories contained in the night sky . . ."

The memories continued coming fast and furious, tumbling over one another, confusing his muddled mind.

"Nothing is more useful than silence . . ."

"That's your favorite saying, Calum . . ."

"Tau."

"It means immortal . . ."

No.

The air exploded between his tightly clenched teeth in a noisy hiss, and he stumbled back a step. His stomach lurched.

Evelina Pruitt.

Little Lena Duchess.

Christ in heaven.

An empty, mirthless laugh burst from his lips. All the signs had been there—right down to those damned glasses she'd arrived with and then conveniently never needed again—but he'd failed to see them. "Of course, I should have known you were a lady," he railed into the silence. He began to pace at the side of her bed—his bed—dragging a hand through his hair. From the moment she'd set foot inside his office, every instinct had roared at him to turn her out. He'd failed to heed his intuition but one other time, and it had nearly cost him his life . . . yet he'd not properly learned. The fact that Evelina Pruitt stood before him now, just a mattress apart, was proof of that. "All the indications were there. Your cultured tones, your knowledge of Greek works," he spat. Her damned regal bearing the queen couldn't copy. *But you didn't want to see it because you were content believing the lie.* Only she was not just a lady . . . He stopped abruptly, and horror brought his eyes closed. *The Duke of Bedford's sister.*

"I should have told you," she said, her voice broken and hurting. Should she be hurt and broken? She'd been the one to enter his club on a lie.

Killing all hint of softening, Calum forced himself to look at her.

"I had nowhere else to go," she whispered, holding her palms up in supplication.

"Why are you in my stables . . . ?"

"I had nowhere else to go . . ."

Of all the damned admissions for her to make, she would echo that exchange when she'd first come upon him in her family's mews. No fear had sent her running; instead, curiosity had pulled her closer. Mayhap it was her penchant for dissembling that made her use those words against him now. But goddamn it . . . for the fact she'd turned him over to Bedford and nearly sealed his fate, there had been a time she'd given him shelter and food. And on the streets a person paid his debts, and he at least owed Eve her piece. Then he could be rid of her. "Speak," he seethed.

"When my father died, he—"

"Settled a dowry on you."

"Yes." She gave a frantic nod. "If . . . when I reached my majority and still remained unwed, those funds would come to me."

"How much?"

"Twenty thousand pounds."

It was a veritable fortune, and it was why Bedford had taken to hunting for her . . . *And she is here, under my roof* . . . He ran cold at the implications of that.

She spoke, bringing him back from the edge of horror. "My brother depleted our family's fortune, emptying the coffers at . . ."

The gaming tables. Calum owned a sizable portion of the man's monies and debt. Over the years, he'd reveled in the truth of what he'd effortlessly wrestled from the nobleman who'd nearly ended him. That had been the extent to which he'd thought of any of the Pruitts, instead content to keep the girl named Little Lena Duchess dead in his memories. "Go on," he said coolly, free of guilt.

Eve cleared her throat, and he damned her remarkable composure when he was one utterance away from splintering. "Gerald is determined to acquire a portion of my dowry, and he . . ." Eve's voice wavered, in her first falter.

He steeled himself. He'd not make any more mistakes where this *lady* was concerned. "I'm growing tired, my lady."

"He schemed with another gentleman to . . ."

To? Calum quelled the question asking to be let out.

"To ruin me. One night my brother had been hosting one of his"— red blossomed on her cheeks, infusing the previously gray skin with color—"scandalous parties."

With Eve under the same roof? He scoffed. Then, having catered to Bedford since the club's inception, and witnessing the level of that lord's depravity, was it a wonder?

"A gentleman entered my rooms." She wet her lips and devoted her attention to the tips of her toes. "Gerald had struck an agreement with him."

And through his fury and unease, a new sentiment was born. A pit settled in his belly. *I don't want her words to matter.* But damn them for doing so, anyway. Calum remained silent, allowing her the time for her telling. Needing to hear the entire bloody story.

Eve's rapid intakes of breath and her broken exhalations filled the quarters. Then, slowly, she lifted her head, meeting his gaze squarely. "He attempted to rape me."

The air stuck in his chest as a red wave of rage seared through his veins.

Eve continued in barely discernible tones. "He . . ."

A growl worked its way up his throat.

She promptly flattened her lips into a hard line and shook her head as if she sought to erase those memories from her mind and her telling. "I clubbed him on the head."

Pride at her resourcefulness, when any other lady would have faltered, filled him. Until she again spoke.

"And I knew I had to leave."

"So you came here," he said tiredly.

"So I came here," she murmured in a soft echo.

And now she had to leave. She never should have been here. The Missing Heiress all of London was speaking of and searching for was, in fact, residing in the Hell and Sin. Calum dragged both hands through his hair.

Christ. He didn't want these imaginings of Eve alone and helpless with a reprobate attempting to rape her. He wanted his righteous fury and resentment for both her past betrayal and the one she'd committed against him now. "Who knows you're here?" he asked the question that needed answering. For the other reality slid in. They now housed a duke's sister in their private apartments. Not only housed her, but employed her, and Calum had made love to her.

"No one," she said on a rush. "Nurse Mattison," she amended.

He unleashed a string of curses.

She moved around the bed, and Calum held a hand out. Eve abruptly stopped. "She is loyal and devoted. She is the one who suggested I go into hiding here, knowing Gerald would never look for me here. She would not betray me."

Did she believe that would bring him any reassurances? "You cannot stay here," he said as much for his benefit as for her knowledge.

Eve gave another one of those unsteady nods. "Yes. Of course. I know."

Damn you, Eve. She'd not even prove her selfishness and fight for the right to remain.

Turning on his heel, Calum stalked over to the door, then froze with his fingers on the handle. "Was any of it real?" he asked hoarsely, not looking back lest she see how she'd shattered him with her lies.

"All of it," she whispered.

"*Pfft.*" He gave his head a disgusted shake. Against his every instinct that screamed to be wary from the start, he'd told himself to trust her. He'd taken her in his arms, in his bed . . . *And I wanted more with her.* His heart spasmed. "What a fool I've been," he whispered to himself.

She moved in a loud rustle of skirts. "You were not a fool," she entreated, touching his arm.

He flinched at that tender caress, and she let her arms fall loosely to her sides.

"I would have you know that everything has been real, and I've wanted to tell you."

"Then why didn't you?" he thundered, and she jumped.

"Because what difference would it have made?" Her lips turned up in a quavering smile. "The result was always to have been the same. For you would have never allowed the girl who betrayed you to remain." That had only been the first crime against her. The other, however—her birthright—was just as damning. "That is what I told myself, anyway, Calum." Tears filled her eyes, turning them into crystal pools of despair.

His throat worked. He'd always been useless with a person's crying. The sight of Eve's tears had always ravaged him, even back when he'd believed himself heartless.

"I entered your club believing nothing mattered more than my own survival." She spoke a sentiment he knew too well. It was one that sprang from desperation and fear and enabled a person to abandon morals and right. She slid a cold palm into his and squeezed. "But then every day that I was here, with you, I didn't think about simply surviving and my security. I thought of you. I—" Recoiling, Calum yanked his fingers free of her seducing touch.

"Enough," he ordered in the same stern tones he used to quell fights on the floor. He'd not have her offer him belated words of affection. His mind shied away from what she'd been one syllable away from uttering.

"Don't you see, I could have still continued the lie? I needn't have mentioned my brother."

He flinched at that additional reminder . . . *You little guttersnipe. Think to steal from me . . . ?*

"But I did because I wanted you to know all."

Another harsh chuckle rumbled in his chest. "My, how very honorable of you." She knew not what she'd done. Nay, worse, she'd not cared. By her own admission, she'd thought of nothing but her own well-being. "You have threatened everything I hold dear," he said on a steely whisper. "My family. The men, women, and children dependent upon me and this club." A lone tear trailed down her cheek, and he steeled himself against the sight of her misery.

Since his brother had wedded a duke's daughter, the club had suffered irreparable harm. Eve's being here now would sound the final death knell if her presence were discovered. *And yet, given the evil I know her brother capable of and what she'll certainly face upon her return, how can I send her away* . . . Nausea roiled in his gut. *I'm going to be ill* . . .

"Calum . . ."

"Not another word, my lady."

Hurt flashed in her eyes.

He gnashed his teeth. How dare she play the part of the wounded party? Casting another disgusted glance up and down over her, Calum stalked out of the room. Fury lent his steps a quick rhythm. He stopped at the end of the hall, where MacTavish stood on guard. "Watch Mrs. Swindell's rooms," he ordered tersely and marched off, calling out for Thomas as he marched belowstairs.

The burly guard came bolting over. "Mr. Dabney?"

"I want you stationed below Mrs. Swindell's window." He spoke in low tones for the other man's ears.

Bowing, Thomas rushed off.

Calum resumed his path to the gaming hell floors. Whether or not Eve Swindell—nay, Eve Pruitt—left now shouldn't matter. The best thing she could do was get herself gone and remove the threat she posed. Yet, he'd be a fool to not carefully watch the lady now. Just as he should have trusted his instincts nearly a fortnight ago when she'd sneaked off with his books and maneuvered rooms. He entered the hell, pausing to study the crowded floor. Where the thick plume of cheroot smoke and clink of coins striking tables always filled him with a calm, today only tumult raged. Busier than they'd been in the recent months, there were still empty places at those once full tables.

And how much emptier they'd be were the fancy lords and gents present to discover Eve's presence here.

"By God, you look like one eager for a fight."

He started as Adair took up a place at his shoulder.

His brother wryly grinned. "And you've taken to startling." His smile withered. "What is it?"

Even as it made sense to tell his brother everything, something kept him from requesting a private meeting to discuss all that had unfolded with Eve. My God, she was Bedford's sister. The girl who'd once been a friend to him, who'd brought him food, and who'd carelessly offered him up to the same brother who threatened her existence now.

"Mrs. Swindell?" Adair accurately surmised.

Yet, Calum had withheld enough. God, even the bloody name she'd assumed had been perfect for her. "She is not everything she seems."

Adair coiled tight like a serpent poised to strike. A thunderous cheer went up, and Calum looked to Lord Cavendish celebrating a win at a hazard table. "You were not incorrect earlier," he settled for. "She is in trouble," he said out the corner of his mouth.

His brother's hushed curse reached his ears. "What manner of trouble?"

He opened his mouth, but just then the burly guard stationed at the front admitted another patron. The Duke of Bedford entered, flanked by Lord Flynn and Lord Exeter. Their boisterous laughter and slurred calls as they made their way through the club hinted at trouble. Drunken lords were oftentimes more dangerous than the lowest base-born brat.

Calum eyed that trio. Was the man who'd attempted to rape her, who'd put his hands upon her and sent her fleeing, here even now? Was it a man who drank Calum's drinks or mayhap a patron he conversed with when he did his rounds of the club floors?

And for his earlier outrage at her treachery, able to think at last, Calum acknowledged the precarious state she'd found herself in that had led her to his club. She couldn't remain, and he would still be wary until she was gone . . . but he understood her silence.

The Duke of Bedford grabbed a passing serving girl about the waist. Her silver tray tumbled to the floor. Cries and shouts went up from those patrons now wearing the contents of those wasted spirits.

"Bloody hell," Adair muttered.

Bloody hell, indeed. "See to it," he commanded, grateful for the diversion that had put an end to talks of Eve and her duplicity. Adair sprinted through the club, with lords cutting a wide swath for him. Barking out orders, Adair shot a hand up signaling for assistance from two of the guards stationed nearby the developing fray.

Calum lingered. He trusted his brother implicitly, but they'd all relied on one another enough over the years to never trust that help wasn't required. Adair immediately calmed the drunken patrons, neatly separating the girl who'd previously been mauled by the duke. The two brothers' eyes caught from across the hall.

"Fine," Adair mouthed.

Fine. He clenched and unclenched his fists. How far from the truth that assurance, in fact, was.

Quitting his spot, Calum wound his way along the same path he'd traveled a short while ago. He took in the men dealing cards and the young women proffering drinks and the former soldiers and street toughs standing on guard. The blade of guilt twisted all the deeper.

These are the people Calum owed his allegiance to. Particularly, his family of five. A few unfavorable words about the Hell and Sin by some pompous lords had already knocked their club down from the zenith of greatness. A duke, even a wastrel and a drunkard like Bedford, could take them down once and for all, with nothing more than the whisper of an ill opinion.

When Calum revealed Eve's identity and deception, his brother would rightfully want her thrown out on her arse. As he bypassed the fray his brother now stood in the midst of, his stare lingered on Eve's brother and the gentlemen he kept company with.

On his best day in the universe as a fledgling merchant's son, he had never belonged to Eve's exalted ranks. And yet, how the universe must be reveling at the irony of their paths being thrown together yet again.

Reaching the back entrance of the club, Calum started past the two guards positioned there. What would have happened if all those years ago, he'd stumbled into some other fancy lord's stables for shelter from the rain and there had never been a little girl he'd called friend. Little Lena Duchess, whom his own siblings had never known of. All they'd known were those nights he'd disappear and return with an armful of bread and provisions. They'd taken those luxuries as bounties he'd stolen from unsuspecting shop owners, and he'd been content to let them believe the lie. In St. Giles, one knew better than to trust a lord or lady. To revisit the same home week after week and meet alone with one of their pampered daughters was a crime far greater than any material theft. Guttersnipes did not mingle with virtuous ladies, and now Calum had gone and done something altogether more dangerous—he'd made love to one of them.

He reached the top of the darkened staircase and looked first toward his office, then down the opposite end of the hall where MacTavish stood on guard.

Each step that brought him closer, strengthened his resolve to cast her out. As he'd told her, she could not remain here.

He attempted to rape me . . . He . . .

His stomach muscles contracted as her words whispered around his mind, bringing forth unwanted imaginings as his mind finished the story she'd not fully tell. Of some nameless stranger scrabbling with her skirts, bringing his weight down over her, exploring her—

She was not his responsibility, this new grown-up Little Lena Duchess he'd known but a fortnight. His brothers and sister and servants and dealers and guards . . . those were the people he was beholden to.

Yet, he could not let her leave. Not unless he was content with the knowledge that he'd be complicit in sealing her fate.

You bloody, weak fool. What was it about Evelina Pruitt that had always managed to shatter his guard? As a girl, reading to him in the stalls, to the woman who didn't give a damn about the station divides between them.

"Bloody hell."

MacTavish jerked his stare over, and Calum's neck went hot over that violent outburst. Striding the remaining distance to her room, he stopped outside and looked questioningly to the guard.

The other man shook his head. "Nothing suspicious, Mr. Dabney. Nary a sound from the woman."

"You're dismissed for the evening."

Dropping a quick bow, MacTavish rushed off down the hall. Calum waited until he'd gone, then directed his attention forward.

He stared contemplatively at Eve's door panel.

Ryker and Niall had forever been the most coldhearted of their lot. When their sister, Helena, had been haunted by Diggory's evil, they'd been incapable of so much as offering a word of comfort. It had been Calum who'd held her through those nightmares. Yet, for the solace he'd given, he'd also never considered himself weak. Particularly not where the overall security of their family was concerned.

Until now.

If Eve were the mercenary lady who didn't give a bloody damn about anyone except herself, she certainly wouldn't have risked discovery as she did with all their trips to the foundling hospital. And therein lay the reason for his tumult. For what she'd confessed about Bedford and his crony's vile goals for her, she still hadn't lived solely for herself. She cared enough about those children she visited and the women who ran the Salvation Foundling Hospital that she gambled with her own safety.

And then there had been him. A man who'd risen from the streets to find a fortune, and he hadn't given a thought about the suffering of those orphans like him. Oh, he'd hired some of the most desperate people on the streets, but even that had not been purely altruistic. Rather, it had largely been a product of club profits and necessity.

How I wish she were someone else, though. But if she were, then would she be so wonderful as this woman who'd held him enthralled? He balled his hands into tight fists. How he wished that she'd not been a lady tied to the peerage, with noble roots that could never be joined with his, not without destroying the Hell and Sin and all those dependent upon it.

He knocked his head silently against the door.

What in blazes am I going to do with her?

Chapter 18

With her valise packed, her gown changed, and her hair neatly brushed and plaited, Eve sat staring at her reflection in the dresser mirror. She cocked her head.

She'd always hated her hair. Most English girls were born and blessed with golden curls. Eve, on the other hand, had been saddled with limp, dull-brown strands that couldn't manage a curl if the Lord set himself to the task of it.

Yet, since she'd blended that noxious recipe and painted her hair, she'd mourned the loss of her natural coloring . . . and not simply because of the odor that clung to her. She'd donned a disguise and lost so many parts of herself. Her name. Her existence. Even those once lamentable tresses.

She touched a reverent hand briefly to the crown of her head. It was an odd thing to sit here contemplating in the time since Calum had stormed out of her rooms. Particularly given that he'd stationed a guard outside her door. "A guard," she whispered into the quiet. Like she was a thief who could not be trusted. Then, what did she expect? Eve let her hand fall back to her lap.

Calum believed it had all been a lie, and the rub of it was, with the exception of her name and the details she'd omitted about their shared past, it had all been real. She'd come here seeking security and instead found him.

I love him.

He'd quelled that admission earlier, and yet that, too, had been the truth. She loved him for being a man of strength who'd risen from his circumstances to become a thriving business owner. She loved him for being honorable and caring about those dependent upon him. And she loved him for entrusting the role of bookkeeper to her, despite her gender. In the end, she'd repaid that gift with a lie.

The door opened, and stiffening, she looked up.

Calum closed that wood panel behind him, shutting them in alone. Silent and stoic, he bore no traces of the affable, grinning man who'd asked her to share her interests with him. He dropped his gaze, and following his stare to her packed valise, terror replaced her earlier numbness. She would return home. To Gerald.

Please, no . . . I didn't . . . What are you going to do to . . .

From the past, she heard the muffled sounds of her own cries, lost to the freezing-cold tub of water as he'd dunked Eve's head under the surface. Her pulse raced as the sting of cold and water burning her nostrils flooded her memory, and she was transported back to that day. A man who'd hurt a child for helping a poor boy from the streets . . . What would he do to a woman who'd thwarted his efforts to secure her fortune?

"Eve." Calum's low murmur slashed across those horrors. Despite the precariousness of her situation, that deep timbre soothed her. It calmed.

Clasping her hands in the model of primness imposed by her nurse-maids, she stood.

When he spoke, his words came unexpected, freezing her. "My brother Ryker was caught in a compromising position with a lady, a stranger to him."

He stared pointedly at her. Did he think because Eve was a lady of the peerage she should know that tale? Where most lords and ladies existed for societal gossip, Eve's world had been far too tenuous to worry after the whisperings of the *ton* or the words splashed on scandal sheets. At her silence, he continued. "Ryker was a duke's bastard, recently titled for saving the Duke of Somerset's life. When he was discovered in a compromising position with the lady, our profits suffered and the number of our daily patrons fell. Ryker and that young lady were forced to wed . . . to save our club."

How these men had given everything for their hell . . . and I put it all at risk. "How very sad for them," she said softly, imagining being forced into a union with one she did not know.

Calum wandered over to the window and stared out. "Oh, they fell in love. Theirs is a happy marriage."

Her heart quickened to hear him so matter-of-factly speak of that grand emotion, when most any other man would have scoffed or yanked at his cravat in discomfort.

"Then they are very fortunate," she said wistfully.

He paused in his telling, casting a glance back. "And were you one of those ladies dreaming of love?"

"Me?" Startled, she touched a hand to her breast. She chuckled. "No. I was far too practical to ever become one of those sorts." When she was nine, she'd overheard two maids talking about Eve's fortune being the only thing that could see an ugly girl such as her married. Calum, however, had made her feel beautiful . . . in every way.

His stare lingered on her face.

Eve's cheeks warmed, and she cleared her throat. "You were speaking of your family." And their marriage to inspire envy in the heart of every spinster lady.

His expression darkened. "My other brother, Niall, fell in love with a duke's daughter."

Another duke's daughter. Eve searched his implacable features. What accounted for this grimness when he'd previously spoken optimistically of Mr. Black's marriage? "Did she . . . betray him?" she asked, trying to make sense of this different telling.

Calum's lips quirked up in one corner. "No." He paused. "She married him."

Given everything she'd withheld about her own existence, it was the height of wrongness to ask Calum for details of his own. Yet, she needed to know anyway. "And you disapproved of the lady?" she ventured tentatively.

"Quite the opposite. She destroyed her own reputation attempting to save my sister from a street thug. The lady is a woman of honor."

A woman of honor. *Unlike me.* That hung in the air, unspoken between them. Was that opinion shared, or was it her guilt that was responsible for that whispered thought?

Eve forced herself to speak. "I don't understand." She shook her head, at a loss. Had she merely imagined his earlier severity? "You did not disapprove of their marriage, then?"

"Me?" He scoffed. "Hardly." His mouth hardened. "*Society* disapproved. The *ton*," he amended. "Polite Society."

She tried to make sense of that. "And yet they approved of Mr. Black's marriage?"

"In terms of membership and profit, our club recovered." From across the room, their gazes locked. "Ryker might have been born a bastard, but he was a duke's son, and titled. Niall is a bastard born to a London street whore. He wasn't some fancy lord's by-blow. He was, and to Polite Society will always be, a guttersnipe."

"Polite Society," she spat. "I'd always found it laughable that the word *polite* should be affixed to the peerage." When those pompous lords and ladies reveled in the struggles of men and women of all stations.

Calum gave her a long look. Did he think she'd commiserate with the *ton*'s archaic thoughts on station? That he might even have such an ill opinion of her, ached like a physical wound.

"To the peers . . . your peers"—Eve flinched—"birthright matters. With Niall's marriage, he crossed an unforgivable line. He dared touch what men such as he, and Adair, and I have no place touching. Gentlemen will happily give their coins and fortunes to bastards born of the streets, but they will not"—he gave a hard, negating shake of his head—"ever permit or pardon those same bastards wedding or bedding a lady."

His vitriolic reaction had stemmed not solely from the harm she'd brought him all those years ago but also from her station. He came here and offered her, the woman who'd twice wronged him, explanations? Her heart filled anew with love for him.

"You cannot stay here," he said quietly, echoing some of the last words he'd given when he'd stormed out. Only, where there had been fury before, now there was a somberness devoid of that seething hatred.

Her throat muscles worked, and she nodded. "I know." Now she knew even more so. To stay here put his club in jeopardy in ways she'd not considered. Because, as he'd accurately pointed out, she'd thought of no one except herself. It surely spoke to the depths of her selfishness now that knowing that as she did, she'd no regrets. She had missed him so very much, and for a brief time she'd a glimpse of who he was now. *How I will miss him . . .* "I would have you know, when I came here, I didn't know you were the owner of this club." Her life for so long had been her father and her family's estates and crumbling finances that she'd known nothing else.

He brushed his knuckles along her jaw, bringing her head back so she might meet his gaze. When had he moved? "Would it have mattered? Would you have not come to fill the post?"

"I . . ." *Lie to him.* "I don't know," she whispered. "If I were more honorable I would tell you that I would not have. I would lie and say

215

that after what my family did to you . . ." He flinched, dropping his hand to his side, and she mourned the loss of the first real warmth she'd known that day. "I could not betray you again as I did," she forced herself to finish. A sad, empty chuckle escaped her. "I am more like my brother than I ever credited because I cannot say any of that." Because she'd always loved Calum Dabney. First as a girl, enamored of the one person who'd seen her and been there, and now knowing him as she did, she loved him with a woman's heart.

He rubbed his hand over his forehead. "What am I going to do with you, Little Lena Duchess?"

That endearment of long ago riddled her heart with warmth . . . and then she registered the resignation there. A cold swept over her. It would be fitting if he repaid her actions all those years ago, in kind. Could a lady be turned over to the constable for invading a man's business and lying to him? No theft had occurred. "I'll leave," she said on a rush. She gestured uselessly at the bag resting at their feet. "If you hire a hackney." She spoke quickly, her words jumbling together. "Well, I can hire the hackney. I've the funds. I'll provide the coin, and I will not mention anything of my time here. You have my assurance."

He eyed her with an inscrutable expression. "You would do that?"

"Hire a hackney?" She frantically nodded. Riding in one of those miserable carriages was the least dangerous of endeavors she'd undertaken in her life . . . particularly when one considered life with Gerald. "You needn't escort me." That way he needn't risk being seen with her in any capacity. She grimaced. Not that he'd given any indication that he would. Particularly not with the peril being seen with her presented.

"How long until you attain your funds?"

At that sudden question, she opened and closed her mouth several times. "When I reach my six and twentieth year. T—"

"Two and a half months, then," he finished for her.

"Look at this, look at this, Calum. The Greeks put candles on cakes to celebrate their birthdays! Candles! We shall put them on yours because yours comes first."

"Don't want any. Seems like a waste of good candles—"

"Oh, fine. Then we shall wait until the end of the month when mine comes."

He recalled her birthday. Another frisson of warmth stirred in her chest. And then it receded, leaving in its place stark coldness. In the end, neither of them had celebrated together. Calum had been carted off to Newgate, and when her birthday arrived, she was alone once more.

"No one knows you're here besides Nurse Mattison." He spoke quietly, his words coming out as a kind of reminder to himself.

Had she not known the gentleness this man was capable of, those cryptic words would have roused terror in her breast. She shook her head.

He released a long sigh. "I must be a fool."

She shook her head.

"You can remain."

She could . . . remain?

Surely with her own hopes, she'd merely imagined that gracious offering?

Calum spoke, and the orders flew fast from his lips as only a man responsible for this gaming kingdom could manage. "Your visits to the foundling hospital are done. I'll hire someone to help them in the interim."

She fluttered her hands about her throat. He would do that?

He leveled her with a look. "Are the women who work there aware of your presence here? Besides the one nurse?"

"No," she said frantically, shaking her head. "I didn't reveal that . . ." Except by his accompanying her, she'd inadvertently put Calum at risk with all those visits to the hospital.

"I don't want you anywhere near the gaming hell floors." Yes, her brother spent more time at his clubs than God did in heaven. "I don't even want you leaving the hell by way of the back door or front door or any other door."

In short, she was to be a prisoner of sorts . . . but one by choice.

"If you require air, I don't even want you ducking your head out the window." She flinched. Which she had done days earlier, putting Calum in even greater peril. "You're permitted to visit the mews, and that is the extent to which you have freedom of movement—until your birthday. And from there, you will leave, and mention nothing of your time here. Are we clear?"

Eve drifted closer to him. "Why would you do this? Why would you help me in this way, even knowing who I am?" *What I did?*

He tugged at his lapels once, the only telltale marker that she'd unsettled him with her direct questioning. "Because you helped me for almost a year and provided food when my family most needed it. I pay my debts, Eve. After this, consider that debt paid."

So that was what this offer was about . . . his misbegotten sense of honor? Bitterness stung like vinegar on an open gash. *Then, what did you expect? That he cares for you as much as you care for him?* "Thank you," she said softly. For his offer might not be driven by what she wished it to be . . . feelings . . . a regard for her. But it was still an undeserving gift he extended.

The muscles of his face spasmed. "Why do I feel like I am making the absolute worst mistake where you are concerned, again, Eve?" he asked, his voice hoarsened with emotion.

"You aren't," she vowed, darting over to him. Eve stopped a hand-breadth away, hovering, uncertain. She ached to take his hands in her own, to twine their fingers together in a warm joining. *He doesn't want your touch.* Not anymore. "I promise you," she said, imploring him with her eyes to see the truth of that. "I'll not betray you or your trust." Not again.

He let his breath slip out through tense lips. "See that you don't, my lady."

With nothing more than that, for a second time that day, he took his leave of her. The quiet click of the door closing thundered in the silence of her chambers.

He'd let her remain.

There should be the thrill of relief and a lightness within.

My lady.

That is how she would forever and only be to Calum Dabney. She would work these next two and a half months for him, and then he wanted her gone.

Tears clogging her throat, Eve picked up her valise and began unpacking, hating that there would never—could never—be more with him.

Chapter 19

Over the course of that week, everything within the club continued on as it had been.

Standing at the mahogany table in the Observatory, Calum alternated his attention between reviewing the reports Eve had drafted and watching the patrons on the gaming floors. For all intents and purposes, it was any other day inside the hell.

For all of Eve's staggering revelations, there had not been any dramatic scandal to rock the club. There'd been no raging duke to storm the hell and lay the final deathblow to their success.

Nor had there been any of the other shared tender moments between them. Damn him for being weak, Calum missed them. He missed the teasing discourse, and their working together at the foundling hospital.

Instead, Eve had become the perfect employee. A barrier of formality had been erected between them where she was his bookkeeper and he her employer, and but for business meetings and topics pertaining to the club, nothing further was discussed.

Her footsteps sounded in the hall. "Enter," he called before she'd even lifted her hand to knock.

Eve entered, somber and silent. Adjusting the ledgers in her arms, she drew the door shut behind her and came over. Wordlessly, she laid several of those folios and ledgers atop his table.

It's my boots. There's nothing else for it.

Frustration broiled in his gut, and Calum grabbed the leather folio. Yanking it open, he proceeded to read her expense report. As he scanned her meticulous columns, she hovered at his shoulder, silent as the damned grave. *Damn you, Eve. Damn you for being . . . what?* What right did he have for resentment? When he'd set out terms under which she might remain, he'd been clear that nothing was to exist between them except the role of employer and bookkeeper. She'd fulfilled her every responsibility and complied with his demands.

And he was bloody miserable.

He glanced over. "And the wheat—"

She handed over another folio, placing it on his desk. "By my calculations," she said in flat tones, "with the adjusted prices agreed upon in my meeting, you'll save an average two hundred pounds each month, and a cumulative savings of two thousand four hundred annually."

It was damned good news considering the money they'd bled since Niall's marriage. Now he felt . . . oddly hollow. "Thank you. That will be all."

Eve dropped a curtsy—a bloody, blasted curtsy—and took her leave.

"Eve?" he called out.

With the smooth, regal grace only a duke's daughter could manage, she wheeled slowly back.

Say something to me. Anything beyond this eternal politeness and formality. "You are well here?" His own sister had eventually chafed at the constraints of remaining solely inside the Hell and Sin. What of a lady accustomed to running her family's estates and going where she would, when she wanted?

"I am well," she murmured. She stared questioningly back.

He cleared his throat. "That will be all," he said gruffly.

Eve dropped another infernal curtsy—and left.

Calum dropped his focus back to the records she'd brought him. Or attempted to. With a curse, he slammed his fist down. Abandoning his place at the desk, he stalked over to the windows and absently viewed the patrons around the club.

It shouldn't matter that he and Eve existed in a solely businesslike state. In fact, it was the only relationship that should have ever existed. Men, of any station, who longed for and lusted after women who served on their staff were scoundrels. Worse, they were fiendish reprobates, and Calum had descended into their ignoble ranks.

Only, Calum hadn't lusted after Eve. Oh, he'd longed to know the feel of her in his arms—and ultimately had acted on that hungering. But there had been more with Eve. For all the guardedness that had existed between Calum and his siblings, with Eve there had been an openness. He'd not felt lesser for laughing with her or worried that it made him seem human when men in St. Giles weren't permitted any weakness. Scarred and broad as he was, women, from the girls who worked in his club to the ladies of the *ton*, eyed him with equal parts fear and disgust. Eve never had.

But then, she hadn't when he'd been a boy of fourteen, either.

He squeezed his eyes shut.

And for a brief time, when only the illusion existed between them, he'd cared for her.

Belatedly he registered Adair's visage behind him.

"You didn't hear me enter," his brother observed, a question there.

"I was distracted," he said, not taking his gaze off the floor.

"As you've been since you indicated Mrs. Swindell was in trouble."

It had been a mistake to storm off that day and blurt out the truth to his brother. Calum gritted his teeth. Nay, the only mistake was in not revealing Eve's identity to the other man. "It doesn't merit a discussion," he said for the third time since his brother had pressed him for details.

"But it is enough that it has you distracted and Mrs. Swindell downcast."

Calum's ears pricked up. "You'd say downcast, would you?" All Calum had seen in their dealings was one wholly unaffected, and perfectly formal. Downcast would suggest she felt . . . something.

A snorting laugh left Adair's lips, and withdrawing a cheroot from his jacket, he lit the scrap and took a pull from it. "Highly unusual for you to sound so bloody hopeful about another person's misery." A glimmer lit his eyes. "I'd expect as much from Ryker and Niall, but not you."

He mustered a chuckle at the other man's jest.

Adair held over his cheroot, and Calum gratefully accepted it, filling his lungs with the smoke. "What kind of trouble?" his brother put to him, relentless.

He deserves the truth, and yet the moment Calum revealed all, Adair would order her gone. "The gentleman she worked for prior had nefarious plans for her," he hedged, offering partial pieces of Eve's existence.

Adair cursed. "Bloody noble?"

Bloody duke. He nodded once.

"And so, she's in hiding?"

"She is," Calum confirmed. Taking one more inhale of the cheroot, he handed it back.

Scrap in fingers, Adair folded his arms and continued his smoke, all the while eyeing Calum through the plumes of white. "Did she steal from the gentleman?"

He shook his head.

"Harm him?"

Calum scoffed. "No." Just the opposite. Fury went blazing through him as Eve's telling resurfaced. "She was wronged," he reiterated. And having been victim to the evil the Duke of Bedford was capable of, he'd no doubts of Eve's peril.

Adair shifted back and forth on his feet. Of course. Calum's explosive defense went counter to the calm evenness their siblings had prided themselves on. Again . . . it had only ever been Eve who'd let him speak without fear of recrimination or judgment.

"You missed your shift," Adair said quietly.

Calum blinked slowly, then jerked his gaze over to the longcase clock. The damning angle of those black handles glared back his error. "Oh, Christ," he whispered on a quiet exhalation.

He, who'd prided himself on putting this club before all, had faltered now twice, and in the most egregious ways.

"It's fine." It wasn't. Adair squeezed his shoulder. "But you cannot be on the floors right now. I have it."

Here Calum had served as second-in-command, always believing himself effortlessly able to slide into the role of head proprietor if the circumstances merited, only to be proved an utter failure in this. And so much.

"Here." Adair handed over the partially smoked cheroot, and his meaning rang loud. Calum needed a break.

"Thank—"

"Don't thank me," his brother said impatiently. "We all serve different roles at different times. It's why we've been successful. There's five of us." Adair started for the door. "Oh, and Calum?"

Shaken, he glanced over.

"A letter arrived earlier from Helena. She wants to meet Mrs. Swindell." With that casual pronouncement, Calum's world lurched again. Following his abrupt departure, he'd not gotten 'round to paying her a visit. Having her here wasn't an option for entirely different reasons. Helena, now living among the *ton*, kept circles with the peerage, and that made any meeting with Bedford's sister an impossibility.

Just one more bloody lie.

"Calum?"

"I'll make arrangements," he said tightly. Helena would have to come here. They couldn't risk Eve going outside. Not with all of London searching for her.

Adair nodded and took his leave. Calum remained at the windows, surveying the crowded floors. He finished his cheroot and tamped it out on the glass window. Dropping the scrap, he stared out as his brother reentered the hell, moving freely and casually as Calum himself once had. Envy sluiced through him. With just one hire of an heiress bookkeeper, his life had become like one of those card towers their former guard Oswyn used to construct—one misstep or faulty movement away from toppling. Adair stopped alongside the edge of the floor, and with his arms akimbo, he was very much king of this empire.

And I'm threatening it all . . .

Swiping his hand over his face, Calum abandoned the Observatory and found his way through the halls, making his way to the mews. For all the darkness he'd faced as an orphan, where his brothers and sister had known zero kindness from the world, for a brief time, Calum had known warmth. The Duke of Bedford's stables had initially posed as a brief shelter from an unexpected rainstorm. In that place, he'd remembered everything he'd lost along with his parents those then nine years earlier. A horse. As a boy of five, he'd had a horse of his own.

After his parents' deaths, in those secret moments he'd sooner have died than admit to his siblings, Calum had allowed himself dreams of more. Of a stable of his own, with a mount like Night. That time he'd spent with Eve had allowed him dreams when his siblings had ceased to think of anything else but survival.

Eve had done that for him. Over the years, with the passing of time, however, he'd not allowed himself to remember anything but his bitter resentment at being turned over to the constable. That dark night had shaped him, so that he learned to trust no one other than his siblings.

But there had been books with her. And laughter. And discussions that hadn't involved death and dying and survival, as it had only and always been with his family.

Entering the scullery, Calum strode past the handful of servants still working at that late hour. MacTavish, stationed at the back entrance, jerked his chin. "She's outside, Mr. Dabney," he said on a hushed murmur for Calum's ears alone. "Been out there for some time."

Calum followed his gaze out the glass panel. With a quiet word of thanks, he exited the scullery, drawn to Tau's stables.

Giving his eyes a moment to adjust to the dark, he entered.

Eve sat against the stable wall, an apple and a knife in her hand. She held out that piece of fruit to Tau, and the enormous creature swallowed it in two loud bites.

She spoke suddenly, unexpectedly. "Do you know, the day we met was one of the happiest ones of my life?" Her words struck like a gut punch, throwing him off-kilter. What did it say about Eve's existence that their time together had been the happiest of her five and twenty years? "You were my first and only friend," she whispered. "In retrospect"—she waved a hand, fluttering that apple about, and Tau made a grab for it—"as a woman grown, I see that to a boy on the cusp of manhood, a nine-year-old girl would have never been considered a friend." Not even one who'd brought him food and kept him company and taught him to smile again.

He had, though.

"For every ill thing you believe about me and the unfavorable opinions you have and are entitled to"—but was he?—"I would have you know before I leave here, that time together meant something to me. You saved me from abject loneliness, and I repaid that gift with betrayal."

He shook his head. "It's done," he said gruffly, not wanting to hash out the past and speak about the darkest moment of his one and thirty years. No good could come of it, and more, coward that he was, he didn't want to relive that terror.

She continued anyway. "That night, my father had been out, as he so often was. My brother, Kit, was away at school, and Gerald had recently returned from wherever he'd been."

At a wicked club. A boy of the streets who'd wound his way about picking those fancy lords' purses, it had been Calum's position to know where to find the most plump-in-the-pockets nobles and who were the easiest marks. It's why he'd made a grab for his watch fob that night.

Eve went silent, and Calum was drawn forward by the need for her to continue. She nibbled the corner of an apple piece and then turned the larger portion over to Tau. She patted him on the nose. "Sometimes, I would go through my book"—that heavy red leather volume they'd both looked over together—"and I would pretend I was one of those mythical figures. The night you were injured, you'd said you would be there. But you didn't come." She lifted her eyes to his. "Of course, I know now where you were." Eve caught her lower lip between her teeth. "As a girl, I was so self-absorbed." She grimaced. "So lonely. I was angry that you weren't there."

"We were going to blow out candles upon a cake."

A sad little chuckle slipped from her lips. "You didn't want the candles. You said to save them for mine."

What a miserable bastard he'd been. Of course, life in St. Giles had jaded him, had knocked most of the niceness out of him. It had been what allowed him to live when men like Diggory would have beaten Calum down for any weakness. Still, he wished he'd been better—for her. He slid into the place next to her so they were shoulder to shoulder. "I'm sorry."

She waved off that apology. "I continued to go 'round to the mews to see if you'd suddenly come, and then I told myself I didn't care if you came. Instead, I played by myself. That night I pretended I was the deity Philotes."

His gaze fixed on the top of her head as a memory whispered forward.

"Let me read this one, of Philotes, Calum."

"I'd rather you read of Zeus, Duchess."

"But you don't know this one . . . Oh, fine."

He stilled. Now he wished all those years ago he'd let a little girl win out and read of that Greek story.

"Philotes was the daughter of the goddess Nyx but had no father," she explained. Just as she'd been without a mother. "She was the deity of friendship, and I loved to imagine myself as her." Eve dropped her chin atop her skirts and rubbed back and forth. "I'd been so lonely until I found you." His heart spasmed. "Then you were there, and I had someone to talk to."

He looked down, giving her a wry glance. He'd been silent and surly and afraid the wrong sound would find him dead. "I wasn't much for conversation then."

They shared a smile.

"Not at first," she concurred with the same honesty she'd shown as a girl, "but in time you were. Until you, there were only stern nursemaids and myself for company." Her gaze grew distant. "I didn't know of your siblings then," she said wistfully.

"No." He hadn't confided in her because the danger would have been too great.

"I'd imagined you were, not unlike me, alone." Eve stopped that back-and-forth movement of her cheek. "I wish I'd known that. I wish I'd known that you had family in your life. Not like mine, people who didn't know I was there, but people who cared about you, because I used to lie abed hating that for you. Hating that you were as lonely as me and on the streets. It was doubly unfair."

"Yes, but then, isn't that life?"

"Unfair? *Hmm.* Who am I to say that? I always had food and shelter and security."

As a child, perhaps. As a woman, she was just as much without now as he had been then. She drew in a shuddery breath. "I was so angry with you that night, because you weren't there. I swore I wouldn't keep checking, but I did anyway, with that little cake I'd cajoled Cook into making." Eve held the remaining part of the apple in her hand over to Tau, and he swiftly consumed it. "And then I found you." Her rapidly indrawn breaths filled the space, blending with Tau's steady munching on the apple. "It was the blood."

I'm not afraid of blood, Calum. They bled my mama.

"There was so much of i-it." Her voice broke. "It was different than when the doctors bled my mother. I came to you that night pretending I was Philotes."

Calum closed his eyes, not knowing what to do with her suffering. Only knowing he wanted to take it away and make it his own.

"One of Philotes's siblings, Apate, was the personification of deceit, the cause of bad." Her eyes darkened, and his arms ached with the need to drag her close. "With Gerald as a brother, I *knew* what he was." She shot her eyes up to his. "Even as a girl of nine. I knew he was e-evil." Her voice broke again, and that evidence of her misery threatened to break him. She shook her head back and forth, and it knocked against the wall. "And I went to him, anyway." Eve covered her mouth with her hand, muffling her hoarse words. "It was my fault you were taken to Newgate."

A piteous sound tore from his throat, and going up onto his knees before her, he forced her up, demanding she look at him. "It wasn't your fault." He'd only ascribed blame to her over the years because it had been easier to live an existence of black and white, and not the nether shades in between.

Eve's shoulders shook with a hideous laugh devoid of her effervescent spirit and cheer. "Oh, come. You remembered me only in hatred and rightfully blamed me. Don't you lie to me now." Then she dissolved into shuddery, noisy tears that shook her slender frame.

Groaning, Calum hauled her close.

He was being kind to her.

Again.

Why was he being so bloody kind? It made Eve sob all the harder. She struggled against him, not wanting this offering. She'd already taken so much from him. Jeopardized his very existence countless times. Eve wrestled in his embrace, but he merely folded her in his powerful arms, quelling her struggles.

His heart throbbed hard against her ear in a steady, heavy beat of his strength and vitality. No longer fighting his hold, she collapsed against him and took the solace he offered.

She cried for the little girl who'd thought him dead because of her carelessness. She cried for all the years she'd spent missing him. And she cried because there could never be a future with the two of them together in it. Not that he'd spoken of wanting more . . . but lying in his arms, feeling the weight of his body cover hers and learning the taste and scent of him, she'd allowed herself to believe . . .

Calum pressed his lips close to her ear, his gentle murmurings lost to her weeping. *"Shh,"* he whispered, rubbing his hand in a smooth, circular pattern over her back. "Don't cry, love."

Love. With his hoarsened, desperate pleading, she could almost convince herself that endearment was real. Eve wept copious tears until nothing but empty, hollow sobs shook her chest and then dissolved into an occasional noisy hiccup. Silence fell in the stable, broken only by Tau's occasional whinny. "After he'd had you dragged off, he came for me." Calum's muscled frame turned to marble against her. "He accused me of helping you. Said I needed to be punished."

A low growl rumbled in his chest. "What did he do?" The deathly promise there was so different from his earlier warmth it sent ice racing along her spine.

He gave her a slight squeeze, and that firm, reassuring pressure brought her eyes closed. Except for when the memories slipped in, she'd not allowed herself to think of Gerald's brutality against her. She bit the inside of her cheek so hard, the metallic tinge of blood flooded her senses, forcing her back to that night. "He ordered a cold bath. I hid. He, of course, found me. When Gerald is bent on evil, not even Satan himself could stop him." *It is why you should leave this place . . .* Because ultimately, his darkness always won out.

"Eve?" Calum urged.

Giving her head a shake, she rushed to be done with her telling. "He dragged me by my hair abovestairs." Her skull ached with the remembered pain of that viciousness as he'd torn clumps of brown tresses from her head. She touched her fingers to those spots and then, belatedly realizing what she did, let her hand fall to her side. "When we reached my room, he shoved my face under the water." Blanching at the remembered horror: the sting of it as water filled her nostrils and burned her throat Choking, gasping. She shook her head. She couldn't paint the details of that act. How she'd been so very certain when the water flooded her nostrils and mouth that she'd die there. "Afterward"—it was safer to start there—"he tossed me into that water." Freezing. It had burned as sharp as the pain in her lungs from that dunking. "And then he left."

A black curse exploded from Calum's lips.

Eve twined her fingers with his, finding strength in that connection. How she'd ached to feel him again like this, even a simple touch, since he'd discovered her identity. How she'd wanted them to return to the beauty of anonymity and pretend. "After that night, he told me you'd died. Taunted me with the story of how he watched you hang and then swing in the gallows, and I knew I deserved Gerald's punishment that night for what I'd done."

"No," he moaned.

Eve covered her eyes with her hands and sobbed all over. "I lied again. I told you I didn't cry."

"Oh, Eve," he said on a broken laugh, once more gathering her close.

"It wasn't your fault," Calum repeated somberly. When she made to speak, he touched his fingertips against her lips. "You were right," he murmured stroking her back. "I *did* blame you because it was easier to blame you than myself."

She struggled back to look at him. "Blame your—"

"I stole your brother's watch fob. I knew who he was. I knew the risk of taking from a man whose home I visited countless times and planned to visit countless others. Every time I lifted a purse, that was the risk I chose."

Eve made a sound of protest. She'd not allow him that. "You were hungry." Never in all the years that she'd thought of him and believed him dead had she ever held him responsible.

"Desperation will make a person do desperate things, won't it?" She opened her mouth, then registered his piercing stare on her. Their gazes locked. "I understand why you did what you did. Then, and now."

Eve ceased breathing as she took his words in, and they were an absolution of sorts.

It was not my fault . . . I had not been the one to cart him off. My only crime had been trying to help him . . . He, the unlikeliest of people, had helped her to see that.

She lay against his chest and drew in a slow breath, letting it fill her.

And in the stillness of the night, in his stables, a calming peace stole through her. Blinking back the residual tears still clinging to her eyes, she caressed the jagged scar by his mouth with her fingers.

Calum caught her wrist in a delicate hold and dragged it to his mouth. Little shivers tingled up her arm as his lips caressed the inseam of her hand. He held it there, close, his breath stirring her skin. "It is why you began working with the foundling hospital," he correctly surmised.

Nodding through the haze cast by his seductive hold, she studied their joined hands. "I first came to London eight years ago. I had one Season." It had been a miserable affair where she'd spent more time watching from the wall than dancing with any interested or uninterested gentlemen. She took care to omit those humiliating details. "When my father tired of London, I was only too happy to leave." She pressed her hand to his side, where the blood had once spilled from. Calum covered her palm, forcing her to stop, and dragged it back. "After all the painful memories associated with that place, I was content to leave it all behind and be the"—she twisted her lips in a droll smile—"*dutiful daughter.*" That grin faded. "Then, my father suffered an apoplexy and lost the use of his legs. He was confined to a bed, and his care fell to me. When he was sick, I took over the bookkeeping. After he . . . died, when I returned to London, I discovered the foundling hospital. Being there gave me purpose and made me feel I was helping . . . if even in some small way."

"You are a remarkable woman, Eve."

She gave thanks for the cover of darkness that concealed the heat cascading over her cheeks. "Do not make more of it than it is. I did not find the children and nurses there until a year ago," she protested, not wanting him to make her into one who'd done anything extraordinary.

"Because you were caring for your father." His mouth hardened, and the gold flecks in his eyes glinted. "A father who owed you his protection."

She'd long ago accepted that her father had ceased to see her when his beloved wife died. "I've forgiven him," she said simply. Just as she'd forgiven Kit for being invisible.

"It is more than he deserved," he said in steely tones.

"Mayhap. Mayhap not." She shook her head. "But no good has ever come from resentment. It just begets more anger and hatred and further darker emotions."

Calum palmed her cheek. "Eve, I—" Leaning toward those words, she silently cried out when he stood. He swiftly exited the stables. "What is it?" he demanded.

"A patron has demanded to see you." Adair's voice carried over to her ears.

"You are acting head tonight."

Eve strained to hear the hushed murmurings. "He's demanded an audience . . . the Duke of Bedford."

Calum fell silent. The earth stopped spinning. And then Calum again spoke, knocking the universe back into motion. "Tell him I'll be along momentarily."

The soft pad of Adair's footfalls marked his departure. Eve slowly stood.

Calum stepped back inside. "Do not leave the stable," he clipped out.

"He's here for me." Her voice emerged threadbare, and she hated herself for that weakness.

"You are not leaving with him."

She gave him a sad smile and shook her head slowly. "Your club."

Calum gripped her hard by the shoulders and brought her up on her tiptoes. He lowered his head, shrinking the distance so their noses touched. "He will not know you're here."

"But what if he already—"

"Enough." He settled her back on her feet. "After I leave, do not answer to anyone. Not even a guard from inside this club. Stay here. I'll return shortly." Calum lingered, halting as though he wished to say more.

And then without another word—he was gone.

Chapter 20

Calum had faced down devils in the street. He'd shared a roof and answered to one of the most ruthless killers and gang leaders in both St. Giles and the Dials. But of all those monsters whose paths he'd crossed, none had he ever wanted to end more than he did Eve's brother.

A short while later, features schooled into a comfortable mask, Calum entered his office.

The tall, elegantly clad Duke of Bedford reclined in the chair closest to Calum's desk. Legs sprawled before him, hands resting on his slightly rounding belly, he personified ducal power. In his very repose, he was a man who acted as though the world was his due and he would expect nothing less.

He'd also been the bastard who'd dunked Eve under freezing water when she was a child and arranged to have her raped when she was a woman.

And Calum, who'd always prided himself on his control, was proved wholly inadequate in an altogether different way. A muscle twitched at the corner of his eye, and he fought to repress the growl stuck in his chest.

"Your Grace." God how he hated using that proper form of address that elevated this man in any way. Feeling Bedford follow his movements, Calum casually collected a decanter of fine French brandy and a glass. "I understand you wished to speak with me." He tipped the bottle, and the clink of crystal was inordinately loud, that mundane sound at odds with the tension thrumming inside this room. He composed himself and turned back. "A drink?" Calum had learned long ago the dirtiest tricks to upend one's opponent. The drunks had always been the easiest to topple. He held the snifter aloft.

The duke's bloodshot eyes went to that glass, and he eyed it the way a starving man did food. Lord Bedford smacked his lips loudly. "Indeed. All business meetings must be conducted over fine spirits."

Carrying the glass over, he held it out. "Is that what this is? A business meeting?" He moved around the desk and settled himself in the familiar folds of his seat. Mayhap it was nothing more than a request for an extension in his credit.

Eve's brother took a long, slurping swallow of his drink. His throat muscles moved loudly in a revolting display of his weakness. While he drank, Calum's gaze went to the other man's lily-white hands. Free of calluses and ink stains, and yet they were large. And those same long fingers had gripped Eve by the hair and yanked her through their home. The imagined sound of her screams pealed around Calum's mind. Laying his hands on the arms of his chair, he curled his fingers, gripping the edge to keep from ripping Bedford's entrails out through his bloody mouth. After he'd finished his drink, Eve's brother released a sigh. He set his empty glass down on the arm of his chair.

"You have something that belongs to me."

Alarm bells went off. Fighting the sudden unease pulsing through him, Calum leaned back in his seat. He tilted his lips up in one corner. "I have a whole number of things that belong to you," he drawled. "Unentailed properties. Your debt. Your former funds."

The duke flattened his lips into a hard line. Leaning forward, he thumped the surface of Calum's desk. His abrupt movements sent his forgotten glass tumbling to the floor with a loud thwack. "Do not make light with me," he snapped. "Where is she?"

There it was, the question he'd have sold his soul not to have heard from this man.

The same mind-numbing terror that had seized all rationale the night he'd been hurled into Newgate struck. He tipped his chin. "If this is about the serving girl you recently accosted," he said coolly, "our establishment no longer deals in prostitution. You'll have to take that manner of business up with Broderick Killoran at the Devil's Den or some other hell. If you'll excuse me," he said curtly, rising.

The duke stared up at him and then broke out into a laugh. "Do you take me for a fool?" His icy smile withered. "My sister is here." He glanced about Calum's office. "You, a worthless guttersnipe, are harboring a lady inside your hell." Eve's brother slapped his fist against his open palm. "And I demand you return her to me."

Folding his arms at his chest, Calum came 'round the desk and positioned himself over the smaller man. "If you lost your sister, those affairs are your own. Now if that is the only reason you've come, on some madcap belief that she is, in fact, here, then you've wasted your time."

A knock sounded at the door.

Grateful for the interruption, he called out.

Adair opened the door. "I was advised by this man that he had business with you and Bedford," he said tightly. At his side, a cloaked figure—a stranger—cowered and shook.

"Ah, splendid," the duke called out, his bravado firmly affixed. "Mattison, please enter. Enter," he boomed, firmly in control and commanding as though this were his office.

Then the name he'd used registered.

Mattison.

Nurse Mattison is loyal and devoted. She is the one who suggested I go into hiding here, knowing Gerald would never look for me here. She would not betray me . . .

Oh, Christ in hell.

Adair gave Calum a probing, silent look. *I've failed everyone. Eve. Adair. Ryker, Niall, Helena. All of them.* Guilt sat like a boulder upon his chest. He gave his head an imperceptible half shake, that slight movement they'd adopted years earlier to signify danger.

Adair gave no outward show.

"Mrs. Mattison, don't hover out there. Come in. You, as well, Mr. Thorne. The more the merrier."

Shoving back her hood, the tall, blonde-haired woman entered the room. She bowed her head, but not before he caught the flash of grief in her eyes.

Adair followed behind and closed the door.

Eve's brother pushed to his feet. "I'm not pleased with the Hell and Sin right now," the duke chided. "Tsk. Tsk. Nor is most of the *ton*. You've earned quite the reputation, you bastards from the streets, of taking up with ladies of the *ton*."

A pit formed in Calum's belly as Adair threw him a sideways glance that demanded answers he'd deserved a week ago. "If you've come here because you've taken umbrage with whom our proprietors have married, then you can cease wasting either of our time and take your services elsewhere," Adair said with a frostiness Ryker Black himself would have been hard-pressed to emulate.

"*Pfft,*" Eve's brother scoffed. "I hardly cared about the ones spreading their legs for you . . . before now." A glacial mask iced the duke's features. "Your brother is bedding my sister." All the air was sucked free of the room, with the only sound being Nurse Mattison's gasp. Then, "My *beloved* sister, whom all Polite Society has been searching for . . . is here." He jabbed his finger toward the floor. "She's your bookkeeper."

The color leached from his brother's skin. *I am so sorry.* Those words, a futile apology, offered nothing. Adair instantly composed himself. "I don't know what you're talking about, nor does my brother."

"No?" The duke hooked his thumbs inside his waistband. "Know nothing, do you? Lady Evelina Pruitt?"

A vein throbbed at the corner of Adair's left eye.

"There's no one by that name here," Calum said tersely.

"Mrs. Mattison?" the duke called out.

The woman gave her head a hard shake. "Your Grace," she implored.

"Mrs. Mattison," Eve's brother demanded, ice in his command.

That nurse slid her eyes closed, and when she opened them, hatred burned from within. She directed that unveiled emotion at Eve's brother. "I sent her here," she said with remarkable cool. "Falsified papers. Arranged the post through the agency you used to find a person for the respective p-position." Her composure cracked, revealing her turmoil. "She's here." That threadbare whisper contained barely a hint of sound, and yet it was enough.

Flummoxed, Adair looked to Calum.

Removing his gloves from inside his blue brocade jacket, the duke slapped them together. "Of course, this is no doubt a dreadful misunderstanding on your part. I expect my recalcitrant, half-mad sister has been passing herself off as a servant." *Half-mad.*

When Gerald is bent on evil, not even Satan himself could stop him.

This is the danger Eve had faced. It was as perilous as any battle Calum or his siblings had known against Mac Diggory on the worst of days.

"What do you want?" Calum asked quietly.

"I want her back." Calum had witnessed on the streets that death was preferable to some of the evil one might face. To turn Eve over to this man would consign her to a living hell. "As simple as that." Lord Bedford tugged on first one, and then the other immaculate white glove with meticulous care. He made a show of wiggling his fingers and flexing his palm. Triumph glittered in the duke's eyes. "You needn't say anything now," he said to his audience's silence.

"What if I say no?" Calum shot back. Adair's curse echoed around the room, and Calum continued over it.

"Why *would* you say no?"

Because I love her. The earth dipped and swayed under his feet. *I love her.* Mayhap he always had. First as the girl who'd been a friend and pulled him from the precipice of complete and total darkness. And then as a woman whose strength, intelligence, and compassion had won all of his useless-until-her heart.

Bedford slashed the air with his gloved hand. "Your club is in shaky enough standings with Polite Society. What will they say if they discover you're the latest of the Hell and Sin proprietors to be bedding a duke's daughter?"

Calum already knew what they would say . . . it was the same thing the *ton* had been saying after Niall and Diana's marriage. *I need more time.* "She's not here," he said quickly.

Adair threw him a sharp look.

"Where is she?" the duke challenged, taking a bold step toward him.

"She paid a visit to our vendors earlier, and then I provided her the afternoon off."

Bedford pursed his mouth. "If I were to call for the constable, you would be found in the wrong. They'd turn your club upside down if I told them you were holding my sister here against her will."

The bloody bastard.

He jutted his chin out. "If you did, then they'd find she is not inside the club." Which in all truth she was not.

Both men went toe-to-toe in a silent battle for supremacy.

Gripping her skirts, Nurse Mattison glanced back and forth between them.

The duke sighed. "You have until tomorrow afternoon." The wastrel lord had slept in the private suites here time enough that Calum knew the bastard would be too drunk to wake up in the morn. "I'll return and gather her. If she's not here, I'll destroy your club." On that, Eve's brother stalked out.

Head bowed, the woman was left alone with Calum and Adair. Calum expected her to beat a hasty flight. Instead, with a remarkable and surprising resilience, she lingered.

As soon as he'd gone, Calum glowered. "*You* are the loyal friend Eve trusted." Giving his head a disgusted shake, he pointed at the door. "Get out."

Tears flooded her blue eyes. "You have to understand," she pleaded, turning her palms up, "he came and had the hospital searched. The constable interviewed the children and threatened them. He vowed to see them thrown in Newgate if I d-didn't tell him where she'd gone, and one of the boys . . ." Her voice cracked, and she continued through it. "Her l-ladyship demanded that they be protected above all others." Even at the expense of her own self—that cryptic conversation Calum had picked up on the first time he'd found Eve at the foundling hospital at last made sense. He dragged a hand through his hair. "I am so sorry." A sob burst from the nurse's lips.

Seething, Adair stalked past him and thundered for a guard. Thomas, assigned to the main suites that evening, rushed forward. "Mr. Thorne?"

Calum stared, more an outside observer as Adair once again served the role of head proprietor while Calum stood completely useless, at sea. He dragged a hand through his hair while the other man barked out orders. Calum couldn't hand Eve over to that man. Bedford would succeed in destroying her where she'd always survived in the past. His gut clenched painfully.

"Escort Mrs. Mattison back to the Salvation Foundling Hospital," Adair was saying. "Remain behind in the event Bedford returns there. If he does, send word immediately."

"Aye, Mr. Thorne." Thomas caught her by the arm.

Still, the nurse lingered. "I tried everything within my power to help her ladyship. I naively believed I was a match for the duke." A tear slipped down her cheek. "I was so very wrong." Her voice caught. "Is . . . her l-ladyship well?"

He wanted to hate the woman. He wanted to turn her out with a cold order to see the Devil in hell. And yet . . . he'd been desperate, too. He knew what that terror did to a man. Calum sighed. He'd not, however, offer false assurances as to Eve's well-being. "The children at the hospital need you," Calum said quietly. "Thomas will escort you home."

She hesitated and then went with Thomas. The burly guard led her from the room, closing the door behind them.

"You knew," Adair whispered, the cryptic softness in his tone more ominous and threatening than his earlier shouts.

Calum pressed his fingertips into his temple, letting his silence stand as a confirmation.

"You knew and you let her remain anyway." Adair stalked over. "With how our club has suffered after Niall and Diana and Ryker and Penelope, you not only let her remain but kept it a secret." He slammed a hand into his chest. "From me?" he roared.

Guilt over his own duplicity turned inside him. "I could not have sent her back to Bedford. Surely you see that?"

"No," Adair snapped, his long-legged strides eating away all the space between them until their toes touched. *"I do not see."* Incredulity seeped from his street-hardened eyes. "I do not see," he repeated in more even, crisp tones. No, he could not. Because even though they were brothers closer than had they shared blood, they'd never discussed what they felt, outside of the hell that had sustained them, whether or not they had dreams and what they dreamed of. Adair frantically searched his face. "My God, man, the duke had you hauled into Newgate, and you'd help his sister?"

"She's no more responsible for Bedford's crimes than we were for Diggory's," he said quietly, willing his brother to understand.

Adair was already shaking his head. "She cannot stay here."

Calum's body coiled tight like a serpent poised to strike. "It is not your decision." He'd be damned to hell once again before he betrayed Eve.

"No." Adair settled his hands on his hips and met his gaze in a primal stare. "It is all of our decision. In allowing her to remain, ya've put all of us at risk." Adair's outrage made him sloppy, and his Cockney slid in, replacing his long-practiced cultured tones.

"I love her."

Voicing that admission aloud knocked him off balance.

Silence hung in the room.

Men of the streets didn't talk of matters of the heart. Mayhap men of any station avoided those topics. Discussions of cards and spirits and business were always fair discourse. Now Calum had plunged them into a murky world that was foreign to them both.

"You love her," Adair repeated, those three words as vacant as his eyes.

For the sliver of a moment he believed that would matter if not most, at least in some small way, to his brother.

"The men, women, an' children who work here call this place home, and you'd threaten all of that. All of them." Calum winced, and Adair pounced. "Ryker, Penny, the babe they're now expecting. Niall, Diana, even ya," he spat with icy condemnation. "Ya'll all be foine . . . ya've your fancy ladies and your purses."

Calum opened his mouth to deny it, but the words stuck there. For in this, Adair was correct. Restless, he stomped over to the window and stared out into those cold streets he'd spent too many years sleeping on. If Calum married Eve, they'd face society's condemnation for the divide in their stations, but he had a fortune enough set aside to sustain them . . . just as Eve herself was in possession of significant monies. What would become of the rest of the members of the hell when—if—the club's reputation was completely destroyed, and their membership disappeared?

"What do you want me to do?" he whispered angrily; his taut features stared back in the crystal pane.

"What do I expect you to do?" Adair scoffed. "You know the answer to that."

Yes, he did. Calum, Ryker, Niall, Adair, Helena—they'd all made a vow to one another years ago. Their family would always come first, before all, and they'd let no person jeopardize one another's security. Frustration and restless annoyance twisted at him, and for the first time, resentment sprang within. Niall had been permitted to love where and whom he would. Calum had supported him in that union unconditionally, and now he himself would be denied that choice?

But then . . . did you not expect Ryker to put the best interests of the club before all? That taunting reminder echoed in the chambers of his mind. It hadn't mattered that Ryker had eventually fallen in love with Lady Penelope. It mattered that Calum, just as Niall and Adair, had expected Ryker to do what was best to preserve the club's reputation. In the windowpane, he caught Adair's retreating form.

He faced him just as he reached for the handle. "How can you expect me to turn her over to him?" he entreated, the question as much for himself as for Adair.

There was a slight softening in the other man's scarred features. "Because if you don't turn her over to Bedford, then you're turning over three hundred and seventy-nine other people in her stead."

Those words hit him like a gut punch.

Adair pulled the door open, and Eve spilled inside.

The only thing that stopped Eve from landing face-first in a damning heap on Calum's entryway was Adair's quick hands and reflexes.

Eve curled her toes into the soles of her boots. Calum had taught her better about listening at keyholes than *this*. "F-forgive me," she stammered.

Both brothers stared silently back. Formidable in their silence, these two men before her were indeed fearless warriors of the streets.

"I was—" She dropped her gaze briefly to the floor. She'd already given this family enough lies that she'd not add one now explaining away her presence. She had been listening. Against Calum's orders, she'd stolen abovestairs and sought out the adjoining office to listen in on that hated meeting. And though the thick plaster had muffled a good portion of Calum's rebuttals to Gerald, her brother, in his typical bois-terous fashion, had been as clear as the bells of St. George's Cathedral.

"If you'll excuse us," Calum said tightly.

Coward that she was, relief took root. "Of course." She dropped a curtsy and wheeled about.

"Adair, my lady. I was speaking to my brother," Calum called out, halting her in her tracks.

My lady . . .

Adair looked back and forth between them, and her skin pricked with the fury emanating from him. Then, wordlessly, he stalked off.

"I told you to wait in the stables," he snapped as soon as the door had closed.

The anger and frustration in those eight words were at odds with the tender lover who'd held her in his arms twenty minutes . . . twenty days . . . twenty years . . . a lifetime ago? *How can you expect me to turn her over to him?* "He's my brother. It was my place to know what terms he'd set." But how she wished she didn't know the threats he'd made against Calum, his family, and the hell. "I took care to use the side entrances and only listened in from my office," she assured him.

He brought his hand down in a wide arc. "Damn it, Eve. Had he ordered the club searched for you, he would have turned you out, proved me a damned liar, and seen you hauled off," he shouted.

He was afraid. When she was a girl, she'd learned early on that Calum Dabney protected himself with blustery shows of temper. And the truth of his worrying ran her ragged inside. It mattered not whether that terror was for her, himself, or the whole of the Hell and Sin, but rather that he knew fear. *I don't want that for him . . .* He'd already known so very much of it. Too much. She watched as he fetched himself a brandy, taking in his swift, uncharacteristically jerky movements while he poured. *He is gone to me. In every way.* Pain cleaved at her breast. "I told you he would not relent until I was returned," she said quietly, when he finally faced her.

Calum flattened his mouth into a hard line. She drifted over. "You allowed yourself to believe that you could ultimately prevail over him, but the moment he learned I was here, nothing would have ever stopped Gerald." She spoke with a quiet pragmatism that roused a rumbling in Calum's chest.

"Do you doubt my ability to look after those in my care?" he put to her on a silken whisper coated in ice.

"No," she said sadly. *Because if you don't turn her over to Bedford, then you're turning over three hundred and seventy-nine other people in her stead.* "But I'm not in your care. I was here of my own volition."

He jerked, but otherwise made no attempt to counter that. And why should he? He'd already agreed that her time here was limited.

"You were only partially right," she murmured, clasping her hands together. "About Nurse Mattison," she clarified when Calum creased his brow. "All people are capable of betrayal, but some are forced to it. She was forced to do what she did to protect the children." She'd not hold the woman who'd been like a sister to blame, just as she'd not force Calum to make a choice between her and his club.

He stared morosely into his drink. "You'd forgive her?"

"Forgive her?" She shook her head. "This from the same man who forgave me for my crime against you. And yet you believe me so selfish that I'd expect her to sacrifice the children inside that hospital?" Eve waited until he lifted his gaze. "Of course I don't blame her, Calum. This is not her fault, and I would never, ever hold her responsible," she said with a quiet insistence, willing him to hear that. Calum was no more to blame than Nurse Mattison.

His throat muscles worked. "If you'll excuse me, Eve?" he said hollowly.

He'd turned her away. She flinched. "Of course. Forgive me." She lingered. "Calum," she called out, and he slowly lifted his head. "I—" *Love you.* Those words didn't belong here now. Not when he fought himself over the decision he had to make. Poor Calum, always in charge of all, didn't realize that ultimately this was and always had been only hers. "I'm so sorry." Eve left him, closing the door softly in her wake. She started down the hall, past that library where she and Calum had made love, and reached her chambers. Eve touched a finger to the curved gold door handle. How odd to have been here but three weeks and to have known more happiness and peace here than she had in the other five and twenty years of her existence.

Chapter 21

Calum had but five hours until the Duke of Bedford returned to the Hell and Sin.

In the end, it was not Ryker, Niall, or Adair who could help him from his situation.

One of his uniformed servants handed over the reins. "'ere ya are, sir."

Accepting them with a murmur of thanks, Calum pulled himself astride. He nudged Tau into a quick trot, and then as he reached the end of the street, Calum gave the restless mount his freedom. Tau bleated his appreciation and thundered onward.

The night's cold still hung in the air, and Calum welcomed the wind as it slapped against his face. His pulse accelerated, pounding a frantic beat in time to Tau's hooves as they struck the cobblestones. Any other time, he would have found calm in this. Riding had always filled him with the same exhilaration as securing a fat purse, and then racing off from those unsuspecting lords and ladies.

Not now.

Five hours. He had five hours before Bedford returned. The same bastard who'd put a knife in Calum's side and seen him in gaol. The vile reprobate who'd given his friend permission to rape Eve.

And I am expected to turn her over to him.

Because there could be no mistaking Adair would hold him accountable when Bedford struck the final death knell on their club. A familiar frustration rooted around his belly and mind, once more. Calum had begrudged Niall not one jot of his happiness, and yet Calum would be expected to make a decision for all, at the sacrifice of his own happiness.

As the dirtied cobblestones of St. Giles gave way to the fashionable end of Mayfair, he flexed his jaw.

It surely spoke to his selfishness that resentment burned strong inside him for what his siblings had that he'd be asked to sacrifice.

Calum slowed his mount outside a familiar white stucco residence. Dismounting, he did a search of the area. Even if the lords and ladies of Polite Society failed to see them, they were always there. His gaze landed on a small boy with a cap pulled low on his head. He motioned to the lad, and he instantly sprinted forward. Yanking out a purse, Calum tossed it to the street urchin, who easily caught it with dirt-stained fingers. "I need you to watch my . . ." His words trailed off as the cap slid forward on the child's head. "Horse," he finished.

For the lad with wide blue eyes and thick, curly blonde hair was none other than . . . a girl. His heart pulled. With her dirt-stained cheeks and tattered garments, she may as well have been Helena, all those years ago, when they'd sprung her free of Diggory.

"Wot?" the girl demanded combatively. She stuffed the purse inside a pocket sewn along the side of her pant leg. *How many times did I don garments like the ones this child wears now?* "Ya aren't lookin' for me to bugger ya," she demanded.

"No," he said quietly. "I'm not. I've a meeting in this household," he pointed to the front door. "When I return, there will be more coin." *I was this child . . .* Near an age to himself when he'd been orphaned and then escaped from the foundling hospital. Her belly grumbled loudly. "Afterward, if you are searching for honorable employment, I am the proprietor of a—" *Gaming hell.* His throat tightened, and the staggering truth of the threat facing that very establishment slammed into him with the weight of a fast-moving carriage. *This is what I jeopardize. Men, women, and children who will find themselves on the street once more.*

"Oi'm not lookin' fur the koind of employment you're talking about," she spat at his feet, jerking him to the present.

"It is a gaming hell. The Hell and Sin. The best . . ." He faltered. For that was no longer true. "One of the finest in London. Your work wouldn't involve you lying on your back or offering any other favors. Think of it," he said quietly.

She narrowed her eyes and met his offer with stony silence. *Smart girl.* That world wariness could only come to one who'd lived on the streets.

Bounding up the steps, Calum rapped hard on the door.

The wide panel was instantly opened by the graying butler there. "Mr. Dabney," he greeted. It spoke volumes of the servant's professionalism that he gave no outwardly show of surprise to the early-morn meeting. Then, mayhap it served as greater testament to the peculiarities he'd come to expect from the Duke of Somerset's family.

"I'm here to see the duchess." How peculiar to go from a girl like the one who now held Calum's reins to a step below royalty and for some . . . like him the stain of the street mattered still.

"If you'll follow me?" The butler turned on his heel and started down the halls of Somerset's elegant townhouse. The servant's unhurried steps and calm stirred Calum's frustration. He yanked out his watch fob, consulting the time. Four hours and approximately thirty minutes.

And I still don't have a goddamned idea as to how to make this right for everyone.

"Mr. Dabney," the butler announced.

Spectacles perched on her nose, Helena glanced up from her desk. Surprise lit her eyes, and she instantly came to her feet. "When I indicated I expected a meeting immediately, I did not . . ." Her words faded to silence. "What is it?" she asked as the servant closed the door behind them.

"There is trouble."

The color leached from her cheeks, and she rushed around the desk. "Killoran's men?"

"No," he silently cursed. He was making a bloody mess of this. "It's—"

"Diggory's henchmen?"

Now three years dead, those loyal to that old gang leader continued to wreak havoc on those who'd betrayed him.

"Everyone is . . ." Except there were different forms of harm, and the existential threat now posed by Bedford was as dangerous as a blade or knife wound. "No one is hurt," he settled for.

Helena slid her eyes closed and mouthed a silent prayer. Then she opened them, the earlier worry back in place. "What is it?" she asked again, motioning to a seat.

Restless, he rejected the offer. Calum clasped his hands behind him and strode over to the window. Peeling back the edge of the gold satin curtain, he stared out.

The little girl holding his horse shifted back and forth on her feet. Occasionally she stole a furtive glance about, and then reaching up, she scratched Tau on the shoulders. She instantly dropped her arm to her side. How many times he'd had to remind himself to present a wholly hardened image to the world. There hadn't been room for weakness or shows of it . . . not even with his siblings. Only in those mews of the Duke of Bedford's townhouse with the young Eve had he been free to ask questions and talk and dream without fear of judgment.

Helena moved behind him, hovering at his shoulder.

"We are in trouble," he repeated again, for himself, needing to hear that and fully accept what Eve's presence in the hell meant. He let the curtain go, and it fluttered back into place. "The bookkeeper . . ."

Helena jerked erect. "Mrs. Swindell?"

He nodded. "She is not who she said she was."

His sister thinned her eyes. "Who—"

"Her name is Evelina Pruitt. She is sister to the Duke of Bedford."

Helena's eyebrows went shooting up, nearly reaching her hairline. "Bedford's sister?" Her expression darkened. "Bedford's sister," she repeated, shaking her head.

His family would only hear the lady's connection to the duke. They didn't know that Eve had provided them food when their bellies had been emptiest or that she'd been a friend to him. They couldn't know, because Calum had kept that part of himself from his siblings. "She came seeking the post because she herself is in danger." Calum proceeded to explain everything from his first meeting the Little Lena Duchess to Eve's interview to her commandeering his books and rooms, to Bedford's arrival. When he'd finished, Helena stared contemplatively back.

"So, in order for Bedford to remain silent, he is demanding the return of his sister," she said quietly.

He gave a brusque nod. "If I do not comply, he'll destroy our club, which has been suffering—"

"Since Niall," she supplied.

Calum started.

With a little chuckle, Helena slapped him hard between the shoulder blades. "For all your intent to keep me safe as a girl and then woman, you never credited me with seeing enough. You still don't." Her smile dipped, and she gave his arm a light squeeze. "It's how I know you've feelings for Lady Evelina."

His throat bobbed up and down. "Love," he said hoarsely. "I love her." It was the second time he'd uttered that profession and the second person he'd given it to, and still Eve had never heard those three words from his lips. Calum dragged his hands over his face. "I don't know what to do," he whispered. "I love her." Calum let his arms fall to his sides. "There is no one I want to be with more, but how do I choose her when everyone else will lose?" he begged, needing an answer that would make all of this right.

"Oh, Calum," Helena said collecting his hands. "Sometimes you cannot make everything right for everybody."

He stared blankly down at her head. No. He could not.

"No matter how much you, just like Ryker and Niall and Adair, tried to make my existence into what you thought it should be . . . you still have not learned that you cannot control life. You cannot ensure the club will always be thriving and successful. You cannot control the decisions of others. Or force Bedford to remain silent even after this. So much is beyond our grasp." She gave his hands a squeeze, forcing his gaze to hers. At just three inches shy of six feet, she was taller than most men he knew. "We cannot even control who we love. Our hearts decide that."

And Calum's heart had belonged to Eve Pruitt long before she'd ever reentered his life. Of all the mews in London where he might have sought shelter, it had been hers because fate had known they were to be joined. "So, what do I do?" he asked gruffly.

"You let love win," she said simply. "For that is the only power you truly have in any of this. You keep her at your side, and face what you will, knowing you have her, me and Robert, Ryker and Penny, Niall and Diana, and so many others now as friends and family."

He briefly closed his eyes.

I want that. I want to be selfish and take that gift she offers.

Adair's furious countenance flashed to his mind's eye. "Adair was not so forgiving."

Helena snorted. "That's because Adair hasn't been in love. He might not understand your decision now, but in time, when some woman knocks him totally on his arse, where he belongs, then he will know." She winked.

"Thank you," he said hoarsely.

"Pfft." She swatted at him. "You already knew the answer when you came to me."

Footsteps sounded in the hall. A moment later, the door opened. Calum and Helena looked as one. Her husband, Robert, the Duke of Somerset, stepped into the room, a toddler cradled in his arms. "Someone is here to see you, love . . . Oh, Calum."

Helena motioned him forward. "We were discussing matters of the club."

"Is everything all right?" the duke asked, coming over.

The duchess instantly tickled her son under his chin, earning an incoherent babbling laugh for her efforts.

Calum stared on, and a wave of envy went through him. So long he'd thought the Hell and Sin was all he needed . . . but this is what he wanted. A family. Children. Love. And he'd found that latter part with Eve. Now he wanted it all with her. "I'll leave Helena to explain. Thank you, both," he added.

He turned to go, but Helena rushed over, blocking his path. "What?"

Helena leaned up and placed a kiss on his scarred cheek. "When the nightmares came, you were the brother who was always there. Let others be there for you now. I trust you'll find the same peace I have in accepting that."

And for the first time since Bedford had stormed his club and put his threats to him, Calum smiled.

Chapter 22

Eve hadn't slept, but oddly, as she'd gone through her morning ablutions and started from her rooms, her entire body stirred with a panicky wakefulness.

It was time.

Or rather, it soon would be. Gerald would return, and somewhere between his departure last evening and this moment, she'd accepted the truth—she could not let Calum make this decision. Because knowing him as she did, the boy in the mews who'd become an honorable man worried after those on his staff would never bow to Gerald's threats.

She stared blankly at the wood-paneled door. Before her courage deserted her, she jerked the door open. Calum's brother stood there waiting.

Eve shrieked and slapped a hand to her breast. "Oh, you startled me."

A gentleman of the *ton* would have replied with his apologies; Adair, however, met her with only seriousness. "My lady? May we speak?" he asked somberly. Gone was the frosty anger he'd directed her way last evening.

She eyed him a long moment, then nodded. Adair spun on his heel, and she followed after him, winding her way down another corridor.

He reached a stark, white-paneled door, and opening it, he motioned for her to enter.

Eve stepped inside and took in the unfamiliar room. Not unlike Calum's office, a sketch of tasteful elegance, Adair Thorne's space exuded that same sophistication. His mahogany desk was positioned off center, in the far left of the room, with two Egyptian Revival–style armchairs neatly positioned at the foot of it. "Won't you sit?" he urged, and she claimed one of those ivory upholstered seats. Unnerved by the intensity in his stare, she forced herself to remain still under his silent scrutiny.

In a surprising move, Adair didn't take a seat at his desk, but rather claimed the chair beside hers. Curving his hands along the edge, he turned it so he might face her. "The night your brother had my brother thrown in Newgate, we only discovered Calum's whereabouts by chance," he said without preamble.

Her stomach lurched at the unexpectedness of both that admission and the imagery painted of Calum in that vile place.

"A boy from our gang saw him being taken away from your town-house and immediately came for us. It took some nosing around, putting questions to your servants, and ultimately paying coin to find out what had become of him."

Eve's mouth parted in soft shock. "They took your coin to answer those questions?"

He nodded, and disappointment filled her. Those loyal servants, many she'd considered closer than family, had taken from children struggling in the street.

"We found him. Cost us more than half the fortune we'd amassed to earn him his freedom. He was weak from blood loss. He couldn't even manage to stagger out on his own feet. I carried him through the cold corridors of that hell." His telling brought her eyes closed. What Adair had undertaken would have been no small feat for even a fully grown man. As a boy, Calum had towered over even her papa and most of the footmen. And how weak he'd been. *Because my brother thrust a blade into his side, and I turned Calum over to his evil hands . . .*

It wasn't your fault . . .

Despite Calum's gruff reassurances, it *had* been her fault. A tear seeped from her lashes and tumbled slowly down her cheek. She hated to reveal that weakness in the face of Adair Thorne's strength through his telling and what he'd actually done that day. Feeling Adair's stare, she forced herself to reply. "He was fortunate to have you," she said, her voice hoarse. Whereas Eve had only brought suffering to him.

"We were fortunate to have one another," he said gravely. "Calum saved my life more times than I deserved. As he did Ryker and Niall and Helena. Because that is who he's always been, my lady. He's been a man who saves people." And now he'd attempt to save Eve.

Eve dropped her gaze away from his penetrating stare. "I neither need nor expect him to save me." Was that a whole truth? *Do you truly believe yourself capable of outmaneuvering Gerald once he carts you back home?* No doubt, Lord Flynn would be lying in wait. She steeled her jaw. What neither of those men could know is that she would never allow herself to be maneuvered into marriage. Even if raped and ruined by the earl.

My half-mad sister . . .

Only Gerald had grown more and more desperate. There was another way he could attain those funds. Her stomach muscles clenched.

Adair leaned back in his chair and folded his hands over his flat stomach. "The day you entered this club, hiding from Bedford, you immediately earned my brother's protection. Calum is loyal. Honorable. He would never turn you out." He looked at her pointedly.

Eve blinked slowly as his meaning became clear. He wanted her to leave. Of her own volition. Of course, that should come as no surprise. What reason did she have to believe he or anyone else inside the club would put all the people here in jeopardy for her? She was an interloper who'd deceived them, whose brother now threatened them. As such, she'd never be deserving of any of their fealty—and most especially not Calum's.

"What do you want?" she asked bluntly, angling her chair to face his so she could look him square in the eyes, making him say it.

His expression grew instantly shuttered, and he put his hands up. "I would not presume to tell you what to do. Calum would not . . ." Would not forgive him for that interference. He coughed into his hand. "This club sustained each of us through darkness and evil you could never understand."

Had he been vile and hurling epithets and accusations, it would be easier than this subtle pleading. Pleading when she suspected Adair Thorne revealed not a hint of himself to anybody. Eve leaned over and placed her hand on his. "I love your brother," she said quietly. Color exploded on Adair's sharp cheeks. "And I never, ever would have asked him to make that sacrifice for me."

A commotion sounded in the hall. Adair whipped his head sideways toward the shouts going up, and calls for the proprietors.

He is here . . .

And for all her earlier bravado, terror clutched at her throat and made it impossible to swallow, to speak. With a slow sense of foreboding, Eve stood.

"Oi said get out. No one gets through these halls without . . ." That gravelly Cockney was met with a loud cry, a thump, and silence.

"Get behind my desk," Adair ordered, surging to his feet as the heavy slam of doors echoed in the hallway. Followed by further commands, shouts, and the loud thump of bodies, met with inevitable silence. "Stay down." Withdrawing a pistol from his waistband, he raced to the front of the room.

A sad smile pulled at Eve's lips. For all of Adair's desire to have her gone, he proved how very much like Calum was. The inherent need to protect and defend was part of who they were.

From his position at the side of the door, he glowered at her. "Behind the desk," he mouthed.

It is time . . . She gave her head a shake and moved to the center of the room, just as the door was thrown open. It bounced back with such force it struck the back wall, and then her brother's hand shot out, catching it.

Eve's breath caught on a shallow gasp, and she stared as her brother pointed a pistol at Adair.

"Put it down," he whispered.

Her brother.

Adair hesitated, then slowly lowered his gun to the floor.

She stared unblinkingly.

And yet—a peculiar humming filled her ears—not *the* brother she had spent all night in terror over, but rather another she'd despaired of ever seeing again.

"Kit," she whispered, taking a tentative step forward, and then another. She stopped. Afraid to breathe. Afraid to utter one more word. Afraid that if she made one false move, this moment would end just like every other dream of him invariably did.

"Evie," he said in hoarsened, very real, and very much alive tones.

With a cry, Eve rushed across the room. He instantly folded her in his arms and pressed a kiss to her temple. "Oh, God, Evie. I'm so sorry. I did not know."

And that rumble of his chest as he spoke and the bergamot scent that was so patently his proved he was indeed real. She sobbed against his chest.

It was over.

Dismounting, Calum handed his reins to a servant and climbed the steps of his club with a peculiar sense of doom and peace mingling.

He scanned the room. At this early-morn hour, the tables were largely empty, with the exception of the most dissolute lords. His gaze landed on Adair.

Stationed beside the hazard table, he spoke to Harpe, one of their oldest dealers, a man who'd been with them since the club opened. Adair spoke with an ease that ran counter to the man he'd left this morning. As he spoke, Calum watched him. Adair had always been a quiet leader of their group. He'd not ruled with the same rigidity and obvious strength of Ryker, but in his own right, he was of equal—mayhap greater—strength. The club would suffer . . . but they would survive, as they always had, and then eventually thrive . . . because that was what they did. And ultimately, they'd one day be stronger for the love and partners they'd each found who had only strengthened their family. In time, as Helena had aptly pointed out, Adair would see that. He might not forgive it for a long time until then, but he would.

Filled with an aching need to see Eve and tell her all, offer her everything he had, he started across the gaming floors.

His brother looked up midspeak, said something else to the dealer, and then fell into step alongside him. "I would speak with you," Adair said, easily matching his long strides.

"I need to speak with Eve first." He'd withheld the words she deserved long enough. A sense of absolute rightness sent heat to his heart.

"She is gone."

Calum passed the guards stationed at the stairway leading up to the private suites when Adair's words registered. He slowed his steps. He'd misheard him. He'd merely imagined those three—

"Her brother arrived earlier and—" While his brother's voice droned on, a loud humming filled Calum's ears. His breath came hard and fast as he struggled to drag air into his lungs. ". . . and so it is settle—"

With a roar, Calum grabbed his brother by the shoulders and drove him into the wall. The guards cried out, and then hovered, wisely choosing to not interfere. "You let her leave." He knocked Adair back into the plaster.

The slightly shorter man grunted. "By Christ, listen to me. It is for the best. She—"

Calum launched a fist, catching Adair in the chin. His brother stumbled sideways and then caught himself. Planting his feet, he held his arms up, prepared for battle. "It is best she is gone."

With a bellow, Calum flung himself against the other man. Except Adair had the benefit of calm on his side, and he caught Calum by the wrist. Wrenching it behind his back, he propelled him into the opposite wall. "We do not fight in the gaming hell," he muttered, one of the longest-established rules of the club.

No, they didn't fight. They *hadn't* since they'd been sparring for the same scraps in the street—members of rival gangs, who'd eventually joined the same front. "Go to hell," he spat. Breathing hard, he wrested free. "How could you let that bastard take her?" He brought his hand back, but Adair caught the blow with his other hand.

They remained locked, two primitive warriors, both refusing to cede a proverbial inch. "I did not send her away," Adair gritted out, his face flushed and red from the strain of his exertions. "She *chose* to leave."

"Impossible." She wouldn't have left. *What assurance did you give her last night that she'd stay . . . or worse, that you wanted her to?* He sucked in a breath. How could she not know what she'd come to mean to him? *Because you never showed her.* He faltered, and Adair instantly took advantage of his distraction.

Panting, Adair shoved Calum away and stuck a finger out. "She chose to leave," he said in an echo of his earlier profession.

Because she was honorable. Because she would not have stayed knowing she'd put his club in jeopardy. She'd risk her own safety with that bastard Bedford and Flynn. An agonized moan tore from his throat. "You know what he'll do to her, and you let her go, anyway," he whispered. Who was this man before him?

Calum made to leave when Adair called out. "You misunderstood." Adair glanced about, favoring their audience with a quelling glare. Everyone promptly returned to their respective tasks. Dropping his voice, Adair gripped him by the shoulder. "Didn't you hear a damned word I said? Her other brother, the one who'd been missing, returned from his work with the Home Office." *Not Bedford.* The affectionate— when present—but absentee brother, whom she'd not given up hope of again seeing.

A wave of relief assailed him.

"It is done," Adair said quietly, lightly squeezing his shoulder.

It is done? "That is what you'd say?" he asked vacantly.

Adair shrugged. "She is safe. The club is well. And we can carry on without fear of discovery."

Did his brother truly believe Eve being free of danger and out of the hell was all that mattered to Calum? Or was it that he cared so little? "I love her," he whispered.

"Oi'm not having this discussion in a bloody stairway." Adair took a step, and this time Calum halted his retreat.

"We'll have this discussion here or on the gaming floors or in my office, it doesn't matter. Nothing changes. I love her, Adair." The other man recoiled. "I love her," Calum said for good measure. "I need you to hear that to understand that nothing will keep me from marrying her." *If she'll have me.*

A vein bulged at the corner of Adair's left eye. "You are mad." That hushed declaration filled the stairway. "You would throw away the safety and security of all these people"—he motioned to the hell behind him—"for a woman."

God help him for being the selfish, grasping bastard that he was . . . "I would," he said solemnly. "We will survive."

"We will survive? *That* is what you'd say?" Adair exploded into a violent laugh, until his shoulders quaked and tears streamed down his cheeks. "And this of the same man who supported Ryker marrying to save the club," he spat.

"I was wrong." He was just grateful that his error had not cost Ryker the happiness that Calum had found with Eve. Helena's assurances whispered forward. "And someday, you'll find you were, too." Calum turned on his heel.

"Where are you going?" Adair called after him.

"To find a candle."

"A candle?" By Adair's consternation, Calum may as well have declared himself mad and headed to Bedlam.

And with his brother's protestations trailing behind him, Calum grinned.

Chapter 23

Her brother had a townhouse.

It was a peculiar detail to fix on given the fear she'd lived with these past weeks, and yet she hadn't known Kit had been in possession of a London townhouse.

Seated on the window bench overlooking the streets of Grosvenor Square, her knees drawn up, Eve skimmed her gaze over the well-stocked library. She took in the floor-length shelving and leather button sofas. Kit was her brother and she loved him, and yet she couldn't even venture to imagine what books he'd have placed upon those shelves. She didn't know what dreams he'd had or who his friends were.

Since Papa had died, and letters upon letters had been sent and been unreplied to, she'd gone from hope to despair to eventual acceptance. For the whole of her life, Kit had been devoted—when he was around . . . The truth had always been that he'd been gone more than he'd ever been part of her life. Oh, she loved him and always would. But he'd represented the closest dream she had to family, and she'd not truly understood that—until Calum Dabney.

Through all the sadness and loneliness that her life had been, there had been one year of her life where there had been someone—a friend.

In those days they'd spent together then, and too briefly again now, she'd revealed more of who she was than she had to any other.

"And I've lost him all over again," Eve whispered into the quiet, for in giving that truth life, mayhap there could be peace. Her heart spasmed. No. It didn't help. Dratted tears blurred her vision, and she frantically blinked.

"May I come in?" her brother Kit called from the front of the room. *Never let yourself be caught unawares . . .*

Frantically turning her head back toward the window, she discreetly dabbed at her eyes. "Of course." What a silly offering, given this was Kit's home. Eve made to rise, but he motioned her back.

His skin bronzed from the sun, and midnight strands drawn back, he bore traces of her beloved elder brother, and yet there was a sharpness to his gaze that she didn't recall. But then, she also had no remembrances of him brandishing a pistol and pummeling burly guards to reach her.

Flicking out his coattails, he claimed the spot beside her. "Evie." He spoke with a trace of nostalgia. Did he also have remembrances of her so very different from the reality that had always been there? "I didn't know what these years have been like for you," he said somberly. "And I should have." His mouth tightened. "I always knew what he was."

"We both did." She spoke softly to herself. Yet she'd made the mistake in trusting him with Calum's care, as a child. She lifted her eyes to Kit's. "What happened to him?" she asked, needing him to make sense of what she'd never understood about their eldest brother.

Kit dusted a hand over his mouth. He let his arm fall back to his side. "In my work for the Home Office, there are men and women who will trade their souls for government secrets. They'll do it for fortunes and fame or prestige. And then there are others . . ."

Calum had struggled and clawed to survive in the streets and had shaped himself into a man who helped others and lived without resentment. And yet Gerald, who'd been born with the world at his fingertips for the taking, existed as this twisted, black soul.

"What could he possibly have wanted in life?" she implored.

Kit gave her a sad smile. "Gerald is one of the others. He's one whom there's no explaining for or understanding. Some men are just born evil, and our brother is one of those." His empty smile withered. "I understand you were living inside that gaming hell." She stiffened at that unexpected shift. "The Hell and Sin. Hiding from Gerald. What did he do?" There was a steely promise there that hinted at death.

For an instant Eve considered telling Kit everything. She considered going back years earlier to the day she'd found a friend in Calum, and then eventually lost that same one with her brother's cruelty. But there could be no changing their pasts, any of them. Telling him the evil Gerald had carried out would not undo it, and would only rouse unwanted guilt. Just as sharing that special bond she'd shared with Calum with Kit, who was more a stranger to her, felt . . . wrong. "He attempted to maneuver me into a match with one of his wastrel friends," she at last settled for. "Nothing happened." It almost had, and would have had Lord Flynn not been more than slightly intoxicated.

Kit narrowed his eyes, and she curled her hands into tight balls, braced for his questioning. "I was on the Continent, Eve," he said quietly in guilt-laden tones. "As a second-born son, I thought there was nothing more important than building a future and fortune for myself." The muscles of his throat moved. "I was wrong," he confessed hoarsely. "Gerald had been intercepting the letters sent by father's solicitor, Mr. Barry. And yours and . . ." He sucked in a ragged breath. "Had I known . . . any of it, what your life had been like, I would have returned, Home Office and career be damned."

"Don't do that," she admonished. Once it had devastated her that he'd been gone. Now, finding he was safe and had been all this time, she also found peace in knowing if Kit hadn't been gone, she would have never moved inside the Hell and Sin. And those days she'd had with

Calum Dabney, she would not trade for anything. "I'll not have you guilty or regret having made a life for yourself, because of me."

"But—"

"It is fine," she said softly, covering his hand with one of hers.

"It is not fine." His hand tensed under hers. "You were my responsibility—"

Eve's patience snapped, and she surged to her feet. "I am not your responsibility," she cried. All her life she'd existed as an afterthought for everybody, a person to be cared for and looked after, and yet she wanted more. She always had. "I'm not anyone's responsibility. I'm not yours. I'm not Gerald's. I'm not . . ." Calum's. "Anyone's," she finished weakly.

Kit opened his mouth slowly, then pushed to his feet. "You are correct," he finally said, offering words Gerald would have sooner cut his tongue out than admit. "You are my sister, and you deserved better than two rotten brothers."

Eve sighed. "One rotten brother. You simply had your work with the Home Office. I'd not begrudge you a life of your own." A wistful smile pulled at her lips. "I simply wished I could have been part of it."

Kit came over. "I am here now, and I'm not leaving." Once that would have been enough. Her brother hovered, rocking on his heels. In this instance he was uncertain when she'd only ever remembered him as self-assured. "What of the gaming hell? Did you come to any harm there?"

"No." The denial burst from her lungs with a vehemence that brought his eyebrows together. She shook her head frantically. "Cal . . . Mr. Dabney," she swiftly amended at Kit's intense stare. "Mr. Thorne . . . everyone there was kind. They respected me, treated me with k-kindness." She damned that silent quaver and cleared her throat in a bid to conceal it. "They provided me safety and security." She spoke of precious gifts and yet how . . . wrong it felt mentioning all Calum had shown her in such sterile terms. Calum and his brothers deserved more than Eve had brought into their lives. "Gerald threatened to expose their club for illicitly hiring a lady. He threatened to tell Society that Mr. Dabney and I were . . ." Her cheeks exploded in warmth, and she prayed her brother mistook that blush for sisterly, ladylike embarrassment. Avoiding Kit's eyes, she coughed into her hand. "It would be the height of wrongness for Calum's club to suffer because I deceived them about my identity."

"I'll speak to Gerald." The icy glint in his eyes served as an assurance that he'd not allow their brother to disparage the Hell and Sin.

An awkward pall of silence hung in the room as Eve and Kit stood, siblings but strangers. "I thought I might explore my new home," she finally said. Home. The Hell and Sin had been more a home than this place or their family townhouse.

"Of course. Can I have my housekeeper show—"

"I promise I am not in need of a tour," she said wryly. "That would take away the fun of exploring. I thought you of all people should know that."

He grinned. "Indeed." Kit dropped a bow and started for the door, pausing when he reached the entrance.

She stared questioningly back.

"Were there any accuracies to Gerald's claims?"

Flummoxed by that blunt, unexpected query, Eve shook her head quickly. Too quickly. She stopped the frantic back-and-forth movement. "No. We were friends," she settled for. "We became friends."

Again, her brother brought his eyebrows together, only this time no further questions followed—and he left. And mayhap she was an ungrateful creature, for with all the years she'd spent missing Kit and yearning for him to return home, she felt nothing but a sweeping relief that he'd gone. She didn't want to answer any more of his questions. As she'd said to him, everything that had come to pass had already come and gone and now served as nothing but a dull pain inside for what would never be.

Numb, Eve moved from the library, through the halls of her brother's townhouse. Smaller than the residences they'd called home, but just as elegant with its dark Chippendale furnishings and dark satin wallpapers, it was very much a bachelor's residence.

And she knew enough that no bachelor, regardless of how devoted a brother was or intended to be, wished to have a sister underfoot. A spinster one, no less.

But then, in two months' time, Eve would no longer be dependent upon anyone's charity—not Kit's, not Gerald's, not Calum's. Those funds that had once represented the zenith of her independence and her hopes for the foundling hospital would at last be hers. So where was the previous thrill that such thoughts of independence had once roused?

Eve reached the end of the carpeted hall and stopped, staring blankly at the wall ahead.

Because independence had been the greatest dream she'd allowed herself. After years of being under her brother's influence and living in constant fear, she'd thought of nothing except those monies that would allow her freedom from it all. She'd contemplated the good she could do with her inheritance with the foundling hospital . . . which she would at last be able to fully do.

Now, however, she'd a glimpse of what life was like with a partner at her side . . . someone who shared her interests and joined her in her efforts at the foundling hospital. Eve drew in a shaky breath. "Stop," she whispered.

"My lady, do you require help?"

A maid startled her from her reverie.

Forcing a smile that she didn't feel, Eve waved off her efforts. "Thank you. No. I was just . . . I am . . ." *Wallowing in my own misery.* How pathetic she'd become. Forcing a smile, Eve continued her trek through Kit's home. She wound her way down the curved stairway, belowstairs. Drawn forward by the buzz of activity in the kitchens, Eve strode toward those familiar sounds.

As soon as she entered, the room drew to an abrupt halt, and then as one, the men, women, and children working dropped simultaneous curtsies and bows.

Eve's cheeks ached from the force of her fake smile. Before one of those too-attentive servants came forward, she pulled open her own door and strode outside into the mews. She sucked deep of the spring air and, not breaking stride, marched toward the stables. Reaching the closest one, Eve let herself inside.

The horse, a chestnut gelding, let out a whinnied greeting. Eve closed her eyes and let a calming peace that she'd always found in the stables claim her. A horse knew not and cared not what station a person was born to. They saw only people . . . and for a too brief time at the Hell and Sin, Eve had been treated in that same light.

She sank down to the hay-covered floor and took support from the wall.

The people at the Hell and Sin—Calum, Adair, the servants and guards—had not treated her as a pampered miss. They'd not dipped their eyes and bowed and curtsied, and she wanted to go back to that. To go back to how it was. And she wanted that with Calum in her life.

The door creaked, breaking into her regretful musings, and she shot her gaze up. She stilled, afraid to move and find that she'd merely dreamed up the figure towering over her. Calum doffed his hat and twisted at the brim, more uncertain than she'd ever seen him in all the time they'd known one another. How perfect that the stables should be the last place she ever saw Calum Dabney. It completed the circle of their meeting and relationship.

"I thought you knew better than to let someone catch you unawares."

She sought out a clever quip and came up empty. "How did you know where to find me?"

He gave a wry half grin. "If I were honorable, I would tell you I'd knocked at the front door as any gentleman would do, and was shown out here by your obliging brother."

A little smile hovered on her lips.

Calum jammed his hat back on. "But I was never, and will never be, one of those fancy lords. I knew after you'd gone, I'd eventually find you here."

Of course. This was where she and Calum had always been meant to be. Only he was so very wrong.

"You were always more honorable than any man with a title affixed to his name." His willingness to help so many people served as testament to that. Then reality intruded. "What are you doing here?" she asked hesitantly, trying to make sense of his presence.

Calum shot a hand out, and she automatically placed hers in his large, naked, calloused palm. He guided her to her feet. "In your haste to leave this morning, my lady, you left something behind."

"I did?" His words were starting to penetrate the haze cast by his unexpected arrival.

"You did. Very many things."

That is why he'd come. "Oh," she said blankly. Her valise and bonnet and belongings. "You needn't have come for that." The cramped stalls suddenly too small for the volatile figure simmering beside her, Eve started past him. She made it no farther than one step outside.

"Me." Calum shot an arm around hers, capturing her wrist in a tender yet determined hold. He brought her around to face him. Some indefinable emotion glittered in his eyes. "You forgot *me*, madam."

Her heart caught. "I don't . . ." She shook her head. "I don't understand," she whispered.

The column of his throat moved. "I returned to find you'd gone, and with you went my heart."

She gasped and clutched at her chest, searching for words.

"My every happiness. My reason for smiling." He continued over her breathy exhalation. "I believed you cared for me." His throat bobbed. "Mayhap loved me even."

"I do," she whispered. "I've always loved you. It is why I left." Surely, he understood that? "All you ever dreamed of was that club—"

271

"Do not presume to tell me what I ever dreamed of, Eve, for if you indeed knew that, you'd know that you were the only dream I've ever had."

Her heart caught.

"And you do not get to decide what is best for me or my club. You don't get to simply walk out as though nothing mattered," he said on a harsh whisper, releasing her quickly.

My God . . . He was hurting because she'd left. "I love you," she tried again, needing him to understand. "But—"

"Do not mention the bloody club now or the next breath, madam."

She promptly closed her lips and tried again, needing him to understand. "I could not let you sacrifice everyone for me." She loved him too much to ever have him abandon his dreams for her.

"Oh, Eve," he said hoarsely. "You have always thought of others. I have loved you since you were a girl taking care of a street urchin—"

"You were never an urchin." She had never seen him in that light. "You were my—"

"—to when you stole my books."

"—friend. You were my friend." She paused. "I did not really steal them," she said achingly. "Your books. I more borrowed them."

"To when I followed you to the Salvation Foundling Hospital."

"You followed me because you didn't trust me," she pointed out.

"Eve?" he said on a ragged laugh. Blinking tear-filled eyes, she lifted her gaze to his. "Can you let me please do this?"

"I don't know what . . ."

"Because I'm not a gentleman, no doubt. Because if I were, I wouldn't make such an absolute bumble of asking you to be my wife."

Eve pressed her palm to her mouth.

"I'm desperately trying to do this properly and making a blunder of it." He reached inside his jacket and fished out a candle.

She cocked her head.

Silence lingered in the mews, broken by the whinnying of horses. "You once told me that the Greeks placed candles upon cakes at the time of their birthdays," he said solemnly.

"And blow those flames out to send their wishes to the heavens," she finished for him, reverently gathering the narrow white wax. He recalled still all these years later those stories they'd shared and read together. "I rejected that offer so many damned times. I want it now." Her heart squeezed at the emotion in his pronouncement. "I want that damned cake, and I want that wish, and I want it to be you."

Eve leaned up and placed her lips to his. "Oh, Calum," she whispered when she drew back. She captured his cheek in her palm. "You never needed a wish. I was yours since you stumbled into those stables, and I'm yours forever."

"I love you, Eve Pruitt." He caught her wrist, dragging it to his mouth for a lingering kiss. "And when I am with you, I am home."

She twined her hand with his. "We are home, together."

Epilogue

Eve had never spent her life dreaming of a fortune, but seated inside her office at the foundling hospital and evaluating the food reports, she had a great appreciation for just all that money provided.

Eve frantically scraped her pen over the page, completing the monthly reports for the Salvation Foundling Hospital.

In the weeks since she'd wed Calum and secured her dowry, those monies had been put to use inside this institution that had come to mean so very much to her.

One number upon the ledger, however, commanded all her notice.

Fifty children. Pausing, she reverently stroked that now dry number she'd inked earlier that day. Only this was solely the beginning. Those children who'd found homes in the expanded space inside the foundling hospital were just the first. Discussing it the night they'd been reunited, Calum had proposed they expand the help they provided . . . to other hospitals and establishments around England.

A quivery smile turned her lips up. With their monies combined, they'd care not only for the children here but also other boys and girls all over who'd been living on the street, as her husband had been. Those young souls would be spared some of the horrors he'd known . . . and for the ones who'd already known too much darkness, now they'd know light.

How many men who ran a thriving business would devote not only their money but also their time?

A knock sounded at the office door, and she glanced up. It was as though she'd conjured her husband from her thoughts. Butterflies fluttered wildly in her belly, as they always did at the sight of him.

Wholly elegant in his repose, Calum lounged against the doorway. "Is my wife altogether too busy to accompany me on a short walk?"

Warmth suffused her breast, and she dropped her pen. "I'm never too busy for time with my husband," she protested as he came over and dropped a kiss on her lips. The heat of that contact fanned her desire. "Just sometimes shamefully engrossed in my numbers," she whispered as he broke contact. Then she widened her eyes. "I missed our appointment."

He cuffed her teasingly under the chin. "By five minutes, Mrs. Dabney. Should I sack you for such an offense?"

A smile pulled at her lips, and she repressed that grin. Setting her features into a teasingly somber mask, she met his eyes. "I have it on good authority that you were kind enough to show one of your former bookkeepers the benefit of the proverbial doubt, and hired her though she was five days late," she said in grave tones.

"Did I?" At the feigned shock lighting his eyes, she grinned. "Well, she must have been a tempting minx, then, who hopelessly captivated me from the start."

Her lashes fluttered, and she tilted her mouth up.

"Uh-uh," he said teasingly, and she pouted. Calum took her by the hand. "We'd a meeting in the mews."

Laughing, she allowed him to guide her through the halls and outside to where the recently renovated mews stood now complete.

"It appears we are to keep meeting like this," she said breathlessly as he brought her to a stop outside a stable door. "First—" Her words ended abruptly as he opened the door of the stable.

She covered her mouth with her hands.

The magnificent old black horse chomped noisily at his hay. A familiar old horse. Tears popped behind her lashes, and she blinked them back. To no avail. "Night," she whispered. The beloved stallion who'd been present for her every meeting with Calum snorted in the quiet. Eve whipped her gaze up to her husband's. Through blurry vision, his loving visage met hers.

He dusted his knuckles back and forth over her cheek in a tender caress. "So many interesting things about the Greeks. I learned much of it from a small girl in a different stables," he said quietly.

A tear slipped down her cheek. "D-did you?" Her voice caught.

"Oh, yes. The Greeks had an idea that the horse could help a person who was hurting or suffering. That they could bring happiness and calm and peace." Another tear joined the first, and then another and another. Calum lovingly framed her face in his hands, and with the pads of his thumbs, he caught those crystal drops and brushed them away. "And given all the happiness we found together among those magnificent creatures, I thought it only fitting that we bring that gift to the children who are—*oomph*." Eve hurled herself into his arms, and Calum staggered back under the unexpectedness of that movement.

Night briefly paused in his chewing and eyed them with equine boredom.

"I love you," she whispered to her husband. "I—"

"I loved you from the moment you entered those stables all those years ago," he said quietly, echoing every thought. "I was yours from that moment on." So much love spilled from his eyes, her heart caught. "We were destined to be together." He held her gaze, and at the piercing intensity there, she drifted closer to him.

Eve lovingly framed his face with her hands. "And now we'll never be apart. Never again," she whispered.

And going up on tiptoe, she kissed him, sealing that promise.

Acknowledgments

To Alison, Lauren, and my entire team at Montlake Romance, I'm so very grateful for all your support. Thank you for trusting my vision as an author and for allowing me to bring the Sinful Brides world to the page.

About the Author

Photo © 2016 Kimberly Rocha

USA Today bestselling author Christi Caldwell blames Julie Garwood and Judith McNaught for luring her into the world of historical romance. When Christi was sitting in her graduate school apartment at the University of Connecticut, she began writing her own tales of love. Christi believes even the most perfect heroes and heroines have imperfections. Besides, she rather enjoys torturing them—before the couple earn their well-deserved happily ever after.

Christi makes her home in southern Connecticut, where she spends her time writing, chasing after her courageous son, and caring for her twin princesses-in-training. For free bonus material and the latest information about Christi's releases and future books, sign up for her newsletter at www.ChristiCaldwell.com.